all
muck and
mullets

Samantha Clark
x

all muck and mullets

Samantha Nash

Matador
9 Priory Business Park,
Wistow Road, Kibworth Beauchamp,
Leicestershire. LE8 0RX
Tel: (+44) 116 279 2299
Fax: (+44) 116 279 2277
Email: books@troubador.co.uk
Web: www.troubador.co.uk/matador

ISBN 978 1783063 932

British Library Cataloguing in Publication Data.
A catalogue record for this book is available from the British Library.

Typeset in 11pt Aldine401 BT Roman by Troubador Publishing Ltd, Leicester, UK
Printed and bound in the UK by TJ International, Padstow, Cornwall

Matador is an imprint of Troubador Publishing Ltd

To my incredible family and JB.
Thank you for believing in me.

CHAPTER 1

May

Four Villages Fete

Milton doubled over just in time to hurl the contents of his stomach clear of his new white trainers, then falling to his knees; he re-filled his lungs before passing out on the muddy verge by the side of the path. He was no stranger to spending the night lying in a pool of his own vomit, but he seldom woke to find himself a few feet away from the village hall car park. In the partial darkness, lit by a solitary street lamp, Craigie and Mick could just make out the shape of two stumpy legs poking out from the hedge in the gloom.

'Bet you five quid that's Milton?' sniffed Mick, scurrying towards the prostrate body.

'I ain't betting with you no more. Course it's Milton, unless a dwarf just moved to Adderstey, who else is it gunna be?'

The two teenagers stood over the contorted figure of an unconscious 24 year old man and gave him a light kick in the ankle. Milton stirred just enough to convince them he was alive.

'Must have started drinking dead early today, it's only 9 o'clock'.

'Uhuh, shameful. Still, a mini-man like Milton only needs a couple of pints to get him rat-arsed.'

'One pint for a pint-sized bloke!'

'He-he-he!'

Milton stirred again, shifting uneasily against the roots of a thorny hedge. As his jacket slid open, a small plastic bag fell from the pocket onto the ground. Craigie picked it up, squeezing the contents and squinting in the poor light. Mick snatched the bag from Craigie's hand and peered at the brown block in the self-seal bag. He opened the plastic and stuck his nose in, taking a long deep sniff.

''Ere, you know what this is don't yer?'

'Hash, you berk. I ain't a moron!'

'Oh yeah. Shall we nick some and smoke it? My Dad has some tobacco and Rizlas we can roll up with.'

'Nah, makes me feel sick. I hate feeling sick.'

A back door into the village hall kitchen flew open and steam billowed out, along with a bright shard of light and the sound of cackling and moaning old women.

'It's no use, it can't be saved Lily, you've curdled your eggs. You'll just have to start it again.' squeaked one of the frail old ladies from the Women's Institute. There was a loud clattering and rattling noise as Lily emptied the cake mixture from the stainless steel bowl into the dustbin outside the kitchen door.

Craigie's face broke into a mischievous grin as he grabbed the hash bag from Mick and scuttled off towards the kitchen door.

'Oi! Wotcha doin'? We can't leave Milton like this'.

'Shhh! He ain't going nowhere. It ain't cold and it 'ent raining. We'll come back for him later.'

They stood close to the wall, watching the W.I. ladies

jostling each other for workspace and meddling with their competitors' cake entries behind their backs. Most had completed their masterpieces and were bragging and preening over the final touches of hand crafted sugar flowers or the smooth finish achieved on their icing, in between consuming huge quantities of tea and biscuits.

Ethel was behind schedule in baking a variety of delicious treats ready to sell on the W.I. cake stall at the Four Villages Fete the following day. She moved swiftly, with well-practised haste, between cutting the gingerbread dough to pouring the beaten eggs into the chocolate brownie mixture that was swirling around the bowl of the industrial food mixer.

There was a crashing noise and some grunting coming from the vestibule at the front of the hall, sending the old ladies into a frenzied state.

'Oh my goodness, it's a murderer! We'll all be killed!' shrieked Ethel, grabbing her weighty handbag as a weapon.

'Get a grip, Ethel.' Marge Henderson said, rolling up her sleeves and marching into the darkness of the hall, 'It aint gonna be any of us what gets murdered tonight!' The meek and the belligerent members of the W.I. each grabbed a kitchen implement and followed her to confront the intruder.

Craigie peered over the window ledge and squinted through the haze of flour and oven heat at an empty kitchen. There were three mixers still whirring and stirring, plus a number of bowls containing various creamy batters and mixes. Mick stared vacantly through the window, watching his friend dash in through the door, glance into each bowl and then crumble a little of the hash resin into the darkest of the mixtures, before scooting back out quickly.

Mick stood for a moment, his brain catching up with events, before running after Craigie, who was already striding at speed around the side of the hall towards the car park.

'Did yer put it all in?'

'Nah. I'll put a bit back in Milton's pocket or he'll think it's been nicked. The state he's in, he'll think he gave it away down the pub.'

By the time they reached the hall entrance, Marge Henderson was physically evicting Milton, who had woken up, staggered into the vestibule and mistaken a cupboard for a urinal. Marge and her W.I. ladies had caught their intruder peeing all over the mothers and toddlers painting pinafores.

'Don't worry, Mrs Henderson,' yelled Craigie, coming to her aid, 'we'll make sure he gets home safely.'

Craigie slid a supporting arm under Milton's elbow and slipped the remaining hash back into his coat pocket.

'Oh you are a good boy, Craigie. I'll be sure to mention it to your mother what a lamb you have been.'

★ ★ ★ ★ ★

Lily was the last to leave the village hall kitchen that night. After helping Ethel box up the cake stall goodies, she sent her home to put her feet up and volunteered herself to secure the building. The bell of a kitchen timer sounded, heralding the completion of her third attempt at baking a prize winning fruit cake. Nervously, she jabbed a skewer into its flanks, which drew out clean. It was done. She turned it out onto a cooling rack and noticed that all the dried fruit had sunk to the base of the cake – another failure. Taking her glasses off, she rubbed her eyes and sat for a moment. The thought of another humiliating year of her culinary attempts not even getting placed in the competition was too much to bear. Wearily, she boxed up her latest disaster and washed the few remaining items of kitchen equipment before locking up, loading the cake tins into her Morris Minor and beginning the short journey home.

Avoiding the pot holes in the lane from the village hall, Lily saw Big Mazzer swaying to and fro, trying to get her key into her front door lock. She stopped the car level with Mazzer's house, wound down the window and called to her. Mazzer spun around and promptly dropped her keys in a puddle. Her breath wafted into Lily's face, making the old woman choke.

'Good evening, Mazzer'.

'Ow do Lily!' she mocked, tugging her forelock and bowing exaggeratedly.

'Had a good night I see?'

'Why deny yoursen a bit o'fun gal? You don't know what you're missing!'

'I suppose you have already finished this year's entry into the competition?'

'Yep, all sorted and packed away'.

'Hmmm. Mazzer, I have a little business proposition for you. May I come in for a while?'

★ ★ ★ ★ ★

Jimmy Earlem, a tall wiry man with the dust from the last scaffolding job still in his hair, pulled on his laceless boots, and fired up the old truck. It skidded in the mud as he tried to reverse from the grass verge outside his mum's house. As his brother Donny clambered in the passenger side, the wheels bit and the truck lunged forward. 'Oi! Yer daft bugger. I ain't in yet,' he said, choking on his first cigarette of the day. 'Whose bloody silly idea was it to give up our Saturday to put up some poxy tent for the Fete anyhow?'

'Yer so public spirited ain't yer! We get a load o' free booze fer doin' it so stop yer whinge arsing,' Jimmy eloquently replied. 'Besides, it'll piss down all day an' you'll be glad of a beer tent.'

The Earlems swung the truck round past the swings and slide of the recreational ground without changing down from fourth gear, and barely missed an Irish Wolfhound that some toff had released to 'do its business' where the kiddies could pick up a nice lot of germs. The truck slowed to a halt with the grinding sound of worn brake shoes on metal. The local garage mechanic had laughed at the very same sound earlier in the week but Jimmy had put him straight, informing him that they had years of wear left. They laboured with their hangovers silently and telepathically with the grace and finesse of a 17 stone synchronised swimmer.

Clive arrived shortly after in his sparkling new Metro at a sensible pace. Wearing his usual royal blue waterproof, he began to pace across the grass towards the Earlems, but finding them throwing small sharp tools at each other to kill the boredom, he decided that a wave from a discreet distance would suffice, before returning to his pride and joy to carefully unload his eight man tent.

Every year since anyone was sober enough to remember,

it had rained on the annual Four Villages Fete and every year, Clive Gellert had pitched his eight man tent so that locals could view his photographic account of the village as it changed, or didn't change, with the years. While the unsuspecting grannies viewed, they eagerly and tirelessly repeated the adage, 'those were the days', and were treated to their annual grope from Clive's uncle, Bert Gellert, who was eighty if he was a day, his new bifocals giving him a whole new lease of life. Clive would wander around in his anorak taking the year's photos of the few villagers who had turned out despite the rain and the incomers taking over, to play on the Wheel of Fortune or hit the headmaster with a sponge. Within the hour, volunteers had arrived and were beginning to set up the stalls while keeping their fingers crossed that the heavens would not open for the umpteenth consecutive year.

Fat Shuggy's 'main man', Tony, was there deputising from the local pub. A decision greatly appreciated by the Fete attendees, as Fat Shuggy was a miserable, unpredictable, cirrhosed man whose idea of customer relations was to give you a clean glass if you were favoured. If you so much as dared to take your out-of-date crisps back and ask for a refund, he would bar you, then promptly forget the conversation through his alcoholic stupor.

On occasion, Shuggy would decide to take a holiday, alone of course, and for two whole weeks, profits would soar. Word would get round that Fat Shuggy had left the country and people from even the next parish would flock. Tony was the exact opposite. A potential nominee for a peace prize, his placid demeanour and easy smile provided a shield from the abuse Fat Shuggy spewed from every orifice. Despite his young years, Tony had the ability to diffuse any hazardous situation, laugh with the customers and keep the books straight. To add to this impossible list of achievements, Fat Shuggy trusted Tony, which is more than he ever did his wife. In the marquee, Tony had set up the barrels and the optics and had instructed the barmaid to serve the Earlems a well-earned early snifter.

It was sometime around 2 'o clock when the fete officially opened, and the chairman of the board of non-locals babbled something into the PA system, hired specially for the grand day. A smidgen of applause faintly echoed from the primary school walls but it was drowned out by the scramble into the beer tent. Big Mazzer could be heard above everyone as she barged and shouted. Old Alf Burrows was knocked flying by the rush, but Big Mazzer came to his rescue, picking him up by his meagre waist band and brushing the mud off his lapels.

'Yer wanna watch yerself, Alf, they're a mean bunch o' buggers. Flip yer over soon as look at yer, they will!' she chastised in a booming voice. She turned round in the confines of the marquee, which was already heaving, a manoeuvre which cleared a large enough space for both her and the tiny Alf to step to the front of the queue. No one attempted to argue with this six foot tall side of a barn, except Milton, a unicellular life form, so named because of his surname, Keynes. Milton would regularly pick fights with anyone he could focus on, and nine times out of ten he would take one swing, completely miss, and pass out on the floor.

Big Mazzer was in no mood for fighting on a day when she was trying to impress one of the band members, an unsuspecting accordion player from Leicester, so she put one hand on Milton's head and pushed him into a seat where he couldn't annoy anyone.

Fumes were wafting out of the joins in the tent flaps as the last of the local contingent squeezed in, just as the grey skies began to issue forth a heavy drizzle. Outside the marquee, tied up dogs and children alike began to whine as the drizzle built into big dewdrops and itched their noses, followed by yells of 'Shut yer chelpin'! It's only mislin' fer Christ's sake!' When these kind words of encouragement failed to arrest the moans, an ashtray of beer and a packet of nuts were pushed through the flaps. It was odds on whether the dogs or the children would get the peanuts.

Elsewhere, Lily, in her capacity as a professional complainer and bore, made a note of the address label on the band's instrument cases, just in case the music later was too loud/quiet/off key/inappropriate or all of the above before making her way to help Ethel. She had already congratulated herself on clearing Clive's Photographic Account Tent of the several grannies in there who were suffering Uncle Bert's advances rather than get their new perms wet in the rain. Even Bert wouldn't dare to grope up Lily. The village couldn't stand the repercussions.

★ ★ ★ ★ ★

A gang of W.I. husbands had collectively hired and raised the Adderstey Parish Women's Institute marquee and were tolerating the continuous prattle and criticisms from their exacting spouses within. The sallow light that penetrated the canvas gave everyone a sickly, pallid complexion and the damp seem to seep up the arthritic joints in their legs. Not even a pot of tea from their gargantuan urn could raise their spirits as they hung their cross-stitch pictures and mounted their crochet cushions on display.

Ethel busied herself setting up her cake stall while simultaneously listening to Lily's perpetual monologue of complaints. Craigie appeared on the scene, in his stonewashed drainpipe jeans and red ski jacket. Blond streaks in his mousy hair glowed surreally as he sauntered up to peruse the offerings on Ethel's cake stand. He clocked the dark chocolate brownies, the date and walnut cake and the double choc chip cupcakes and then turned around to see more dark coloured sponge cakes being unwrapped on the competition stand. He sidled casually back out of the tent and found Mick sitting on the playground swings.

'So?' Mick said impatiently. 'Did you figure out which cake has got the stuff in?'

'Hmmm, nah. There's a load of dark coloured cakes in there. It's gunna be harder than I thought.'

'Well, how many bowls did you put it in?'

'Four or five I reckon. I picked the mixes which looked the darkest, but all those cakes in the old biddy tent look bleedin' dark!'

'You said it'd be easy.'

'Yeah yeah, gimme a chance, I'll think of summut. Stay here.'

Craigie re-entered the marquee and made a point of examining the crafts on all the competition stands, stalling for time. He picked up entry cards and squinted at the exhibits which were furthest away and nodded sagely at the jams and preserves. Ethel stumbled behind him, almost dropping a Tupperware container of shortbread biscuits.

'Oh, Miss Loosely! Are you alright? Here, let me give you a hand.' Craigie seized the opportunity and grabbed the box, guiding her by the shoulder back to her stall. 'Good grief! You must have baked yourself to a standstill! There are so many delicious things here for sale.' He didn't give Ethel the chance to refuse his help, grabbing at the tins and serving plates and promptly unpacking the cupcakes.

'Use the tongs, young Craigie, not your dirty hands'.

He smiled angelically and continued to flit about in the hope she would be distracted enough for him to take a couple of the darkest cakes, but Ethel's eagle eyes missed nothing.

'Not there, dear, place the cake stand over here.'

He was beginning to lose faith in his plan until she offered to let him sample a cake of his choice to thank him for his help. He took a good look at the selection and concluded that there were no visible clues as to which of them had been doctored. He would have to choose randomly.

'Do you sample your cakes Miss Loosely?'

'Well, er… no, not really. I just stick to my recipes and hope for the best.'

She stopped what she was doing for a while to think about it, her nervous insecurities bubbling to the surface.

'Forgive me, Miss Loosely, but if you don't try them, how do you know if they taste nice?'

'Erm, well, I don't know. Oh goodness. Do they taste horrid then? People have been buying them from me for years. Perhaps I should, well, you know, try them… ' Ethel was flapping again like the canvas beer tent after everyone had enjoyed several helpings of Mazzer's three bean stew.

'If I eat one of each cake or biscuit I shall be sick. Not to mention the dent it will put into the profits for charity.'

'I see your point. You could sample some of them and then the rest next time you bake? How about we share them, then they won't go to waste?'

Ethel thought for a while. She got the feeling that she was being scammed out of free cakes, but couldn't understand why Craigie would need to. After all, his mother, Big Mazzer, made the best cakes in the district.

'Hmmm, let's see'. She broke open a cupcake, pulling the gooey fondant topping apart in gloopy strands and handing him the larger half. 'We can share one, and then I really must get on with my signs and open the stall.'

The moist chocolate sponge slipped down in no time at all, and Craigie crossed his fingers behind his back that she had chosen wisely and that in a short time, the dreary day would become a whole lot brighter.

★ ★ ★ ★ ★

Trev Cooper, a 37 year old leather clad biker, had left his mother Fubbit Cooper, in control of his enormous rottweiller, 'Lemmy', while he limbered up in the beer tent for an afternoon brawl. Fubbit, God only knows where the name came from, had used her Dentugrip and felt confident that her teeth would remain in place while she screamed at Lemmy for dragging her across the fete on her back and pinning small children in the play area.

Thunderous footsteps shook the sodden earth as the village's answer to Giant Haystacks made his way past the primary school. Lily's grandson, one of many, Beefy Underwood, had smelt the beer tent and was parched. Making a minor detour, he launched his hulking mass towards the kiddies play area.

'Stop it, Lemmy, bad boy, put the child down. Nanny's going to be very cross!' persisted Fubbit.

Beefy stepped up to Lemmy, picked him up by his collar with one hand and punched him out cold with the other. Lemmy's tongue lay limp on the ground, collecting mud while Fubbit chased after Beefy, wagging her finger and threatening to tell Wayne what he'd done to his precious dog.

'Shut yer bleedin' hole woman!' was the best you could hope for from Beefy and with that he barged into the beer tent, displacing several smaller locals in the process. Tony, being above average height, saw the people part before his eyes and a fist the size of dinner plates thud on the makeshift bar. He quickly poured Beefy a pint of his usual and settled him down.

Jimmy Earlem was feeling playful. He'd been drinking in the tent since before it had opened and now it was time for a little action. He slithered over to Beefy and muttered in his ear that Big Mazzer had been looking for him earlier in the day and was disappointed that he hadn't shown up earlier. In fact, Jimmy reckoned that Beefy was 'on a promise'. Beefy squirmed and guffawed in a cross between embarrassment and anticipation. Jimmy slapped his back as a final gesture of male bonding then sneaked quickly away to watch the results of his meddling.

★ ★ ★ ★ ★

Ethel's self-doubt rose again a little later that afternoon. Across the marquee, she watched her close friend Lily fussing over an impressively iced fruit cake, adjusting its decorative ribbon and checking the stability of its stand. Frowning, Ethel turned her attention back to her own work.

'The brownies are not selling too well today', she mused to herself, 'maybe I should try out one of those?' The thought was fleeting, the action immediate. 'That one tasted just fine. I wonder if the date and walnut cake is okay?'

Some W.I. husbands moved the heavy screens across the competition stands and the judges ushered the remaining women out of the area for their deliberations. By the time Lily brought a refreshing cup of tea over to Ethel's stall, she had 'sampled' a great many of her own cakes.

'Ethel dear, you have a smudge of chocolate on your chin'.

'Hmmm, you should try these Lily.' Ethel garbled through a mouthful of muffin, before shoving a lump of cake as big as your fist into Lily's face. 'It's rea-a-a-ally good!' She was spitting soggy globules everywhere.

'What on God's Earth has got into you woman?'

'Roll up, roll up! Come and try some of my delicious cakes! All for a jolly good cause!'

Clive Gellert entered the marquee and took his camera out from its protective polythene cover and started taking his snaps of the competition stands, a concession made by the judges who had almost completed their task. Satisfied that he had a full record of the winning entries before they were announced, he slipped past the screens and into the main area of the tent, which was set out like a café. Marge Henderson was in charge of the beverages that were supposed to wash down the cakes that customers purchased from Ethel.

'Hmmm, I never noticed Clive Gellert's bottom before,' pondered Ethel out loud. Lily stood transfixed, wondering if her friend had been body-snatched by an alien. 'Don't you think he has a lovely, pert little bum? Couldn't you just give it a big squeeze?'

Before Clive could even ask Marge for a cup of tea, Ethel had stripped off her apron and flung it at Lily, before dodging the tables and chairs, and scurried over to where Clive was queuing up. 'Take over for a while, won't you Lily my dear?'

'Have you been drinking woman?'

'Oh what a marvellous idea!' She grabbed a very perturbed Clive by the arm and gazed up at him. 'Be kind to an old lady, Clive, and escort me to the beer tent, won't you? I have a terrible thirst'. Sporting a 'rabbit-in-the-headlights' expression, the poor man was too shocked or too gentlemanly to refuse, and so Ethel lead him back out into the rain.

Mick and Craigie were hovering in the doorway, trying to decide which of the cakes to buy with the remaining money that Mick hadn't spent on cigarettes. They stepped sideways politely to allow Ma Earlem to enter the marquee before continuing their discussion.

'If you had just smoked the bleedin' stuff when we first got hold of it we wouldn't have had all this soddin' trouble!'

'I told you before, it makes me feel sick!'

'Look, you said you tried the cupcakes and nowt happened, yeah?'

'Yeah.'

'Then it's either the brownies or the date and walnut cake, cuz there ain't much else left what's brown!'

'How much cash we got between us?'

'Enough for one of each cake'.

Craigie and Mick purchased their cakes and retreated to the corner of the marquee and got themselves comfortable on the dry grassy floor.

Ma Earlem, who had overheard their entire conversation, quickly bought the rest of the brownies and the last of the date and walnut cake, with a view to getting her husband so stoned that he would be too wasted to make his usual Saturday night unwelcome advances towards her after closing time at the pub.

Mick wolfed down the entire piece of date and walnut cake before Craigie could stop him.

'You stupid arsehole! We were supposed to share it!'

'Yeah I know, you got the brownie, I got the date and walnut.'

'Jeeezus you are dumb. What if it's not in the brownie? We were supposed to share them both!'

The crackling P.A. system squealed into life, proclaiming that the winners of this year's competitions had been decided and requesting that interested parties should make their way to the W.I. marquee to hear them announce the results. The screens were drawn back and the judges stood in front of the competition stand, clipboards in hand, waiting for the crowd to gather around them. Clive had sprinted from the beer tent to capture the moment and was gradually making his way through the blue rinses and twin sets, closely followed by Ethel, who was still clutching a small sweet sherry in both hands.

The judges began with the prizes for the most original pickles and preserves and the best knitted 3D object, then the cushions and needlework. By the time they got to announce the baking contests, most of the ladies were tapping their feet and tut-tutting impatiently. Ethel stepped up to receive a highly commended award for her 'Black Forest Gateaux-style trifle' and had to have her sherry taken from her forcibly to enable her to take her prize.

'And now the contest for which you have all been waiting, the Best Iced Fruit Cake Award goes to entry number 151, which was beautifully crafted by… ' The judge looked down her clipboard list to the name next to the number. 'Um, and the winner is… Lily Underwood!'

There was a stunned silence for a second too long then a feint smattering of mistimed applause.

'Oh my goodness!' Lily exclaimed, 'well I never did! Thank you so much.'

Clive stepped forward to take Lily's photograph as she accepted the award from the judge with a handshake. He focussed the lens, told them to say cheese and clicked just as Ethel shot up to pinch his pert bottom, making him jump like a vasectomy outpatient on a space hopper.

'Miss Loosely! Do you mind?'

'Not one bit, Ducky,' she replied with a wink. There was a general hubbub and murmuring that grew louder until Marge Henderson piped up.

'Didn't Big Mazzer enter this year then?

Her question was met with further murmurs and shrugs. 'Hey Craigie!' Marge beckoned him over to them. 'Why didn't your mum enter the competition this year?'

Craigie looked directly at Lily and smiled.

'How would I know? It's not as though I was with her while she baked till the early hours of the morning, now is it? He tilted his head to one side as he said it. Lily's mouth fell open in realisation. He was still staring directly in her eyes as he passed her shoulder on his way back to Mick in the corner, who, in Craigie's absence, had helped himself to the chocolate brownie and was lying on the grass whistling Kylie's 'I should be so lucky'.

'I'll be seeing you soon Mrs Underwood.'

★ ★ ★ ★ ★

Big Mazzer returned from 'having a slash' in the primary school loos, smoothed down her tousled locks and readjusted her workman's cleavage so a little less of her bum was displayed. Beefy also smoothed down his tufts of hair and readjusted his crotch to a more comfortable position. All this was timed to coincide with the band's performance. Mazzer planned to make lustful looks and jeers at the accordion player from Leicester, and win him over, whereupon she would probably sling him over her shoulder and drag him to her place while her husband, Mad Patrick, was away from home.

It was Donny Earlem's turn to play the little tinker. Lighting up his 56th cigarette of the day and still coughing, this picture of health, wove between the raised elbows, holding his breath to beat their wafts of body odour, to reach a small cluster of geriatric bikers, whose greying crew cuts glistened in the artificial light. 'Wayne', nodded Donny.

'Ay-up, Don mate,' Wayne sniffed, trying to look mean. Donny could remember quite clearly Wayne's first day at school, when he had been too scared to ask the teacher if he could go to the toilet before assembly and so halfway through, the whole school was treated to wailing screams and tears as the class made fun of the boy who wet his pants on his first day. Donny, even now, had to stifle a cackle as he thought about the spectacular height this man had reached.

The band tuned up nervously as Mazzer took up her prime position at the front, blocking the views of at least four other people. Beefy stubbed out his fag, hitched up his jeans and made his way up to her. The bikers had formed a mean semicircle to the left of Mazzer and Donny lit the touch paper.

'So Wayne, I hear Beefy laid out your dog,' Donny sniggered as the band struck up with the introduction to 'Delilah'. The veins started to bulge on the side of Wayne's forehead as he turned to enlist the help of his biker mates. Beefy made a lunge for Mazzer, who had been wolf whistling the accordion player. He tried standing on tiptoe to reach her mouth, but she clapped one hand over his face and shoved him away, straight into Wayne's fiery friends.

The old and experienced placed their cigarettes in their mouths and a hand both sides of their beer glasses and strolled out of the marquee and towards Clive's Photographic Account Tent. Those graced with little or no sense became embroiled in the most impressive fight the village had seen for donkey's years. Noses that had been broken were realigned, knuckles were shattered on Beefy's jaw and the delicate sound of tearing leather filled the atmosphere. A few minutes later, Beefy was seen crawling along the ground looking for the rest of his pint, Alf was making his way to the pub in time for last orders, Wayne and his chums were laying in a heap with Lemmy, Jimmy and Donny could be seen sitting on the primary school fence throwing empty beer bottles at each other and the accordion player was running for his life.

Lily Underwood was the only one left, standing over Beefy, for once, silent with disgust. She grabbed hold of one bleeding ear and pulled him moaning to his feet.

'Shane, you're a bitter disappointment to this family.' She screeched with a tear in her eye, 'You'll end up just like your father,' and with that The Four Villages Fete drew once more to a close, complete with its photographic record for posterity.

CHAPTER 2

June

Superstud

The grubby windows of the kitchen were just visible behind the mountain of crockery that balanced precariously in the sink waiting to be scrubbed.

'Bucket!' Dunny yelled to his precious daughter, hacking up his lungs, 'Ave you fed them chickens yet?!' As he regained control over his mucus linings, his son Notch wandered in.

'She ain't here Dad. She went up Nan's fer a fag.'

Dunny was lying in an arm chair square in front of the 1970's TV with his forerunner to the remote control, a seven foot bamboo cane balanced between his gout ridden toes, which he used to change channels and hit small children with. Yesterday's gravy, swathed in body odour, adorned his greying vest, and his even greyer Y-fronts poked through the broken zip of his jeans. He was a short, beer gut on legs with the collective sense of a small shoal of amoeba, almost pleasant when sober and a total incoherent psychopath after sniffing the barman's apron. His nickname, 'Dunny' was acquired after a particularly heavy drinking bout when he slipped and got wedged under the gents' urinals and was extracted kicking and screaming after last orders. Even then, while he could barely co-ordinate his legs to walk, he boasted his prowess at fist fighting and offered to take on half a dozen of the rescuers. The name stuck simply because his real name, Marvin, reduced even the most po-faced to fits of laughter.

The Underwood Family gene pool was not fairly or evenly distributed. It could be argued that a group of chimpanzees would possess more intellect and beauty than the Underwood household, but as it was, Notch acquired the greatest part of the meagre rations of intelligence and, as for beauty, let's settle for rugged. Notch developed his athletic ability from an early age, dodging the blows from his father and elder brothers while they raged over possession of the last can of beer in the fridge. He could also be seen vaulting the stacked paving slabs, Cortina axles and broken chest freezers in their back garden, trying to escape a good beating from his current girlfriend, who had undoubtedly discovered his penchant for anybody's younger sister.

Notch was the second youngest of the family. Bucket, the only daughter, was the last hurrah for this less than idyllic family. As Notch carefully combed his hair in the remaining shards of mirror hanging near the door-frame, Bucket shuffled in and punched him in the arm.

'Aaaharr, cow!' Notch exclaimed, 'Wha were that for?'

'Fer nicking me last fag yer git!' she said, in her finest, daintiest tones. 'I 'ad to go up Nan's fer one coz I ain't got any money iver'.

Bucket had the basis for a very good figure but little justice was done to it by clomping around hunched over with a thunderous scowl and a cigarette dangling limply from her lips.

Dunny whined feebly again about the chickens, then jabbed the cane into a TV button to change to the news. Dunny had reached an unfamiliar era in his life where the balance of power was subtly changing. As master of a house full of small children, he could terrify his offspring into submission. Housework and garden chores could be shared under his strict supervision, pocket money could be indefinitely withheld and severe punishments could be administered under general anaesthetic, namely Ruddles County with a Jack Daniels chaser.

After many years of Dunny's tyranny, the young Underwoods noticed several trends to his behaviour which could be manipulated, under Notch's guidance, to their advantage. Dunny would rant and rave about the serious and the banal than slam the door and drive off at speed to find a pub in which he had not yet been barred. On his return he would find all of his offspring vanished and none of the chores done. A short time later he would pass out in front of the TV and the morning would begin the pattern again.

Dunny had been following this routine for so long, he had not noticed the two eldest boys, Ewan and Beefy growing to gigantic proportions. One day, during one of Dunny's rages, he had hit Ewan clean in the face with little or no provocation. Without flinching Ewan, who by this time was six foot and built like their outdoor privvy, picked Dunny up and slung him down the stairs. Both sons stepped casually over him and out of the front door, leaving Dunny to clear up his own blood.

This afternoon was much the like any other Saturday. All the kids busied themselves in their various pursuits. Ewan was off courting his first cousin Alma; Beefy sat in the pub garden counting the hairs on the palms of his hands; Notch went up to the Big House to help the youngest daughter with some creative haymaking in her daddy's stable and Bucket sat and scraped the stubble from her legs with an instrument akin to a scythe.

It was a couple of weeks after the Four Villages Fete brawl and, thanks to most of the participants having the memory capacities of goldfish, things were immediately forgotten and back to as normal as the village ever got. Dunny had heard on the grape vine that Fat Shuggy, the landlord at the local pub, had gone on holiday and The Bull was now open all day. As a mark of respect for such an auspicious occasion, Dunny had a bath and put on a clean shirt. The day was so hot and humid that within half an hour, large sweat stains were growing beneath his arms and down his back. He wet his hand under the tap and smeared the few strands of hair he had left growing from his left ear over his bald head. Oozing sensuality, he picked up his car keys, kicked the cat out of his way and swaggered over to his car.

★ ★ ★ ★ ★

'And smile once more for me please, Mrs Underwood, very good, that's a nice one' the photographer from the local town newspaper said, winding the film on his camera forward before starting to dismantle the flash and reflective umbrella.

Lily's cheeks flushed as red as her Yardley's lipstick as the lady reporter read back to her the list of achievements and activities that she was involved with in the village.

'Let's see, apart from the W.I. events, you are the Sunday School teacher, you arrange flowers and clean for the church, have become a governor at the Primary School, are involved in the amateur dramatics, are a long standing Parish Councillor and now a prize winning baker of cakes. Good grief, Mrs Underwood, you seem to be on a one woman crusade!' The reporter took a deep breath. 'Are there family members who can help you with all these things?'

'Well, both my son and my daughter live on this estate and I have six grandchildren. You missed my granddaughter just a while ago, she wanted to borrow a fag… ahem, she um, came to see if I was ok, such a thoughtful girl.' Lily corrected, remembering that Bucket was only fourteen and was supposed to be giving up smoking.

'So, Mrs Underwood'

'Call me Lily, dear, please.'

'OK Lily, where did you get your recipe for that amazing winning fruit cake from? Is it something handed down through the generations or was it something you just cooked up?'

'Yes it was um, my mother's recipe'. She glanced furtively towards something moving past the front window.

'And is there a secret ingredient? I managed to taste some at the fete. How did you get it so moist and sweet without being cloying?'

'Umm, it's well, it's a secret.' The shadow passed across the window again, and it seemed to be wearing a baseball cap.

'Awww, come on, Lily, please tell me?'

'It's um,' the baseball cap stopped and rose to reveal Craigie's grinning face peering through the open window.

'Grated carrot, isn't it Mrs Underwood?' Craigie leaned right in and squinted till his eyes readjusted from the bright sunshine in the garden to the comparative gloom of Lily's sitting room.

Craigie wandered around to the side of Lily's house, let himself in through the back door and strolled into her sitting room.

'Oh, is this one of your grandsons?' The reporter enquired innocently.

'No it's a, um, local lad who helps me around the garden sometimes.' Lily beckoned him in, trying desperately to hide her displeasure. 'Shall I make more tea? Craigie, you'll lend a hand, won't you?'

He shrugged at the reporter and followed the old lady back into the kitchen.

'What's got you all rattled? Guilty conscience by any chance?'

'What are you doing here?'

'It's time we had a little chat about your new found culinary expertise, I reckon.'

Lily pondered for a while, assessing the likelihood of escaping from her web of lies unscathed.

'I have no idea what you are talking about boy. Go and bother someone else!'

'Hmm, and I thought you might be an honourable old biddy too.' He shook his head, disappointed. 'I was prepared for you to come clean and give my mother the recognition she deserves.'

'I'm sorry, I really have no idea… ' He cut her sentence short.

'I was with her when she made that cake. There is no denying she should have won the competition.'

'Ah, well, um. Your mother and I had an arrangement and I will thank you to say no more about it.' She hissed in hush tones.

'I'm sure that nice reporter would love to hear about the 'arrangement' you made with my mother'

Lily sighed. There was no wriggle room.

'How much?'

'A tenner for now.'

'A tenner? I am a pensioner! I can't afford that!'

'Don't give me the 'poor old grandma' routine. Everyone knows your old man was loaded before you nagged him to death. I need a tenner to get me roots done. Mind you, you look like you could do with another blue rinse an' all love.' She glared at him then rummaged in her bag for her purse. Thrusting the ten pound note into his hand, she warned him that it was a one off payment or she would have to tell his mother that he was a twisted little blackmailer. Craigie watched the old woman warm the pot before adding three spoons of tea leaves from a caddy and an extra one for the pot. She unwrapped a parcel of Ethel's white chocolate and raspberry cookies, laid them neatly on a plate and Craigie carried the tray into the sitting room. Lily thanked him for his help and suggested he hurry home to his mother, who would be worried about him. He declined, with a wry smile, announcing that he would take her up on her kind offer of tea.

'Are these biscuits your creation too?' the reporter asked, scooping one up and munching on it eagerly. 'They are delicious!'

'Aren't they Miss Loosely's speciality biscuits, Mrs Underwood?' Craigie was stirring again.

'Er, yes. Yes they are. She is a tireless fundraiser and bakes them for charity. The least I can do is support her by buying them from her.' Lily glanced back at Craigie smugly.

'My editor is very keen to promote the country living section of the paper and has asked me to offer you a weekly column in *The Herald*. He has even thought of the title, 'Just like Granny used to Bake'. What do you say?'

'Oh no, I don't think I would have time for anything like that dear.' Lily fidgeted in her chair.

'Go on, Mrs Underwood,' Craigie goaded. 'The whole county ought to share in your amazing talents.' A derisive snort escaped involuntarily, making the reporter frown at him, perplexed.

'It's just with all my other commitments, and besides, I haven't got a typewriter even.'

'You wouldn't need to type anything, Mrs Underwood. You must have notes, recipes jotted down and such-like, you simply select one per week and telephone it through to our copyist. She will type as you read it out.'

'Would Mrs Underwood get paid for her column?'

'Of course, young man, we can't expect her to divulge her secrets for nothing!'

Craigie's mind figured 50 percent of something was better than 100 percent of nothing.

'Come on, Mrs Underwood,' Craigie urged, 'You MUST have your incredible recipes noted down somewhere, just like my mother has… '

There was a long pause and some oddly furtive glances

between the old woman and the boy, followed by him nodding his head exaggeratedly.

'Um, can I think about it?'

'Yes, certainly. But don't leave it too long or my boss might offer the column to another.'

A short time later, Craigie and Lily stood respectfully by the side of the road, waving goodbye to the reporter and photographer as they turned the top corner of Wesley Drive in their Ford Cortina and disappeared. The air had turned still and humid and the sun was finally beginning to dip low in the sky. Lily turned savagely to the youth.

'How dare you come round here and threaten me like that!'

'Hey! You are the one committing fraud, lady! Don't be giving me none of that 'holier than thou' crap either. Look, let's not be enemies, Mrs Underwood. I think we can do very nicely out of this if we work together as partners…' Taking her by the arm, he led her back into the kitchen to discuss his proposal.

★ ★ ★ ★ ★

At the pub, it was like the parting of the Red Sea. Instantly recognisable on entry, Dunny's arrival sent folks scampering away into inglenooks even the landlord was not familiar with. A thriving bar could be bankrupted in a matter of days in the presence of this infamous character. Tony was managing The Bull in Shuggy's absence and was very experienced at dealing with this difficult character. Detecting imminent trouble, he swung an unsuspecting trainee bar girl around by her apron strings to face Dunny's leers. Dunny licked his lips, rattled the fried bacon out of his false teeth in approval and grabbed the girl's hand. She shrieked but was frozen to the spot.

'Hello my dear,' he gushed as he kissed her hand, 'and what's your name then?' She pulled her hand away and ran off to scrub it with some Dettol.

Tony sighed, fixed his best grin and went to serve Dunny the first of his innumerable pints and to listen to the interminable list of achievements that he would boast about. His favourite was the day he threw up on Harold Wilson's feet whilst being AWOL from the Navy. Dunny had been there for a number of hours without picking a fight with any of the brave or foolhardy locals that remained in the bar, probably because it was early summer and his thoughts were of love, or lust at the very least.

The barmaid was plucking up courage to leave the safety of the bar to retrieve some glasses, but with tom cat instincts Dunny was at her side trying to impress her. With admirable strength of will she made her way undaunted around the pub collecting empties and cleaning ashtrays, followed by a lascivious lump of lard pirouetting around her, tangling his UPVC grey loafers in every barstool that lay in his path. When it came to the end of her shift, the barmaid jumped into her car, sped home, ransacked the bathroom cabinet for a handful of her mother's Valium and carefully considered Voluntary Service Overseas.

His ego a little bruised at this rejection, he declared that 'she must be one of them 'Lezzies'' to Tony with a wink and wandered from the bar to the lounge in a huff. Through the gaps in the stone walls either side of the fireplace, the remains

of a large buffet was laid out. Spilled white wine wrinkled
the red paper tablecloth and tore it into ragged holes beneath
the foil platters. Dunny was drawn by the sausages on sticks
and tripped clumsily up the quarry tile steps to investigate.
Standing awkwardly, he grasped his crotch and yanked at the
material to release his discomfort before leaning on the table
and grabbing a handful of triangular cut ham sandwiches that
were curling at the corners.

Some of the youths sitting at the furthest end of the long
table froze, trying to blend in with their surroundings. He
made a lunge for a cheese vol-au-vent and slowly they
shuffled along the banquet benches and hid behind a floral
arrangement. By this time, Dunny had moved onto drinking
rum. Throwing the last of the mahogany liquid down his
throat, he looked about him for anything else that he could
scavenge and spied a half full bottle of house white next to
the birthday cake.

The statuesque daughter of the village's big house,
Araminta, paused mid-sentence, leaving her drooling
entourage of young admirers transfixed. She briefly scanned
the room for Notch Underwood, who was nowhere to be
seen, then took a deep breath before striding confidently on
her Italian heels towards the embarrassing gate crasher and
relieving him of the bottle of wine as it moved perilously
close to his nicotine stained mouth.

'Oi!' He focussed on the Amazonian beauty towering
above him in her jade silk dress, which clung in all the right
places, and was stunned into silence. The vapours from his
Brut aftershave stung her eyes and violated her taste buds,
and taking a deliberate step backwards, she attempted to

cautiously charm him out of the pub lounge and away from her best friend's birthday party.

'Mr Underwood,' she smiled politely, a half smile employing no more than the corners of her mouth. Any other such smile might be misinterpreted as allurement. 'Are you a friend of Jocelyn? Were you invited to this party?'

'Eh?' Dunny was staring directly at her cleavage.

'Mr Underwood, it really isn't the done thing you know, helping yourself to other people's food and drink.'

Dunny heard a garbled sentence that reminded him of his ex-wife when she would find him laying paralytic on the kitchen floor with one hand in a box of cereal and the other down his Y-fronts. He turned back to the buffet and scooped up a few strawberries that were decorating the cake.

'There is plenty to entertain you in the bar area, Mr Underwood. I hear they are planning a darts tournament in there. Wouldn't you prefer...?' she persisted, but Dunny had spotted his son Notch, who had returned from the gents and was ensconcing himself in the snug with a small group of teenage girls.

'Whoa, Notch my boy!' He bellowed, and pushing Araminta aside, he stumbled down the snug steps towards them.

Notch squirmed uneasily as his father attempted to perch on the end of the bench next to the birthday girl. One buttock connected with her lap and she screeched just as Dunny regained his balance.

'Hotch up then girl!' he demanded, threatening to sit entirely on her knees. She moved rapidly then looked imploringly at Notch to rescue her. Popping another strawberry into his mouth, he masticated slowly, making stomach churning slavering noises.

'These could do wiv a spot of cream,' he leered. 'Do you girls like a bit o'cream?' He cackled bawdily.

'Dad! Don't!' Notch pleaded.

'Wha'?' He held another strawberry by its stalk and dangled it above his tilted face and then tickled the end of the fruit suggestively with the tip of his tongue. Raising his eyebrow at the young lady beside him, he asked if she would like his last strawberry. She declined vigorously, her face contorted in disgust, her hand covering her mouth as if she were about to be sick.

There was a moment of quiet, Notch and the girls horrified and struck dumb by his performance. Finally noticing their distress, he dropped the fruit and took the delicate hand of the young lady by his side in his. He was surprisingly gentle and calm, his lewd persona put to one side as he twisted his body to face her, deep sadness in his eyes.

'Do I embarrass you, little lady? Do I? I really didn't mean to upset you, honestly.'

She held her arm rigid, fearful of what he might do next. As his grip loosened she quickly pulled her hand away defensively. 'You don't want an old fart like me around, do you?' The girl shook her head briskly.

The bell was rung, last orders bellowed and all the empties were loaded into the dishwasher behind the bar. Dunny climbed into the front seat of his silver Granada, which was so far reclined that he could easily have had root canal work done while driving. In the sultry and oppressive darkness, with only one headlamp working, the car made its own way home instinctively.

Neighbours surrounding Dunny's house were all in bed, listless in the heat, windows wide. All that could be heard for miles around was Dunny's numerous attempts to reverse his car between his battered gateposts and into his drive. After three more attempts and the loss of his left tail light, he gave up and left the car on his lawn, then dragged himself through the obstacle course at the rear of his estate to shut the hen house up. On his return, he slipped and fell face down in the mud, filling his nostrils with grass, corn and chicken excrement. Undeterred, but an inestimable time later, Dunny found himself in his bedroom. His thoughts fixated on amour, he switched on his illegal band CB with one hand and extracted hen food from his orifices with the other. A regular user of the device, Dunny hoped he might catch a caller that he had managed to strike up an interesting conversation with earlier in the week. He tuned the radio into a channel he knew that she used and began the ritual of asking who might be out on the airwaves.

'One four for a copy, one four for a copy.' The CB crackled and hissed. 'One four for a copy, one four for a copy. Anyone got their ears on tonight?'

More static on the line, but he thought he could hear a muffled response. He heaved himself up from his bed and increased the volume. Sweat poured down his neck and saturated his collar. Dunny threw open the windows, fumbled with his shirt buttons and sank back down on his unmade bed. He lay down, positioning his sore feet carefully, then holding down the handset button he tried calling again, before promptly passing out.

'Superstud?!' said the CB, 'are you still there Superstud?' she persisted. 'It's your 'Fallen Angel'! Talk to me Superstud!' Her words echoed around the street and into the residents' houses. Initially, they were amused, each coming to their bedroom windows to hear the commotion more clearly, but Dunny's new 'handle' soon grew old and infuriating when Fallen Angel and her girl friends continued to party over the airwaves at full volume.

Two doors down, a young couple were trying to pacify their children and dogs as the dulcet tones of Fallen Angel continued trying to rouse a drunken Superstud. Helen, who had only achieved three hours sleep in the past 48 hours nursing their baby through colic, burst into tears. Her husband, Peter, tried in vain to comfort her, but his efforts failed to assuage the sobs from Helen, the moans from his children and the howls from the two mongrels.

'I'm going to call the Police,' Peter stated calmly.

'Don't be silly,' sobbed Helen, 'They won't come out to noise pollution.' His mind set, he pulled on his jeans and trainers and thought how best to tackle the problem.

Peter kissed his wife and then crept down the stairs and out of the front door. It was only a short walk to the village phone box and the place was utterly deserted. With only the welfare of his family on his mind, he grabbed the receiver and dialled 999.

'Fire, Ambulance or Police?' said the operator in nasal tones.

'Police, please,' Peter breathed.

'And what is the emergency, sir?'

'There is such a racket at number 6 Wesley Drive,

Adderstey, I think someone is being murdered!' He rushed the sentenced to feign an urgent and concerned air.

'Can I take your name please sir?'

'I'm not getting involved!' He squealed and slammed down the phone. Even at speed, it took 15 minutes to drive out from the town, so Peter strolled back home, taking in the sweet air on his way.

Peter was just climbing the stairs, removing items of clothing as he walked, when he heard the low grumbling purr of a Rover squad car driving past Dunnys' house. Helen and Peter stood in the darkness looking out of the open window as the squad car turned around and parked.

'How did you manage it?' whispered Helen.

'Tell yer later!' He smiled and pecked her cheek affectionately. Helen could see the curtains twitch in the houses opposite as the whole street watched the proceedings.

The two officers climbed out of the squad car, adjusted their caps and, frowning to give the impression of authority, swaggered through Dunny's gate and up to the front door. They tapped lightly at first, but no response was forthcoming. Helen chuckled as she watched the officers lose their patience and begin to kick at the door, their loud thuds accompanying the calls from 'Fallen Angel' and her friends.

'Come on Superstud!' snarled the officer, as he pounded viciously on the bowing door, 'get your lazy arse out of bed!' The police were close to kicking the door down when Notch appeared from around the corner, dishevelled and pulling straw from his hair. Zipping his fly up, he walked towards them cautiously.

'Something wrong officers?'

'You could say that,' the younger of the officers said sarcastically, resting his hands on his hips in an impatient gesture. 'You live here son?'

'Um, yeah, I do. I guess you would like to speak with my father?'

'Uhuh, that's if Casanova can spare us a moment of his time,' the elder officer muttered.

Notch produced a Yale key and allowed them to enter the hallway first. They mounted the stairs and into the offender's bedroom. A nauseating mixture of odours from unwashed bed sheets and vomit made the hardened officers wince and retch but one of them bravely approached the bed. Dunny's pale protruding stomach rose like a beluga whale cresting the waves before diving back beneath the sheet with each slow and noisy breath.

'What's yer dad's name, son?'

'Marvin Underwood.' Notch grinned and backed out of the room. Turning on his heels, he could see his sister had opened her bedroom door a tiny sliver so she could peer across the landing at the commotion.

'Mr Underwood!' the mature officer said loudly. 'Mr Underwood, wake up!' He leaned over the bed and rattled Dunny's shoulder. Dunny stirred, moaned in his sleep and farted.

'Eurrgghh, gross. I'm not paid enough,' the younger one said. Dunny's swollen and purplish toe took on a garish glow in the light of the street lamp outside his window. Unable to rouse the comatose reveller, the elder officer took off his cap and used it to take a hefty swipe at the malodorous and diseased foot.

Dunny screamed in agony and shot vertically out of his bed as though he had been harpooned by Poseidon's trident. Literally hopping mad, he tried to focus his bleary rum soaked eyes and saw the black uniforms trying to grab his arms to steady him.

'Get off me, who the bleeding hell do you think you are? Get out of my fucking bedroom you trespassing bastards!'

'Calm down, Mr Underwood! You are in violation of... '

Dunny's arms were flailing around as he tried to square up to them, his grunts alternating with whimpers each time his foot connected with the floor.

'You really don't want to be doing that, Mr Underwood, just turn off the CB radio... '

'Get out of my house!' The younger officer moved towards the CB and tried to locate the power button. 'That's my property, don't touch that you... ' Dunny staggered forward and threw an ineffectual punch at the baby-faced constable, knocking his hat off his head and folding his ear backwards. The Sergeant grabbed Dunny's flabby arms, holding them firmly behind his back before pushing him face down onto his sweaty bed.

'Shut that infernal racket off constable.' The young officer replaced his hat and disconnected the CB radio, silencing 'Fallen Angel' and her gang for good.

'Sarge, this is an illegal band radio, shall I bag it up and confiscate it?'

The sergeant nodded, then addressed the perpetrator, whose muffled groans were getting fainter with pain and exhaustion.

'This is the situation, Mr Underwood. You have an

illegal device causing noise pollution and making you very antisocial in a residential area. You have attacked a member of the police force after we were invited into your home by your son. By rights I should arrest you now and take you to the cells, but frankly you stink and I don't want you puking in the squad car.' More muffled moans. 'Consequently, we are taking the radio and we will send you the time and date in the post that you will appear for your formal caution – and make sure you have a bath before you come.' He released Dunny's arms, allowing him to fall sprawled across the divan, and made his way back out of the room following the constable. Looking back at the pitiful sight, he couldn't help a parting shot; 'Time to hang up your G-string and retire, Superstud!'

The residents of Wesley Drive breathed a sigh of relief and clambered back into their beds as silence fell once more on the airless summer night.

★ ★ ★ ★ ★

Craigie cleaned up the last of the empties from the tables at The Bull and stacked them in the dishwasher. It was later than usual as Tony had struggled to expel the remaining drinkers, who were taking advantage of Shuggy's absence and Tony's good nature and had spent half an hour trying to persuade him to agree to a series of 'Lock ins' after hours. Craigie bid his farewells to Tony and left via the car park entrance, taking deep gulps of smoke-free air on his moonlit walk home. He turned the corner of the jetty leading to the Village Hall and stopped in his tracks, seeing his mother draped awkwardly over a man bearing no resemblance what-so-ever to his father.

Sighing, he sat out of sight on a neighbour's doorstep and waited for his mother to fumble with her keys and then fumble with the man before scrambling up the stairs, dragging the chap to her marital bed. He watched the light in her front bedroom go on briefly then off again. He waited a few minutes more then let himself into the house. Bawdy giggles and creaking floor boards assured him that it he would not be disturbed as he dragged the step stool over to the kitchen shelves and reached high for his mother's ring binder containing all her personal recipes, collected over her many years of training and professional cooking.

Producing a notebook from his back pocket and a blunt pencil from the 'odds and sods' drawer beneath the counter, he leafed through her handwritten notes and recipes, jotting some of them down in the notebook to sell to Lily. Turning towards the back of her folder he was drawn to a clear plastic wallet containing white and brown envelopes. He was familiar with this kind of mail, envelopes with sinister little windows at the front and warnings stamped in red next to the stamp. His heart sank. Closer inspection confirmed his fears that his mother had not paid any of the utility bills and was in arrears on the mortgage again. The bank's letter was very curt in reply to her request for additional time to pay the debts as their kindness had been prevailed upon for too long already. They very much regretted to inform her that unless she made at least their suggested contribution and discussed payment plans and terms that they would be forced to foreclose on her mortgage by the end of July.

Craigie cradled his head in his hands and choked back the bile rising in his throat. For all his bluster and bravado, the sum total of all his childhood insecurities rose and overwhelmed him and he sank sobbing to the floor. The relentless noise of worn bedsprings gradually diminished from above and was replaced with loud echoing snores, which he recognised as belonging to his mother. He lay on the kitchen floor for more than an hour, the chill from the tiles cooling his salt stained cheek. Staring vacantly, his empty head started to fill with nebulous thoughts, each one taking an ethereal form that rushed before his glazed eyes. The bailiffs arriving to take their TV and furniture, his mother spending their last remaining pounds on cigarettes and booze and the ridicule he would suffer at school when he was finally taken into care. Mental and physical exhaustion carried him into sleep around 2am. He woke with a start when his mother's folder slipped and fell from the work surface and dug into his hip, corner first. The metal clasps securing the pages cracked open and spilled the contents across his body.

Craigie moaned, more from surprise than pain, peeling his face off the floor tiles and twisting himself till he sat upright. Momentary bewilderment gave way to the memory of why he was on the kitchen floor in the early hours of a summer's morning. He began gathering up Mazzer's recipe pages and threading them back onto the metal rings, hoping that they had not been filed in some specific order. The plastic wallet of menacing threats he secured carefully at the back and, flicking the pages in reverse order, he spotted some drawings and notes scribbled on the back of some of the recipes. Head cocked to one side, he peered at the faint pencil

41

scrawl and concluded that the notes and labels surrounding the diagrams were not in his mother's handwriting, but still vaguely familiar. It looked old, like the style of writing you see next to sepia print photographs from the turn of the century, swirling script that was difficult for him to decipher. It showed a large metal container like a tea urn drawn carefully with its capacity noted in gallons, connected to a series of tubes and glass pipes that appeared to run through a bath containing iced water. A heating element was fixed beneath the urn and there was a series of temperatures circled in Fahrenheit next to a diagram of a thermometer. Below the drawing was a recipe, but it didn't look like anything his mother would have cooked: for one, the main ingredient was potato peelings.

CHAPTER 3

July

Guffner's Demise

The forensics van drove up Wesley Drive and parked on the top corner obstructing the traffic. Valerie was scrubbing the specks of dust from the shiny roof of the little red Nissan in her pink shorts, which rode up her behind and exposed enough cellulite to make even a plastic surgeon weep. The heat from the tarmac refracted the light and disturbed the vision of the children as they persisted in their game of kerby. Their premature frowns and grazed knees eclipsed in the excitement of their first week of the summer holidays. In a week or two they would be kicking cans around the pavement and complaining to all adults who would listen, of boredom. For now they were content to bounce a slightly deflated basketball at a kerb, just inches from Valerie's car. Normally she would move the children on to a less sensitive area, such as outside old Pa Earlem's place, but today there were more important things to do. She watched as white suited men hoisted a steel trolley from the rear of their van, mounted the kerb and dragged it towards the house on the corner opposite her home. By this time, the children had deemed the van and its contents far more interesting than kerby and were bearing down on the trolley wheelers.

'Oi! Mister!' one yelled, 'Wotcha got in there?'

'Bugger off! Nosey bleedin' kids.' One of the men in grey overalls swept a butch arm across the chest of the larger kid, pushing him aside.

Valerie pulled the wedgy out from between her buttocks and leaned on the back doors of the white van, peering in.

'Madam, this is police business! Kindly step aside and let us get on with it!' he said in more courteous tones than he used to the children as he ushered her away from the area.

'Do tell me what's happening! I am the Neighbourhood Watch Co-ordinator, I have a right to be informed!' Valerie persisted, the last sentence being shrieked as she paced backwards in response to the man's slow, advancing steps. A few moments later the curtains of the house where the trolley had disappeared into were being drawn and a loud, deep, incessant barking began. The two men who had entered the house were now vacating the premises at speed, followed closely by a large grinning German Shepherd dog. The first man was fast and shut the gate behind him, the second man was just vaulting the fence when Rex sank his teeth into the man's Doctor Martin's boot, bringing him cascading to the floor. Cecil, a World War II veteran of some considerable proportions, appeared in the doorway and growled something incoherent at Rex. Panting in the heat, the dog slunk away, leaving the man to examine the shards of rubber dangling from his boot. Eventually, the Scene of Crime Officers wheeled the black zipped up body bag into the white van. With little or no ceremony, the corpse of Eileen Brown, alias Guffner, was driven away for examination. Guffner's husband stood unshaken and unmoved in his pristine attire, watching the police to-ing and fro-ing about his home in their own detached fashion.

★ ★ ★ ★ ★

Craigie sat on the middle green at the top of Wesley Drive, leaning his back against the sycamore tree trunk, watching the spectacle unfurling at the Browns'. His interest in proceedings waned rapidly as his thoughts drew back once more to the discovery of his mother's repeated financial catastrophes. From his cross-legged seat on the grass, Craigie was able to see virtually all the houses on the estate, from Dunny's place at the bottom of the Drive, round past the Earlem's in the far corner and back to Lily's house, adjacent to Valerie's pink frilly home. Pulling out the sheets of notepaper containing this week's crop of recipes, harvested from his mother's personal file, he briefly contemplated asking Lily for a greater share of the profit made from selling the recipes to the local newspaper, but it was pin money compared to the amount needed to clear his mother's debts. Pot washing and clearing up at the pub was all the work he could legitimately get till he turned eighteen and that barely covered his own expenses. There had to be another way to get more money. He peeled his baseball cap off his head and used the sleeves of his T shirt to wipe away the sweat that had built up from the hat band. Scratching at the thunder flies in his hair, he watched as Bert Gellert shuffled down the pavement, away from a visit with Pa Earlem, clutching a brace of pheasants swinging from their tied feet. One of the pheasants was big and fat with scruffy plumage and bald patches, the second was smaller with curiously pale feathers and its throttled tongue lolling from its beak. Craigie reflected wistfully on how his mother's and his own fate might look very similar in the coming months if neither of them acted upon it.

'Craigie.'

'Hello Uncle Bert.'

'Chin up boy, you look like a wet weekend in Scunthorpe!'

Bert hobbled across the road to where Craigie sat and struggled to his knees beside him.

'What's up with yer leg, Unc?'

'Ah um yeah, I sort of fell out of a window'

Craigie looked scornfully at the old man.

'Have you been sniffing round Mrs Longfield again?' The dapper old man grinned mischievously.

'Jed came back from The Bull earlier than anticipated. Got me laces caught in the trellis under her bedroom window. Fell down the last few feet.'

'Well it serves you right, you dirty old man!' Craigie shook his head with feigned disgust.

Bert laid down the pheasants and shuffled around till his back was against Craigie's tree.

'Quite a view you got here'

'Uhuh, they carted her body off about 10 minutes ago. Dunno why they are still ferreting about in the house though.' Bert nodded slowly.

'A bit fishy then.'

'Uhuh.'

★ ★ ★ ★ ★

Cecil and Eileen had met by chance one night in the local town some 50 years ago, when the world was gripped by an impoverished state of panic and patriotism. Hitler had assembled his men in Poland and France and the Allied Troops were in a frenzy to get married off before being isolated from sanity in a transit camp on the South Coast. Just before these young men could risk their lives for a tireless bureaucrat in London, they were allowed a weekend's leave. Cecil, having no family to call his own, spent his leave on a stag night in the very town where Guffner and Fubbit Stanley were revelling.

'So many uniforms and so little time,' Guffner thought, as she and her sister paraded up and down the bar, their tea stained legs and crooked pencil lines smearing with each splash of beer. Neither girl was a reputed beauty of the region but both sported ample bosom and shapely thighs and, provided they kept their mouths closed, they could be considered a catch. Such were the times when a young squaddie had few hopes of returning alive, let alone a hero, that it was a must to at least declare an intention of marriage, if only to get your leg over before facing Jerry.

Cecil was a proud, forthright young man, who rarely got drunk and thought that loss of self-control was an unpardonable sin. His slow paced sips of real ale could never leave him wanting for un-slurred words or the ability to walk in a straight line. His friends, or rather acquaintances, for few people ever really knew Cecil well enough to consider him a friend, thought that his pompous self-righteous attitude ought to be excused for the evening. With each round of real ale, the Bridegroom's drink was not the only one being regularly spiked with gin.

In a new, but not unpleasant state, Cecil spied a raven haired beauty singing by the piano. Her voice, like gravel on a washboard, came to him as light and melodious, her tinkling laugh rattled the horse brasses off the walls and her sunken eyes wept with every lewd joke her sister regaled her with. In an unprecedented move Cecil, deprived of his good sense, wove his way over to her. He stood next to her in silence, puffed out his chest and smiled a lazy grin. Guffner and her sister were just finishing the final chorus of 'White Cliffs of Dover' as her hand reached over to the top of the piano where a line of cherry brandies sat – gifts from each squaddie to prolong their performance. She downed a drink, put the glass back in line and turned to Cecil.

'Got a request, luvvie?' she smiled, showing the gaps where teeth once lived. Cecil grabbed her and kissed her deeply without much of a fight. The bar was a seething mass of laughter and calls of 'Wey Hey lad! Give 'er one for me!' his acquaintances, the loudest of all.

She shoved him gently away. 'Oh you saucy beast you!' she declared, pushing her Marcel Wave back in place before grabbing him again for an encore. That night, unbeknown to him, Cecil had sealed his fate. He left Guffner early the next day, but not before she had secured a postal address of the transit camp in Sussex where he would be posted for a few weeks. Her letters to him were met with groans of despair as he recalled the morning he awoke next to something akin to Godzilla.

Within a few weeks Guffner declared a suspicion of impending parenthood and urged a response in favour of marriage. Being a basically decent man he applied for compassionate leave and took the train to her town. As he walked the five miles from the station to Guffner's home he felt the evil grip of doom cast a shadow about him. His only hope was a heroic death in battle.

Just two weeks after the wedding, while Cecil was stationed in Cairo, he received a letter informing him of the false alarm. Part of him was incensed at the injustice, while another part was relieved that Guffner's genes would not be passed on. With such a fate awaiting him in Adderstey on his return, Cecil threw himself into his duties, determined that he would be the perfect soldier. He took on kami-kazi like missions and braved the most arduous conditions. He regularly turned down leave and wrote to Guffner with fabricated excuses that denied his return.

'The Army is such a cruel, evil beast!' she told all her friends and relatives.

On a particularly dull day in Cairo, where no newsworthy events took place, Cecil was ordered to drive a wagon loaded with medicine and first aid equipment to an encampment south of the city. It was a normal enough journey with no special detours and a route that was so well used as to be considered safe. His friend, Wilbur, was to accompany him on his journey.

Near the final leg of their journey, Wilbur was baiting Cecil and his prudish opinions with a flash or two of a porn magazine he had purchased in Cairo. Cecil wavered from the main drag of the road a little and swerved near the verge, directly across a landmine. Wilbur had been killed immediately. Cecil spent the next year in a convalescent home in Leicestershire, learning how to walk on a wooden leg. It was hopeless. Cecil had no chance of escaping Guffner. The Front would have been more preferable to a life with one leg and Guffner's nagging.

In the few years that Cecil had been away, Guffner had grown into a wizened prune of a creature without an ounce of compassion. Cecil's untimely return to the country had put a halt to her unstinting war efforts with the remaining farm hands and unsuspecting Americans. She had selflessly devoted her time to the raising of morale. Once the war pension had kicked in, Guffner had insisted on the white picket fence, new car and any other luxury his money would run to. Rather ironically, the laws of nature decreed that Guffner could not have children and with each passing year they both grew more bitter and twisted, hating everything that dared to cross their paths.

To reduce their contact time and the number of occasions during the day they were required to speak civilly to one another, they kept a series of pets. As each passed away, from a lack of will to live in their presence, Cecil bought a more vicious breed of dog to intimidate potential callers and any small children who dared to pass by. Rex was the latest and obviously most vicious and nasty of all, except Guffner.

★ ★ ★ ★ ★

'So what's got your goat then boy?' Craigie's Great Uncle Bert enquired.

'Mum's in trouble again.'

'Money or the old bill?'

'Money.'

'Right. That's a bugger.'

'Uhuh.'

Bert fished in his pocket for his tobacco pouch and pipe and began the ritual of cleaning out the bowl and refilling it.

'I guess I could write to Dad at the oil rig and ask him to send more money or come home and help us,' Craigie said desperately. He had no liking for his unpredictable and occasionally violent father, but desperate times called for desperate measures.

'That what your mother told you? Your Dad's away on the rigs?' He scraped his penknife deep into the sooty recess of the pipe, scouring it clean.

'Ain't he then?' Craigie scowled, one eye closed against the shaft of sunlight penetrating the sycamore's canopy.

'No he en't boy. Unless Parkhurst's in the middle of the North Sea.'

★ ★ ★ ★ ★

The police took their time rummaging through cabinets and cupboards and asking a myriad of intimate questions, searching for anything untoward. Cecil effected shock with the skill of a Shakespearean actor, even bringing himself to the point of tears. He heartily shook the inspector's hand as he left and saw the police to the gate. Cecil watched the squad car turn at the bottom of the road before he limped back to the house.

Across the street, Valerie was busy in verbal combat with Lily Underwood. They were stunned into silence after they observed Cecil draw his curtains wide, fling open all the windows and turn his stereo on full blast.

'Well I never!' squealed Lily, almost drowned out by the noise of a Radio One bubblehead introducing the next song.

★ ★ ★ ★ ★

'This is certainly a lively location, boy! Better viewing than *Coronation Street* I reckon!' The old man sat puffing away on his Digger Flake, nudging his great nephew in the arm animatedly. Craigie's elbow slipped off his raised knee, making him drop the papers containing his mother's stolen recipes. One of the sheets flipped over before landing on the grass beyond his feet. There was that drawing again, the one with tiny notes in the margin of temperatures and water baths and peculiarly coiled metal devices. Bert glanced down at the pages strewn on the cracked earth and scooped up the sheet with the complex diagram. Turning it upright and thinking for a moment, he chuckled.

'Gunna start yer own bootleg business young Craigie, eh?'

'What do you mean?'

'Shine, lad. Potcheen, liquor, hooch, call it what you will.'

'You mean Moonshine?'

'God, you're slow to catch on boy. What do yer reckon I mean? You're the one with the recipe and instructions to make a still!'

'I am?'

'Bleedin' 'ell. Don't they teach you young 'uns anything

at that fancy school of yourn? I'd best get these birds gutted and plucked or they'll start stinking up the place.'

Bert leaned heavily against the tree trunk to haul himself upright. Craigie jumped to his feet and started after the old man.

'Wait, Uncle Bert. Can you teach me? I mean, can you um, help me?'

Bert swung around to face the boy and glared, dipping his chin to his chest.

'Ain't it bad enough for your mother to have your father in the clink, without you trying to join him there?'

'I reckon the coppers around here have enough on their plates without noticing the likes of you or me, don't you?' Craigie raised his arm, waving a gesture towards the strange carryings on before them.

★ ★ ★ ★ ★

The women watched with baited breath as Cecil appeared on his doorstep carrying a large bundle of ladies clothes and limped decisively into his back garden, followed closely by the alsation.

Valerie, who knew nothing of tact or decorum, grabbed Mindy, their deaf Jack Russell, by the collar, hooked her onto a lead and dragged the poor dog with bulging eyes and tongue distended with the strain, past Cecil's house and down the footpath which ran adjacent to his long garden. Just a thin length of chain link fencing prevented Rex from gobbling up Mindy in one bite, his fur so high on end Rex could have joined the Sex Pistols on tour.

Despite her thighs chaffing with every stride, Valerie could walk surprisingly quickly. She slowed her pace to view the goings on through the gaps in the hedge, where Rex was on guard, but could only hear a crackling sound above the perpetual noise of Cecil's stereo. Rex was bordering on psychotic, dashing to each gap in the hedge, snarling, barking and shoving his hulking mass against the flimsy chain link fencing that surrounded Cecil's garden. Mindy ran, choking on her lead and pulling her owner towards the comparative safety of the recreational ground at the end of the footpath. It was not long before Valerie noticed the thick black smoke billowing up into the clear blue skies behind her. On closer examination she found a chuckling Cecil, fuelling the fire with forks full of Guffner's clothes and other belongings. Cecil wiped the sweat from his brow with his hankie and settled on a garden chair to sup the remains of his pint of real ale. Next to him, on a small bench, lay Guffner's makeup bag, her best friend to the very end, which Cecil tossed into the flames with great joy.

Valerie ran as fast as her flip-flops could carry her, back to her house to ponder on the next course of action. She tripped up the step on entering her garden, Mindy's lead tangling around her ankles, throttling her slowly. Valerie was helped to her feet by a passing neighbour of Amazonian strength and stature. Despite Valerie's girth, she was relatively small and easy to lift. This man mountain, or rather woman mountain, a much more likable version of Valerie. All that knew her said that Marge Henderson was a nosy old cow, but her heart was in the right place.

Marge pumped Valerie for any intelligence on Guffner's

demise. Valerie brimmed with pride as they stared at the black clouds of smoke filling the sky.

''T ent right , is it?'

'Yer right Val, it ent! He oughta be locked up. 'An' that dog 'an all!' With no further information to be gained, Marge stomped up the road, the pavement cracking with each step.

Marge was collecting the village tote money, a charitable raffle in aid of the village hall repairs fund. This monthly collection afforded her the vehicle with which to claim the title of grand master of the village grapevine. After her meeting with Valerie, Marge decided on a circuitous route and headed post haste to Fubbit Cooper, née Stanley's house at the top of Wesley Drive.

Fubbit's house, in correct mourning procedure for her dear departed sister, was in darkness, the curtains drawn. Out of respect for his aunt, Wayne had stopped revving up his motorbike and locked up Lemmy, the Rottwieller, in the barn. Lemmy heard Marge's footsteps and reared up at the window barking wildly.

'DOWN BOY!' bellowed Marge. Lemmy, silenced, rolled over in submission. He had never been the same dog since the village fete and his encounter with Beefy.

'Coo-ee,' called Marge, like a signature tune.

'Come in Marge,' said Wayne with due respect, 'Mum'll be in 'ere in a bit!'

Taking advantage of the situation, Marge sat quickly at the kitchen table, awaiting the offer of a cuppa. Wayne already had the teapot in his hand and was too slow witted to think of an excuse to be rid of Marge. Skinhead biker aside, Wayne was dragged up with country manners and so he offered politely.

Fubbit, who had a fascination with amateur dramatics, gushed in wearing what looked like Victorian mourning clothes. Seeing Marge, Fubbit raised her lace hankie up to her eye and snivelled. Marge felt a sudden pang of remorse and jumped up to give her a bone-crushing hug, while Fubbit sobbed her dry tears. Wayne dutifully placed a plate of Hobnobs on the table along with the tea things and went to join Lemmy in the barn.

After the obligatory words of sympathy, Fubbit poured the tea and stuffed her face with Hobnobs, while Marge updated her on the latest gossip. When Marge had finished informing Fubbit of the disposal of Guffner's possessions, a genuine tear began to well up. Fubbit swallowed hard and poured another cup in gratitude to Marge.

'So wha' do yer reckon of it Fubbit?' Marge asked indelicately.

'I reckon 'ees done away wiv 'er!' Fubbit whimpered.

'You can't be serious gel! Why would ee?' said a stunned Marge.

''Coz 'ee had 'er insured fer a small fortune! AND, AND he never liked 'er iver.' The snivelling had given way to anger. 'It were about 'er 50th Birfday, when Guffner 'ad that bad do wiv 'er heart.' She explained. 'While Guffner lay in hospital, staring death in the face, Cecil was arranging life insurance. He said that 'eed 'ad 'em both covered at the same time, just to be sure, but you can bet your arse that her premiums were larger than his!'

'Did she always have a bad heart?' persisted Marge, who was trained in interrogation by the KGB.

'Well, after the 'eart attack that time they put 'er on these pills which cured 'er but then she 'ad summut wrong wiv 'er fyroid gland. They gave 'er pills fer that 'an all. I reckon he thought she wouldn't make old bones and were counting on 'er popping off sooner. Still, we'll find out if the git's dun 'er in at the inquest!' Fubbit was still ramming Hobnobs in her mouth and wet crumbs were flying out and ricocheting off the table as she spoke.

'If yer want, Fub,' said Marge hopefully, 'I'll come wiv yer to the inquest.'

'Oh that is good of yer Marge, fanks,' and with that Fubbit lapsed into her well rehearsed hysterics.

★ ★ ★ ★ ★

The following morning, Craigie rose early and went to call on his Uncle Bert. It had taken a lot of persuading to get Bert on board with his venture, especially as it would take a quiet, unobserved location and a lot of hard graft to set it all up, not to mention a constant supply of water, electricity and ingredients to keep the still running. After a sleepless night of fretting and worrying, Craigie had solved the problem just as dawn broke at 4.30 that morning. Assuring his uncle of the perfect location, he dragged the old man from his breakfast table, up the main road and out of the village, branching left at the first copse to the Old Folks' Home, where his mother worked as a catering manager.

'Oh you're not serious, Craigie! Not here!'

'Why ever not? The grounds man has retired and they en't replaced him yet. His barns are perfect for the job. He's got a workshop, water, leccy, tools, the lot. He's even got a telly and a sofa to have a kip on at lunchtimes. Well, knowing him, he probably kipped most of the day away and I can get all the spud peelings we can carry from the potato peeler in the scullery. It's the dog's bollocks, Unc!'

'And how do we explain our constant visits to the place, eh?'

'Well, I thought of that. I'm always up and around here to see mum, so no one will bother about me. You could either say you are thinking of applying for the ground keeper's job or you could be visiting one of your old crusty mates up here!' Craigie's cheeky grin reappeared for the first time in days. Bert clipped him around the head lightly, and then rubbed his stubbly chin for a while, pondering the possibilities. He sure could do with some extra money. His pension simply didn't stretch as far as it used to and the odd luxury wouldn't go amiss.

'Show me this sofa you mentioned and I'll think on it.'

★ ★ ★ ★ ★

The long stretch of blistering days and clammy nights broke with a series of spectacular thunderstorms, drenching the parched earth and felling the power cables, plunging the village into darkness. Bert lit a candle and placed it on a table next to the sofa in his newly acquired workshop. Donning his coat, he nipped out into the torrential rain and wrestled his soaking bicycle into the workshop for the night. 'Ent no way I'm gonna ride home in that!' he said to himself, before bedding down for the night.

It turned out that enquiring about the ground keeper's

job with the Manager was enough of an interview to secure the part time position. After this fortuitous piece of luck, neither Bert nor Craigie had rested on their laurels and so they had begun to gather the materials necessary to forge their still.

It had rained persistently for several days in the lead up to the inquest, which was attended only by police, medical experts, Cecil and Fubbit's entourage and the Judge, who heard the evidence from the inspector that had arrived at the scene first. His report was detailed and thorough and included a description of the shock suffered by Cecil.

The coroner's report was next, from a wild haired and disorganised man, who kept losing his train of thought and asking for prompts from the counsel regarding which question he was attempting to answer. The court clerk provided him with a copy of the document and he read out the summary of blood toxicity and cause of death.

Next up to give his statement was Cecil, in an immaculate grey suit with a black arm band of mourning. On his jacket lapel, he wore the coloured strip denoting all the medals he was awarded during the last war. Cecil stood tall and well groomed in the courtroom and with a wavering voice he described the routines which Guffner had followed for the last 20 years or more.

Cecil explained how Guffner had been taking a balance of heart and thyroid pills since she had been diagnosed in her fifties. He emphasised how upset he had been during her stay in hospital and how he had gone to great lengths to ensure that his beloved wife had not over-exerted herself from that day on. He was questioned on his motives for taking out insurance policies immediately after her diagnosis, despite the large premiums that were set by the insurance company. Cecil had clearly rehearsed his answer. He told the courtroom that her spell in hospital had made him face his own mortality and he suddenly realised that if anything were to happen to him, Guffner would not be provided for or looked after in her ill health. At this point, he managed a slight break in his voice and a pause long enough to compose himself. He said that together they had discussed their situation and both had agreed to make financial provision if the worst happened. The judge was assuaged by the supporting documents that stated a similar financial pay out would have been afforded to Guffner if Cecil had died first.

Cecil continued to tell the court his well rehearsed story, being very frugal with facts and neglecting to mention that he had encouraged Guffner to partake of a small nightcap in her cup of tea to aid a restful sleep. He also failed to inform the court that it was he who prepared the nightcap and the pills that she would swallow every night before sleeping. Guffner had stopped taking notice of the colour or number or the frequent changes to her medication, but Cecil monitored them closely. The label dictated that two white pills and one pink pill were to be taken twice a day. Cecil would deliver the tray with her tablets already laid out for her, supplemented by an additional pink pill from an older prescription. Cecil also failed to declare the odd extra pill dissolved in her nightcap. After the evidence from the medical examiner, the verdict was declared – death by accidental overdose of prescription drugs. Fubbit's sobs and wails could be heard echoing throughout the wooden panelled courtroom as the case was closed.

★ ★ ★ ★ ★

Craigie rose early, and with new found entrepreneurial spirit, pulled on his orange cagoule and scurried towards the workshop, dodging puddles as best he could. Finding the door unlocked, he entered cautiously to be confronted by two steaming feet clad in grey woollen socks with a big toe protruding through a hole in one of them. A blanket covered the body attached to those feet, but it failed to muffle the trumpeting bottom or contain the over powering stench.

The still in the opposite corner of the room was silent and the heat which drove the process, extinguished. Pop bottles of all different shapes and sizes were lined up in a row at the edge of the room. Craigie reached down and selected the bottle with the widest neck. Unscrewing the cap, he dipped his finger into the clear liquid and withdrew it. The liquor coated his index finger in a syrupy death grip. Stealing himself for the worst, he took a deep breath and sunk the finger into his mouth.

As the thick liquid made contact with his tongue, instantaneous burning triggered a reflex gagging and eye watering cough which startled Uncle Bert into consciousness.

'Jeezus Christ Boy! That's too raw to drink!' Bert did his best to leap to Craigie's rescue, arthritis permitting. 'That's fit for nowt but paint stripping.' He snatched the bottle from his nephew's shaking hand. 'That were the first attempt. I did another batch late last night'. Bert gestured towards an open cardboard box, the bottle tops just visible over the top of the sofa. 'It ought to be left to stand a while, take the edge off like. It's strong enough to put Jed Longfield on his arse with one swig.'

Wiping involuntary tears away with the back of his hand Craigie finally found his voice.

'How will we know if it's fit to drink? I mean, we don't want to blind or kill anyone.'

'I followed the instructions very carefully and didn't let the temperature vary one bit. It won't be poisonous or owt, just a bit um… strong.'

Bert put the kettle on and scooped two spoons of leaves from the caddy into a teapot. Craigie sat down heavily on the sofa and sighed. 'I don't wanna hospitalise anyone, Unc, an' if it tastes rank no one'll buy it either.'

'Yeah I know. Wha'd yer reckon on letting the old folks have a couple of samples?'

Craigie's mouth dropped open.

'On their meds? You are kidding, right? They're barking enough as it is!'

'Precisely! At least they have nurses to hand if anything goes um… pear shaped, and if they are more barking mad than usual, they'll blame the weather for stirring them up.'

'We can't let 'em drink it neat, Unc, it'd kill them.'

'Uhuh, but they could splash a drop or two into their afternoon tea to pep it up a bit.' Bert winked.

'They do have their Saturday sing-a-long this afternoon.'

'Right then, I'll go and see my mate Ted a bit later then.'

They supped their tea in silence, apprehension growing thick in the air.

★ ★ ★ ★ ★

The sun broke through the black clouds around 3pm and beat down onto the steaming wet surfaces. The birds sang out their relief and gobbled up the rising worms on the lawns of the Old Folks' Home as Big Mazzer wheeled the afternoon tea trolley into the conservatory. Cream cakes, scones with homemade plum jam, lemonade, orange biscuits and little triangular sandwiches were carefully laid out on a long table at the side of the dining hall. Small puddles of spilled tea pooled on the oilskin tablecloth, as a porter slammed down 2 large teapots full to the brim, before shoving the upright piano over the threshold of the dining hall and into the conservatory.

Craigie, feeling guilty about Uncle Bert's plan, volunteered to help his mother with the catering, an act which made her deeply suspicious, but not so much that she declined his offer to assist. Uncle Bert loitered outside clipping a box hedge by the patio, just within earshot of the open French windows. A large teak grandfather clock chimed a short echoing ding at the stroke of 3.30pm as the antiquated lift shuddered to a halt in the foyer, delivering its first load of rheumatic octogenarians. Each held onto things of great importance; Beryl – her handbag, Stan – his Zimmer frame, Maureen – her hairpiece and Frank – his flies, as they shuffled towards the buffet table. By the time they had filled their plates with food, the second load had alighted from the elevator and a few of the more able bodied hobbled down the staircase to join them.

Within half an hour, most of the old timers were assembled in their favoured seats, the frail wheelchair bound were positioned near to the French windows, while those more fleet footed amongst them, sat huddled in little groups, pushing the high backed wing chairs into exclusive clusters so they could gossip behind the backs of others.

Uncle Bert's good friend Ted offered to wheel the tea trolley around the room and serve teas and coffees from the giant pots. With his back towards the staff, Ted was able to shield his hip flask from view as he poured small splashes of the moonshine into cups of those who consented.

'Wha'do yer say Beryl?' Ted wiggled his flask in front of her, 'It'll put hairs on yer chest.'

'Go on then,' she giggled, 'I've got hairs everywhere else so it won't make a lot of difference.'

'Good on yer gal. What about you Maud? Fancy a little snifter? We could have a bit of a boogie later on an' all if yer up for it?' Ted winked.

'Awww give over, you smarmy git!' Maud said, lifting her outstretched cup towards his flask.

One of the porters began playing the same old tunes as every other Saturday, with the manager trying hard to start the singing off, without much success. Before long, Ted had been relieved of his flask, which was being passed surreptitiously between residents who were eagerly doctoring their own drinks and tucking into the cakes and puddings with gusto. Some of the old biddies started cackling at Stan's rude jokes and Frank did an impression of an alien possession by squelching green jelly out of his mouth between his dentures. One of the nurses smacked his wrists like a child and scolded him, to which the entire group of residents fell about in raucous laughter. Frank guffawed so fiercely that he spat his green false teeth out and they landed in Maureen's wig making everyone cackle and splutter even more.

'Ooooh, I can't remember the last time I had such a good laugh!' Frank remarked, 'Warms the cockles of yer heart!'

'And yer legs. I reckon I just pee'd meself again!' Maud said, her incontinence pants leaking their heavy load.

Frank tried to extract his teeth from Maureen's hairpiece but managed to knock it off centre, sparking a row which the porters had to break up. Out in the conservatory, Arthur was cramming his sixth chocolate éclair into his mouth before the nurses remembered his diabetes and tried to wrestle it from him, shooting splattered cream on the best party clothes of everyone nearby.

A short time later, the ambulance crew arrived, wheeling the steel trolley through the foyer and past the stairs where two old cronies were necking like teenagers. The old woman was fumbling with Stan's zipper, trying to shove her hand inside his trousers.

Stan pulled away from her incessant kissing for a moment and said, 'You're flogging a dead 'orse there gal, ent been any signs of life down there for years, but I admire your spirit!' Then he re-engaged for more tonsil hockey.

Craigie groaned audibly at the sight of the paramedics giving Arthur a shot of insulin and wandered outside to find his uncle.

'It's a bleedin' disaster, Unc!'

'Ah, wait and see. No one died did they?'

They turned round at the sound of someone shouting from the French doors of the conservatory. It was Ted, beckoning them towards him as he strode across the patio.

'Hey Bert… the boys wanna know if you've got anymore hooch stashed, and if so how much?'

Bert and Craigie grinned and nodded triumphantly.

'Oh, and the old gals mentioned any possibility of you getting hold of 'Ethel's Happy Cakes'? I was told that Craigie would understand what I meant?' Ted looked bemused at Craigie's astonished expression.

'Um… Yes, I'll er… See what I can do!'

★ ★ ★ ★ ★

The news of Guffner's inquest sent shockwaves through the village of Adderstey and the surrounding areas. The post office and the bus stop were buzzing with excitement and disbelief as the gossip passed from one wife to another. Suspicions were heightened still, when just a week after the verdict a 'for sale' sign appeared on Cecil's house, a new car was parked outside and Rex disappeared after a trip to the vets. To add to this, Cecil was seen in the town, arm in arm, with a blousy peroxide blonde of fulsome figure.

Cecil moved to a large modern bungalow on the outskirts of the village with his new 'companion' and a hefty sum in the bank. Few locals acknowledged his presence or behaved any differently towards him than before. He was a mean, rude, miserly man before Guffner's death and people always routed for the honour of the local, even Guffner.

Cecil was seen purchasing many new and expensive gifts and toys, such as his music centre and large sit-on mower to assist his gardener with the half acre lawn to the side of his bungalow. He was even spotted, by Valerie as it happens, in a travel agent, booking a cruise to somewhere Valerie could not pronounce.

On the day Cecil and his companion were to set off on their cruise, Cecil was knocked down by a Guiness lorry as he crossed the main road to post a letter. His death was prolonged and painful and his stay in hospital was attended by none. His funeral was a short and uncomplicated affair, arranged by the solicitors who were handling the distribution of Cecil's new found wealth to distant relations Cecil had always despised. One small bunch of hand-picked flowers was laid at his graveside, from Father Bruce the vicar, who pitied everyone.

CHAPTER 4

August

The Telethon

Tony had finished straightening up the books, Maeve had finished bottling up, Fat Shuggy had coughed up a lung and half his liver and it was time for the Bull to open for the lunch trade. Just five minutes after opening, the local farmers would arrive in their tractors and diggers, park them in the car park and order a vast lunch to sustain them in the fields till darkness.

Tony had been working at the Bull for two years and it was chiefly down to him that takings remained constant, for when Tony was not working, Shuggy would take umbrage at all his clientele and bar everyone in sight – so far as he could see that is. The Bull was an important focal point for the village, especially for the male work force. The pub had recently been refurbished, which initially alarmed locals and attracted incomers and foreigners alike. When it had been completed, it was soon apparent that the bar had retained the spit and sawdust decor that folks were proud of and it was the lounge which sported the red dralon upholstery and pictures of hunting, shooting an' a fishing. Non-locals did not dare to enter the bar but instead huddled in the lounge for protection, after all there was safety in numbers.

Shuggy would always serve the incomers, being one himself, as he could not cope with the sharp tongues or wits of the likes of Big Mazzer and Jimmy Earlem. Tony would invariably serve at both bars while Shuggy slunk off to bolster himself with a couple of port and brandies to wash down his prescription drugs.

It was mid August and the grass of the chapel lawns was parched and brown and large cracks were appearing in the packed clay soil. Never content with the weather, the farmers filed in, chucked their hats on the bar and moaned about the lack of rain to fill out the grain. Tony supplied their drinks and placed their lunch orders in the kitchen.

Old Jed Longfield entered, his footsteps accompanied by a few bars of 'Oh Rose Marie', one of three songs that Jed would regularly wail as he pranced around the bar. He was a big man who would back down from no-one except his formidable wife, Esme. Esme had inherited two large farms within the parish from her father. They spawned two children, both boys, who grew up to fear and respect their mother and laugh and drink with their father. Jed was a friendly man with a cheery disposition and a big red nose. He often shouted the bar drinks and ran a tab for himself and his boys which always ran into hundreds of pounds by the end of the month. As three very valuable clients, Shuggy avoided contact with the Longfields to assure their custom.

Like most sons in the district, they both had the measure of their father, who could be swindled out of large sums of money to pay off insurance claims and police fines. Larger possessions, such as old farm cottages belonging to Esme, could be won on the turn of a single hand at poker – a game at which Jed was notably poor. Such easy wealth enabled them to continue in their eccentricities unchallenged.

The younger son, who had stopped at the village post office on his way to the village pub, was tracing a finger across the text of the town newspaper as he read out loud to his brother.

'The – in – depend – ent – television – station – will – be – holding – the – greatest – 24 – hour – char – ity – event. People – are – needed – to – under – take – fund – raising – efforts.'

'Those adult literacy classes are paying off,' thought Steven, listening to his brother Rueben read.

Esme had insisted on naming Rueben, when he was born, after an old boyfriend she had tried to elope with. Unfortunately for the original Rueben, Esme had dropped him while trying to carry him down a ladder one night. His amnesia was found to be incurable when Rueben realised the advantages of not remembering who Esme was. Jed was less fortunate in that he was brought up in a bungalow.

Jed was just starting up the next round of 'You're a star' when Big Mazzer walked in, wiping her cuff beneath her nose.

'Wha'd hoe Tone,' she exclaimed, 'just a pint of bitter, ta. I gottoo work up the old folks' home sarter-noon. I wanna keep a clear 'ead.' Mazzer downed half the pint in one slurp and shuffled over towards Rueben and the newspaper. Mazzer was quite well educated by village standards and was a superb cook. Mazzer was content to heat up vats of baked beans and slop them over thick toast for the mad folk up at the home. Surprisingly enough, most of those elderly at the home were imports from other districts. Adderstey adhered to the principals of care in the community and left their own mad people to their own devices. What did it matter if old Fred Reilly wanted to flush his teeth down the loo or walk naked down the street at midnight? Who was he harming anyhow?

'Let – the – Echo – know – if – you – have – any – events – to – be – publi – publicised!'

Rueben finished with a satisfied sigh. Steven, his older and broader brother, gave him a slap on the back.

'Wha' were that?' Mazzer said, her moustache hairs mingling with the froth from the beer.

'Fund raising event,' said Steven assuredly. 'Might even get on TV! So the paper says'.

'I always wanted to be on telly. What can we do?' she fidgeted.

'I aint doin' no sponsored run, Steve,' said Rueben anxiously.

'Yer wanna do summut yer good at lads,' said Tony, smirking, 'like drinking!' He said it in jest, but from the vacant expression on all their faces he knew that it was a definite possibility. Tony thought he heard a customer in the other bar and ran off before he could be dragged into any disastrous schemes.

Rueben's eyes twinkled. 'Can we Steve, eh?'

'It 'ud cost us more than we'd raise, yer daft sod!' said the voice of reason.

'Not if yer did a sponsored pub crawl,' Mazzer boomed, 'and yer can collect money in buckets on way round an all.' The idea was there and they were willing. All they required was someone to organise it and a few more volunteers.

Looking around them, there was no shortage of well qualified amateur and professional drinkers, but Mazzer decided that they should all be young and handsome to get the punters to part with their cash. That narrowed the field somewhat.

'Tony my sweet!' Mazzer called through to the lounge. A shudder racked his very spine, but Tony skipped sprightly through to the bar in response.

'You know how you're the most 'andsomest bloke this side o' the Nene?' she cooed. Tony had to agree or Mazzer might have snogged him into submission.

'That were easy,' she crowed, 'who's next?' There was only old Jed and Alf Burrows in the bar, along with a couple so old that their wrinkles masked their faces from recognition.

They sat at the bar for a further hour, or as long as it took for Jed to stop singing and stuff his face with roast beef and Yorkshire pud, and there they agreed their targets. They had a couple more drinks to christen the idea, then the Longfields returned to their tractors and Mazzer hopped in her Reliant Kitten and zipped back to the place of gnashing teeth and incontinence.

Billy Smith was in his dad's spare room up Wesley Drive, pogo dancing and chanting the words to The Jam.

'And the public gets what the public wants!' spat Billy, kicking and headbutting 'til he was dizzy. Collapsing on the bed panting, he was contemplating having the word DEATH shaved into his crew-cut when there was a knock at the door.

Leaving the music blaring and his dad's bull terrier howling, he answered the back door. There stood a tiny woman in her early twenties, her hair in a pony-tail and welly boots just stopping beneath her denim shorts.

'Hello Billy!' she exclaimed, 'Can your Dad use these cucumbers up? I've cut ten already today and the fridge is full.'

'Thanks very much, Ann. I'm sure he'll love them,' replied Billy smiling politely.

'How long are you home for, Bill?' she enquired.

'Just a couple of weeks' leave. I'm being posted to Belize next!' he said with pride.

'Don't forget to take some sun cream, Bill! You know how badly the sun gets you!' She tittered as she made her way down the path away from the house.

Billy rushed back upstairs to pour himself into his jeans and put his new earring in his left lobe. He stretched his Union Jack tee shirt over his head, left his Dad a note and walked down to the Bull. As he turned the corner near the phone box he saw Beefy Underwood staggering in the same general direction. Billy ran to catch up with him, which did not take long as Beefy's pace was hindered by his hulking mass and his inability to stop his knuckles grazing the pavement as he walked.

'How did you get the gash on yer 'ead Beefy?' Billy dared to ask.

'Me sister!' Beefy replied matter of factly.

'Oh,' said Billy, no further explanation necessary.

A short time later Beefy and Billy reached the Bull, only to find Milton had arrived before them. Swaying in the breeze and fiddling with the small change in his pocket, it was obvious to all that he'd been drinking before leaving home. Earlier that day, Milton had argued with his mother when she declared that at the age of twenty four it was time that her son had grown up, cut down on his excessive drinking and got himself a job. This proclamation had wounded Milton deeply and after she had left the house to get a haircut, Milton had raided her drinks cupboard for solace. On her return he promptly staggered out of the front door, knocking over a dwarf conifer in the process, and went straight to the Bull.

Mazzer had already taken up residence there for the evening session and in desperation had asked Milton to join the sponsored pub-crawl. He readily accepted, but Mazzer was resolved to the fact that she would have to ask him again tomorrow.

'Great idea ennit?' he professed to Beefy, whereupon he toppled, took a step and squashed his face on Beefy's chest. Billy righted him and spun him round to face old Alf Burrows, who was in mid flow on the subject of these new fangled Wonder bras.

'Shouldn't be allowed! They give a chap false hope!' Alf ranted.

'What's Milton wittering about Mazzer?' Billy said, watching the stool buckle beneath Beefy's weight.

'Well my dears,' she replied, as though she was about to begin a session of *Listen with Mother*. 'There's a chance I could – we could – get on telly. If we raise enough money. An' clever old Tone 'ere thought of a sponsored pub crawl. Are yer up for it chaps?' She leaned towards Billy as she said this

74

and fluttered her eyelashes – the only feminine wile she had – precious little else could recommend her as one of the fairer sex. Beefy grunted consent, a smile just visible beneath the handlebar moustache that almost rivalled Mazzer's.

'When is it, Mazzer? I have to go to Belize soon,' Billy shouted so that even Alf could hear, without the use of his hearing aid.

'Oh a week or so Bill. Come on lad, you'll come, won't yer? Yeah! That's settled, yer in!' He didn't get the opportunity to argue the point and that was final.

Beardy was coerced into agreement, as was Rick the Shop, who agreed provisionally. He had to do battle with his wife the post-mistress. Despite being new to the village, Rick's wife, Felicity, had adopted the same belligerent attitude to her husband's wanderings as most females of Adderstey. If it was an act to fit in, she excelled at it.

'Boys, boys!' Mazzer slurred as she disembarked from her barstool and greeted the Earlem brothers into her open arms. They glanced warily round the room, all eyes fixed on them. 'How would you like to be on telly?' Don and Jimmy looked at each other and silently nodded consent, bringing the total to eleven. Mazzer bullied little Norris, an old gentleman friend of hers, into driving the minibus and Olivia from the big house with her friend Maeve, to help with the details.

Rick went home to the village shop that night and tried to butter up his missus. After all it was for a good cause. He cleaned his teeth, slicked his thinning hair back into a pony tail and broached the subject. He spent the next five minutes running around the bedroom deflecting projectiles from his person. A pot of Ponds cold cream smacked him right on his forehead, leaving a nasty bump, so Rick concluded that her answer must be in the negative.

The date was set, *The Herald* newspaper informed and Maeve and Olivia were set to drive ahead of the minibus to set up the beers, thus aiding a speedy turnaround. A route was planned to incorporate as many village pubs as possible, terminating at the Bull for last orders. Maeve and Olivia took charge of the slush fund to pay for drinks, but as most inns were given prior warning of the team's arrival many landlords declared their beers on the house.

Rick had sneaked out of the shop when Felicity was not looking. She immediately sussed something was wrong when his purple shirt vanished from the ironing basket and the shop reeked of Rick's 'tottie lotion'. If you could be sent to hell by mere thoughts of evil doings, Felicity had already assured herself of an asbestos throne next to Beelzebub himself.

Rick ran to the Bull car park, jumped into the back seat of the minibus and hid behind the seats in case Felicity should see. One by one all the merry crew gathered. Each had consumed a hearty meal and a pint of milk to line their stomachs and for once they were all sober. Norris handed out large charity tee shirts, which they wore over their clothes, except Beefy who couldn't get his over his head. Olivia, always prepared for everything, rummaged in the first aid kit and found two safety pins to attach the tee shirt to Beefy's back.

Tony saw his life flash before his eyes as Norris put his foot to the floor and got them, ahead of schedule, to the first port of call – the Grand Britannia. Maeve had chosen this pub first as it was full of young, good looking people later in the evening and situated next to the canal. After one pint they could easily be prised away from the place, but whilst drunk, a page three model would have trouble, enticing them away. The buckets were shaken, the landlord fleeced and Rick the Shop could have been arrested for molesting underage girlies, but they left on schedule without too much fuss. Beefy had volunteered to consume the first Stein at 'The Brit', a large jar of ale containing just over two pints, to be downed in one. Still sober and itching to partake of more now that their appetites had been whetted, Norris swung round the corners with the skill of Nigel Mansell and on to the next three pubs, which all passed with little or no hassle. Jimmy Earlem, Rueben and Milton all downed their Steins at each pub respectively, the rest downing their pints or halves.

Tony could smell trouble ahead and slyly tipped his half pints in flower pots or Beefy's pint glass while he was concentrating on breathing. The team was just getting warmed up by their fifth pub, which was to be found in the middle of a leisure park. Many years ago it had been an ideal location for the extraction of gravel, but when the pits had been exhausted a local wealthy landowner purchased the pits and allowed them to become lakes. After extensive landscaping and development, the leisure park attracted thousands of holidaymakers. These people had obviously never visited the area before or they would have packed gas masks to combat the smell from the adjacent sewage farm.

Olivia and Maeve had bought the drinks in (no freebies at this place, the landlord squeaked when he walked) and, on spotting the crew, they zipped off to the next location. Milton went straight to the gents and then sank his pint before sprawling across their pool table mid-game. It was Beardy's turn to sink the Stein. He got halfway and spluttered. Sensibly admitting defeat, Beefy, ever conscious of environmental issues, finished it off for him. Rick the Shop and Billy ran off in pursuit of two scantily clad holiday makers with pineapple hairdos and Jimmy and Donny were to be found negotiating entry into the leisure complex disco – 'Voulez Vous – The greatest seventies night you'll ever experience!'

Tony was trying his best to round them all up but with little success. He turned to find Milton picking a fight with the two lads from Birmingham, who had been playing pool when Milton so rudely interrupted them. Mazzer, who had put some lipstick on in honour of the occasion, went over to smooth things out. She stood directly behind the lads from that city beyond spaghetti junction and clasped a hand heavily on their shoulders. Towering head and shoulders above them she said, 'Now then lads – it's all in a good cause!' Putting sizeable donations in her bucket, the Brummies scarpered. On returning to their fair city, they boasted to their friends that they had nearly fought with a six foot four transvestite called Mazzer.

Jimmy and Donny had gained admission to the disco by taking off their tee shirts advertising the pub crawl. Rick, Milton and Beardy were now in hot pursuit, but were stopped by two rather meaty bouncers. Jimmy could already be seen tangoing to 'Don't Blame it on the Boogie' with a poodle haired, 18 year old who was bouncing out of her lycra bra top.

Milton was getting aggressive again with a bouncer twice his size. Tony, who was not so much psychic as sober, ran over to explain that their tight schedule necessitated him retrieving Jimmy and Donny from their teenage heaven. While bouncer number one physically restrained Milton, his arms flailing wildly, Tony ran around the disco and prized the brothers away from grope corner.

At the Bull, preparations were being made for their arrival, hopefully before last orders. For the last two weeks, punters had been encouraged, using the strongest possible methods, to sponsor the team, by the number of pubs successfully attended, or a Stein being emptied per pub. Posters were displayed in reference to the worthy cause, but few ever focused long enough to read the details.

The whole parish had turned out at the Bull to witness the arrival of the completely obliterated team. Shuggy was at a loss as to how to cope with such an influx of customers without Tony to deal with it all. He had a double port and brandy and hid in the kitchens, leaving little Craigie, the 17 year old glass collector, in charge.

'If anyone asks?' shook Shuggy.

'I'm 18, Mr. England!' replied a bemused Craigie.

Back on the pub crawl, the team had reached the Black Lion, a rival pub to the Bull since it had opened 150 years ago. Old Alf Burrows could recall his grandfather telling stories of how his father would get beered up at the Bull and then a gang would walk the three miles across the fields to beat the Lion drinkers senseless on a Saturday night. The following Saturday, the Lion drinkers would walk to the Bull for a re-match. To this day, it was still wise not to admit your origins if you strayed into the others' territory. Since the crawl was such a good cause and the Lion drinkers were given fair warning, a truce was called.

The Longfields wandered in first and found Olivia and Maeve clutching a stein and several pints along the bar. Rueben fancied some honey roast peanuts, which set everybody off on the munchies. In the spirit of the truce, the landlord declared the round on the house, which was followed by loud cheers and chanting as Billy stood, or rather swayed to down his stein.

'Down in one! One! One! One!... ' the pub chanted in mass hysteria as Billy finished the last dregs of the stein and tipped the empty glass on top of his head, just as the others had done before him. Rueben called to Billy and fired a peanut at his face. Miraculously, Billy caught it in his mouth. After a few more attempts, Billy felt a strange gurgling sensation in the pit of his stomach.

Milton was, again, prostrate on the pool table and Steven was in the process of impressing the local ladies with his one handed press ups on the other end of the bar. Mazzer was locked with Beardy in an arm wrestling contest and Tony was explaining the age differences of most of the girls in the bar to Rick the Shop. Billy did one enormous belch and pebble dashed the bar hatch with liquid peanuts. The landlord turned to Jimmy and Donny, who had narrowly missed the involuntary facial and said, 'If I give yer 30 quid will yer all piss off?!' And with that, they took to Norris's trusty chariot and made off for the next pub.

Beefy sat at the back of the bus and held Billy by the scruff the neck over the speeding tarmac, and as Billy did some exotic pavement art from the backdoors of the bus, Steven molested and slavered over the young lady he'd picked up before Bill's untimely yawn. There was one more pub on the route before reaching Adderstey, which passed in minutes. Beefy had been charged with dragging Billy around and helping him tip his half pints of bitter down his throat. Steven sunk his pint and ran back to the minibus where his new bit of fluff was waiting. Rueben was chatting up any female present so as not to be outdone by his brother.

'Do yer wanna feel me muscles?' Rueben said, staring through blurred eyes.

'You cheeky little sod!' Valerie shrieked, 'Seth – get him off me!' she wailed.

After a couple more pubs that were not on the defined route, they limped back to the Bull at ten to eleven, where their beers were awaiting them. They were received by cheers and yells and a line up of regulars to assist them into the bar. Hearing the cries and whoops, Shuggy re-appeared from the kitchen, pulled his trousers up high and went to shake their hands.

'Well done lads! Brilliant achievement! Bravo!' he snorted. Mazzer considered herself 'a lad' anyway and was difficult at the best of times to offend.

'Whose turn is it for the Stein?' asked Shuggy as sociably as he could. They all turned to look at each other; slow motion had kicked in for all but Steve, who had worked off his drunken confusion in the minibus.

'Tony!' he said joyously, followed by more wails and cheers.

Tony took centre stage next to the bar, the crowd

silenced. Tony was renowned for staying in control and practically sober. It suddenly struck the team that Tony was the most coherent of them all.

'Go on then lad! Don't keep us in shushpension,' Mazzer slurred, back on her favourite barstool. Slowly, Tony raised the stein with both hands and tipped the lot over Shuggy's head. The Bull shook with the screams and howls as Tony offered his hand to Shuggy. In good stead, Shuggy shook it heartily and as he waded off through the puddle to peel his clothes off before they set, he said, 'You're bleeding clearing it up, Tone!' More amazed than entertained, the crowds applauded this single and only gesture of goodwill displayed by Shuggy since he had taken the Bull over.

Pa Earlem strolled out to the gents with the express intention of relieving himself, only to discover that the drain for the urinals had been blocked and the only cubical was occupied by Billy Smith, who sat on the yellowing tiles, cuddling the bowl while Rueben and Steven tried desperately to extricate him. Pa made the sensible decision to nip out to the car park for a pee and a quick cigarette. He walked to the end of the car park, past the kiddies' climbing frame and unzipped his fly. He quickly shook himself and adjusted his clothing before starting back up the tarmac. Parked beside Big Mazzer's Reliant Kitten was Norris's steamed up minibus, which was rocking from side to side. 'Christ, that old van's seen some sights tonight, that's for sure!' Pa said to himself, taking a quick peek through the gap in the window, and chuckling as he headed back to the bar.

★ ★ ★ ★ ★

Few people were visible the following day. Billy was still examining the contents of his stomach, Tony was mopping out the Bull, Beefy was comatose in Dunny's back garden and Rueben was trying to stop his brain banging against his skull while Esme gave him a severe tongue lashing. Rick the Shop had awoken to a frighteningly pleasant Felicity and a detached ponytail lying on his pillow beside him. Jimmy and Donny had gone out on a scaffolding job still viewing the world in time lapse photography. Donny always believed his balance would be better while drunk anyway. Beardy was gargling disinfectant after finding himself sharing a double divan with Mazzer. He later sank two partially dissolved Alka Seltzas and took vows of celibacy with Father Bruce, the parish vicar.

Jimmy and Donny, in a moment of Samaritan behaviour, had offered Milton a job and had taken him with them to show him the ropes. Milton looked at the ropes and bedded down in the back of their pickup. Steven wasn't spotted for another three days. He had been participating in his own kind of marathon with his pink angora clad beauty.

It was a full week before Mazzer had prised all the sponsor money out of the tight pocketed locals, and added to the cash collected on the crawl, the amount raised had reached the incredible total of £2000, give or take a couple of pounds. Ever eager for her 15 minutes, or even seconds of fame, Mazzer telephoned ITV Central office who diverted her call to the Telethon organisers. On a 'pass the parcel' trail, Mazzer finally got hold of the number of the East Anglia department, responsible for outside broadcasts.

Armed with the date, venue and time of the live broadcast, Mazzer tracked down each member of the team to inform them. All but Rick the Shop and Billy were able to attend. Rick was close to divorce proceedings over his severed ponytail and Billy had taken his sun cream to Belize.

On a misty Saturday morning, Mazzer woke early and heaved herself out of bed and into the shower. Mazzer, who had borrowed her daughter's hot brush to make her new hairstyle even bigger, was wearing a dress she last wore at her cousin's wedding in 1974. She added the finishing touches to her baby-blue eye shadow before jumping in her orange Reliant Kitten, the suspension of which clunked as she sat in the driver's seat. With a serious lean to the right, the Kitten was driven flat out to a meeting place in Belvoir Park. Mazzer's eagerness and heavy foot had given her an extra half an hour to wander around the park, watching the preparations for the spectacular television event.

A hot air balloon in the shape of Bugs Bunny was bent double over the dewy grass, just partially inflated. 'Got a bit o' Patrick's trouble,' she sniggered to herself, 'brewers droop!' Mazzer was just unhitching her frock from the perimeter fence when Tony wandered over to help.

'Bloody 'ell, Mazzer! Didn't recognise yer!' he spluttered.

'Bet yer didn't know I 'ad legs, did yer Tone?' She laughed, slapping his arm and ripping her dress in one action.

Before long the rest of the team had arrived at the meeting place, including the Earlems, who had brought Milton in the back of their pickup. He had probably lain there all week.

'You don't seriously let Milton up the scaffolding do yer?' Tony asked.

'We prefer to think of him as the ground crew!' Donny coughed between puffs on his cigarette. Jimmy threw an empty beer bottle into the back of the pickup which landed right in Milton's expanding gut.

'Whooargh!' came the response, followed by, 'Anyone got a fag?'

Beefy arrived, grinning like a schoolboy and shuffling his feet. He had been over to the funfair area, where a dog agility team had been warming up for a display. A Staffordshire bull terrier had dragged its owner right across the events field and attacked Beefy's leg, snarling and growling viciously. The plump girl on the other end of the lead tried her best to drag 'Cuddles' away from Beefy's leg but to no avail. She smiled distractedly at Beefy, who melted instantly in her gaze. To Cuddles' surprise, Beefy reached down and patted the dog so ardently he released Beefy's trousers and was pinned to the floor. The girl continued to chat, but the only response was a fixed grin. She took a pen from her bag and neatly wrote: 'Meet Agnes at 4.30 at the hot dog stand' on Beefy's arm. She could easily have fitted specific directions on his mighty forearms but she hoped it would be enough of a reminder.

Rueben was trying his hand at the coconut shy, hitting several coconuts, which had been nailed to their posts.

'Ere, what a con!' he bellowed, vaulting the stall and grabbing the attendant by the throat. The Adderstey crew gathered around looking menacing, Mazzer being by far the most intimidating. Steven stopped Rueben from trying to ram the ball down the attendant's throat and handed a coconut to each of the kids who had been trying to win for the last hour.

'Rueben! Put him down!' Steven said authoritatively, and Rueben did.

Jimmy whispered, 'Sit boy! Roll over! Walkies!' Donny sniggered.

'Wha' were that, Jimmy?' Rueben said rather agitated.

'Nowt lad!'

It was almost time for the live broadcast and crowds were gathering around a large contingent of ITV soundmen, cameramen and directors. In the middle of all this was a young lady who, despite having connections with non-locals, was born in Adderstey. She was one of the village's few success stories. Caron Alderly had been born the eldest child to a couple of incomers back in the 1960's. They were a relatively wealthy family and chose to send Caron to a private school on the borders of the county. Her brother was considered too stupid to waste a public school education on and was sent to the local comprehensive school to be ridiculed and pilloried until the chip on his shoulder had grown to a whole potato.

Caron, with a good education and a BBC English accent, landed herself a cushy job within the Anglia News Team. An English rose complexion and wide eyed innocence made her a great success and, as luck would have it, for Mazzer at least, she was to be the main presenter for the live broadcast. Caron stood in her lacy pastels amidst the cameras and crowds, fending off autograph hunters, when Mazzer clumsily approached her.

"Ere Caron! You don't remember me do yer?!' She beamed. Although Caron was only a minor celebrity, she couldn't remember everyone she had met, so she tried her winning smile and turned away. Mazzer swung her around again to face her. 'It's me, Big Mazzer from Adderstey!' Still Caron, looked puzzled. 'I helped with the catering at yer wedding luv!' Mazzer explained. Politeness kept Caron rooted to the spot, listening to the team's achievements. She showed Caron the giant cheque for £2000 and emotionally blackmailed her into giving the team a spot for the broadcast.

Just before going on air, Caron had lined the lads up behind an Indie Car worth £350,000, which had been involved in a sponsored rally. To the left of the lads was the dog agility team, Agnes and Beefy's eyes still locked in a peculiar gaze. Jimmy and Donny held the cheque high, obscuring Milton entirely, and Mazzer was standing next to Caron in anticipation.

The director and sound crew mimed the '3,2,1 and go!' and Caron sprang into action introducing the town, the event and herself with consummate ease. The hot air balloons were rising in the background and all was timed to perfection. Caron briefly introduced Agnes, who explained about the sponsored agility event, but she faltered with nerves, halfway through her rehearsed lines. Beefy gave her hand a little squeeze, that would have crushed anyone else and she finished her lines with no more hitches.

The next story was the rally event, which had run concurrently with all the renowned tracks across Britain and had raised £100,000. Big cheers and applause was written on a cardboard sign and held aloft by a crewman. The audience complied.

Mazzer took a deep breath and jiggled with excitement

as Caron made her way over to introduce the team. Thinking only of viewing figures and who she fancied most, Caron walked straight over to Tony and asked him to explain his particular event, all the time obscuring Mazzer from the TV cameras. Tony, who was a little surprised at first, warmed to Caron's giggles and flirtation and he began to explain Mazzer's part in the event. Jimmy and Donny passed the cheque along the row to Caron who said to the camera that such a sum deserved a kiss. As she turned to kiss Tony, Mazzer, who was getting extremely angry, shoved Caron out of the view of the camera. She knocked into Beefy who toppled like a domino across the team, hurling Rueben, a 15 stone dead weight, directly onto £350,000 worth of Indie Car.

The director mimed cut rather frantically and picked Caron up from the mud. A massive dent in the shape of Rueben's posterior marked the close of the broadcast.

'Steve? We'd better ask Dad if he wants a game of cards tonight!' said Rueben, scratching his head.

CHAPTER 5

September

Harvest Madness

It was misty and wet underfoot at 6.30am up Jacket's Gully and Jacket himself had woken early. Fuelled with the desire to recoup his losses from last night's poker game before Jill, his wife, found out, he decided to load up the van for his vegetable round. He dragged the sacks of late variety potatoes from the ripped polythene tent he called a greenhouse and lugged them onto the tailgate of his clapped out VW van.

Jackets' health had never been 'A1,' but his tolerance to alcohol had built to a level where his liver quietly groaned and had begun to fade with no warning signs such as the evil hangovers suffered by most. At the age of 78 his pace of work had not wavered since he was a fit and healthy 20 year old, simply because it had never been more than the speed of an asthmatic slug.

Jacket wiped the sweat from his three day beard with a grey hankie then blew his bulbous nose, before shoving the soiled rag back into his ripped corduroy trousers. From the breast pocket of his coat he pulled out a battered and grimy hip flask and took a deep slug of the liquid from it. Gasping, he saw a wellington-booted figure appear from the gully and turn towards the VW van, which was parked at the edge of the five acre smallholding. Jacket fumbled and panted but managed to return the hip flask to its hiding place just before Jill reached him. Her sight was sufficiently poor for Jacket to remain undetected in his pursuits.

Jill was an honest and God fearing woman who preferred to be ignorant of Jacket's sly carryings on rather than have to atone for them. She was only a couple of years younger than Jacket, although many years working the land had sculpted her face into that of a very old woman. Jill had carried a basket of freshly cut cucumbers from the garden at the rear of their house, which faced their smallholding. A well worn footpath ran through their rented land, which was accessed by a grassy passageway from the road to the field, overgrown and muddy with tractor wheel impressions.

'Better get them wotsits loaded up Jacket,' she ordered. Jacket instinctively turned to load the crates of eggs by his side. 'Wetaminute!' she snapped 'Where did yer get em from?'

'Same as always, my beauty' he chirped. She glared at him for a moment then wandered off to cut some spinach.

For years Jacket had been selling free range eggs from an old lady in the next parish but when demand increased, Jacket found an alternative source, namely the local battery farm. Jacket could not see any harm in the swap and so neglected to mention it, particularly to Jill. While Jill emptied the Victoria plums from the greengrocer's box, Jacket smeared mud on the battery hen's eggs and upped the price on the label.

Jill swung the final box of vegetables into the van and joined her husband in the cab. Pulling out the choke, he turned the ignition and pumped the pedals, but the van emitted no signs of life.

'P'raps battery's gone, boy,' Jill said slowly. After years of purgatory living with Jacket, Jill had been numbed to acquiescence.

'T'aint the bloody battery woman. Wha'ud you knew bout it anyhow?' he snapped, then jumped out of the cab to lift the bonnet and give the starter motor a good thrashing with a rock. Jill pulled a copy of *Woman's Own* out of the dashboard and settled down to the crossword, while Jacket ranted and raved, tweaking leads and smashing up various bits of the engine.

'We only had it a little while an' all!' he puffed, bent double, his fried breakfast causing him great discomfort.

'Try 20 years!' Jill grumbled before turning to the pullout knitting pattern in the centre.

'Wha?'

'I tell yer it's the battery!' she persisted.

Sometime later, Jacket concluded that it must be the battery and so reversed his old Massey Fergusson up to meet the van's bonnet.

'Is that wise, Jack?' she warned, 'you know what happened to Pa Earlem's Volvo last time you tried that.'

'Rubbish! It were his own bloody fault, that were.' Jacket attached the jump leads from the 24 volt tractor battery to the 12 volt car battery and kept his fingers crossed.

Amos Parting ambled up Jacket's Gully, talking to his Jack Russell, Ben the fourth. His former pets, Ben one, two and three, all met with unfortunate accidents. One such accident involved the poor dog's inability to sit in the front basket of

Amos' motorbike. After negotiating a particularly tight corner around Wesley Drive, Ben had fallen and had been promptly flattened by a 3 inch radial tyre.

'Ay up lass!' Amos chirped to Jill through the open door of the van.

'Ello Amos. 'Ere! Get your dog off my spring onions!' she screeched.

'It wun 'urt gell! 'E's only fertilising 'em. Save yer a job 'e will!' Amos leaned in further and winked, 'Ere lass, does your Dad work at Tesco?'

'Bugger off Amos!' she replied curtly, before returning to the problem page.

Amos gave up on Jill and without enquiring after Jacket, whose head had been wedged near the cam shaft, he made his way past the allotments and through to the posh folks' houses. After a loud bang and the smell of burning had subsided, Jill began unloading the van and hitching up the trailer to the 1950's tractor with its key stuck in the ignition. 'Shall atta do the round on the Fergie, 'an that's that!' Jill remarked fatalistically.

★ ★ ★ ★ ★

Lily Underwood was standing at the bus stop with Ethel Loosely watching a council worker wire up a speed monitor across the main road. It had been one of Lily's campaigns to get those posh speed 'calming' measures fitted throughout Adderstey and after three years, 26 phone calls and 12 letters, the District Council had agreed to assess the situation. Two rubberised wires across the width of the road were anchored by the computerised box and then padlocked to the school road sign. Bursting with pride, Lily said, 'Well it's about time too!'

'Good work Lily,' squeaked the tiny Ethel, 'I always knew you'd do it!'

'Persistence my dear,' Lily gloated, 'we must keep the pressure up though Ethel, the job's not done yet.'

'Yes, yes but surely with all the mad men speeding through our village they'll have to do something.'

'It's our job to see that they do!' Lily hitched up her bosoms, Les Dawson style.

The slow, deafening growl of Jacket's Massey Fergusson grew louder as Jacket pulled out of the lane turn onto the main road, narrowly missing the butcher's daughter on 'Panther', her unpredictable mare. Jill hung on to the tail flap of the trailer as she was thrown about with the courgettes and tomatoes. The worn grooves on the tractor tyres tangled the partially fitted speed monitor wires, dragging the connections free from the steel box the workmen were clutching. Completely oblivious, Jacket pushed the accelerator to the floor, throwing Jill horizontal in the trailer, as he headed straight for the old folks' bungalows.

'See yer Sunday, Lily!' Jill yelled as the trailer mounted the pavement for the second time.

'Alright Jill, yeah,' was the reply. 'You know Ethel, Jill's bin tryin' to get old Jacket to Church for donkey's years. She'll ne'er do it. Not while he's in league with the devil she won't!'

Jacket reached the old folks' bungalows, or 'Death Row' as it was affectionately termed, just as the Adderstey cronies were edging out of their hallways like snails on a rainy lettuce patch, their Zimmers rolling away from them down the concrete ramps to the car park. Between the gaps in the bungalows, Jacket could just see old Amos building a bonfire in his garden next to Benny Boy, who was frantically chasing his tail.

'Are these eggs fresh?' Adolf said, waving his stick at a belching Jacket. Adolf, a militant pain in the rear and a crashing bore, would turn out to all the village functions in full military dress uniform and display various historical artefacts that he had collected from his rambles in the fields.

'Laid yesterday, Captain,' Jacket sniffed, his nose growing a little longer.

★ ★ ★ ★ ★

At the Longfields' farm, Steven and Rueben, who had moved back into Esme's farmhouse for the harvest effort, had finished their lunch of fried potatoes, beans, eggs, Jordan's sausages and fried bread. Rueben pulled his boots back on and began to make his way across Esme's kitchen.

'Get yer muddy feet outta here – yer little sod!' she raged, holding a large skillet in her hand. Esme restrained herself from taking a swing because Rueben had always been her favourite. If it had been Jed, on the other hand, he would have been picking fried egg out of the wounds for a week. Rueben climbed the step of the hired digger to return to the hedgerow he had been grubbing up before lunch.

'Where're you goin', Steve?' Said Rueben, puzzled. Steven was hopping into the pickup in his best jeans and navy blue shirt. He reeked of Blue Denim and had forced a parting in his wiry hair, which had partially sprung back to its original cows lick.

'Gotta go to the bank fer Dad,' Steven yelled as he fired up the pickup and roared off before Rueben's brain could catch up with events.

The morning greyness had burned off during the course of the day and the clear blue skies had the whole parish out amongst their fields, gardens and thickets. Rueben returned to the top field before the forest to remove the last traces of a 400 year old hedge. The new combines were so huge that safe passage into 'Dry Dell' meant the destruction of miles of nature's corridors. Despite numerous housing estates springing up on land that dissolute offspring had been bequeathed and subsequently sold off to property developers, the parish was still known by the original field names. Those that were renamed, to suit the tastes of the middle class incomers moving to the district, were referred to by original titles despite protestations. Locals used this minor gripe to firstly amuse themselves and annoy the non-locals and secondly as a form of code with which they could happily discuss dodgy land deals down the pub in front of the unhappy recipients.

One particular favourable deal, made by a local, was the sale of the vicarage land. A doctor and his family, who originated in Leeds, had occupied 'The Old Rectory' for a number of years. Their grounds were, however, not part of the sale. Outline planning permission was sought for a few, very select, luxury homes on the land. The meadow was very picturesque and was bordered by the village brook and mature willow trees. Every local within a 20 mile radius was aware that the meadow would flood every winter and yet, somehow, the building developer, estate agents and unsuspecting new residents remained blissfully unaware of the fact. These high class materialists extended properties, built extra garages and landscaped their meagre gardens, only to find that they needed flippers to enjoy a game of tennis on their own courts.

'An' they reckon we're the dense 'uns!' Pa Earlem would laugh in the pub on a Sunday. 'They dun the same thing up the Chase an' all!'

While Rueben was steaming in the cab of the digger, Steven, who had driven straight to Olivia up at the big house, was working up a sweat himself. He had arrived with cheap champagne, the only bottle Rick the Shop had in stock, and a bunch of flowers from the garage on the main road. On his arrival, Olivia had thrown the flowers and champagne on the sofa and dragged Steven straight upstairs to show off her new jodhpurs and whip. Olivia had embraced local life with great enthusiasm when she returned from Roedean. Her only employment was maintaining Daddy's stables up at his Manor and seeking pleasure amongst the Young Farmers Club at the Bull.

Harvest time always whipped the young ones up into a frenzy and letting off steam was a necessity with which Olivia was only too pleased to help. The older farmers had usually worn themselves down to a slow pace by late summer and spent a great deal more time in the pub than in the fields.

Jacket spent a great deal of time in the pub too, although he could never quite be classed as a farmer. Jacket was born the only child of a local lady of ill repute. It was said that his father had been a sailor, after Jacket's mother had been on a holiday to Blackpool. Others said that there was a striking resemblance to Pa Earlem's father, but then most of the residents of Adderstey were genetically linked somewhere along the line. In the absence of a role model, Jacket became a wild youth, stealing more than ever he earned, which was taxed by his mother to pay for her nicotine and alcohol addictions.

Jacket briefly went to the village school to learn the three R's: Reading Writing and Roughing people up, where he met a farm boy they called Dinky. Dink and Jacket were inseparable and all that they learned was hardly part of any school syllabus. Dink was a short, stocky lad with Robin Hood morality. Jacket had little sense and no morals but his actions were tempered by the sobriety of his young stoic friend. Jacket would always call for Dink just before suppertime, knowing full well that Dink's mother could not bear to see a child's mouth void of food.

At dusk, Dink and Jacket would don their old coats and walk across to the Manor grounds to set their snares. Even at the tender age of 13, Dink was proficient at poaching and knew all the perfect runs in which to set their snares. Jacket, on the other hand, was talented at very little, but was content to wander around after Dink, carrying the wires and jam sandwiches. When the snares were set, Dink would often suggest a quality morsel to bait. For a little variety, Dink would sometimes go pheasant hocking up the Slipe. Between adjacent lands, there was often a narrow piece of land which was too wide to be a cart track and too narrow to plough or run livestock in. Bordered by shrubs and trees, this strip of land leading to another, the Slipe, was a perfect, undisturbed breeding ground for pheasants.

Dink would shove Jacket into the hedge and go and sit, completely motionless in the Slipe. Whether Dink positioned himself downwind of the birds or whether he had some mystical powers, it shall never be known, but Dink would always return laden with game. Being a fair lad, Dink would halve the evening catch with Jacket and return to his family with meat for the larder. Jacket would always sell his share to the local butcher and buy his weeks cigarette's before his mother could extract it from him.

As Dink and Jacket grew older, Jacket became fixated with gambling and drinking while Dink, ever the cautious one, stayed at the parental farm and assisted in the management of the Land Army Girls. Eventually, without the sensible influence of Dink, Jacket reverted to his old ways and became embroiled in all sorts of nefarious affairs.

After countless close shaves with the Law, Jacket fell for a Land Army Girl who was working at Dink's Farm. Jill had been posted to Adderstey as a young woman from Hackney. Her brother, a military parson who followed in their father's footsteps, persuaded Jill to take the Lord's word to Adderstey via the Land Army. This big city girl was in great demand by all the young men who remained behind during the War.

Jill was 'courted' by many of the local lads, from Dink to Pa Earlem, but all were repelled by Jill's holy overtures. Once Jacket had set his mind, he was determined that Jill should be his. Taking picnics into Old Hubie's Meadow, Jill would read passages from the Bible to Jacket as he slumbered undetected beneath his hat. She spent hours trying to coax the heathen into church on a Sunday, but each time he would decline. 'My God ent confined to no poncy barn, girl! I worship 'im in the fields, me darlin'.'

Jacket never failed to walk her to and from the church, rain or shine, every Sunday, since her best dress revealed shapely legs that were concealed for the rest of the week beneath her overalls. Jacket would sit on the headstones outside the ancient church smoking his woodbines and picking at the threads hanging from the cuff of his best coat. Eventually, Jacket proposed to Jill by moonlight up the same Slipe that he and Dink had frequented for many years.

'How are we going to get married if you won't go in a church?' Jill wailed.

'Ah! That's different gel! You gotta have a vicar an' that to make it all legal 'ent yer? No I don't mind church then.' Barring funerals and weddings, Jill never did get Jacket into church again.

After marriage, Jacket's 'dealin's' had to be even more guarded. Occasionally Jill would get wind of a risky deal, like the time Jacket tried to sell some 'rustled' beef to the local constable. That event had Jill burning the church candles till midnight and praying till she contracted housemaid's knee.

★ ★ ★ ★ ★

Finishing the round, Jill and Jacket returned to the smallholding next to the allotments. Jacket had decided to grow a few 'exotics' this year after going to the supermarket and noting the high price that a bell pepper fetched. Setting a few seeds in trays, he potted up the seedlings and grew them on until a whole poly-tunnel was filled with healthy pepper plants. Charging Jill with their care, Jacket watched the flowers set and fall and tiny green nodes swell to perfection. The kind weather and Jill's TLC ensured a tunnel filled with luscious, plump, ripe peppers, ready to harvest.

Emptying the remains of the day's vegetable round into a shaded hut, Jacket padlocked the door and made his way over to the poly-tunnel. Jill had visited the kitchen of an exclusive restaurant on the borders of the parish and offered them first refusal of the pepper crop. Having received top class vegetables from Jill before, the chef agreed, but stressed urgency in the deal. Jacket rubbed his hands at the prospect of paying off a few gambling debts as he entered the doorway of the poly-tunnel. Taking out a razor sharp penknife, he clipped a shiny red pepper from its stalk and gave it a good sniff. 'Don't smell o' much,' he said to himself, 's'pose I'd better try the taste of 'em, since I've grewn them an' all.' He continued in his solitary dialogue.

Piercing the flesh with his knife, the pepper gave way under his heavy hand and split open revealing the arches of white pith and tiny flat seeds. 'Ere Jill! Come quick lass!' Jacket wailed, picking up a second pepper to dissect. 'They're all bleedin' holla! The whole bleedin' lot of 'em!'

'What you chelpin' on?' she said, pounding across the parched soil to the tunnel.

'Ere!' sobbed Jacket, shoving the squashed pepper under her nose, 'See for yersen!' Totally stunned, Jacket threw the pepper to the floor, closed his penknife and wandered away.

'Tread 'em in for me Jill, me old beauty. They'll rot afore next season'.

'Where you goin'?' she jumped gaily up and down on the plants.

'See a man 'bout horse!' Jacket, weary with disappointment, climbed up on his Massey Fergie, trailer still attached, and trundled off to the Bull.

★ ★ ★ ★ ★

Rueben had decimated the 400 year old hedgerow, dug a drainage ditch either side of the field's entrance and was busy stacking the stumps and branches into a bonfire. The light breeze had dropped and the evening sun still beat down on him, making sweat trickle down his back and soak the waistband of his shorts. Tired, hungry and dehydrated, Rueben decided that the bonfire could wait for another day and mounted the steps of the JCB. He turned on the stereo to entertain him as he bounced in the cab down the three miles of country roads back to the Bull.

At a steady 10 miles per hour, Rueben sung along to Radio 1, holding up two Mercedes, an Aston Martin and a spotless Range Rover. Rueben was toying with the idea of driving around aimlessly, as slow as he could to annoy the non-locals who had commuted to London and had consequently been sitting on the M25 for an hour after work. Hunger forced him to pick up the pace a little. Passing the big house, where Olivia lived and with whom he had spent the last month or so in a blissful relationship, he glanced over to try and catch a glimpse of his beloved. Steven was standing on the doorstep, his navy blue shirt loosely draped over his shoulders, in a farewell embrace with Olivia. Steven turned to leave as Olivia clipped his buttocks with her riding crop. Swerving to miss Steven's pickup, which was parked on the roadside next to the drive entrance, Rueben felt his head pounding as the blood coursed around his body.

★ ★ ★ ★ ★

'How's it goin', Jacket?' asked Tony politely.

'Don't ask lad, just don't'. Supplied with his regular pint, Jacket slunk off to a corner of the bar and sat mumbling to himself. Amos ambled in, looking a little shaken, and ordered a double Jack Daniels, which he promptly sank. Mazzer slid off her bar stool and shuffled over to Amos. Towering over him she boomed, 'What's up Amos?' Amos opened his Jacket wide to reveal a blackened waistcoat, still smouldering.

'Got a bit close to the bonnie with the petrol gel!' Mazzer slapped his back and laughed.

'You silly old sod!'

''Ere darlin'?' Amos said, returning to his old form, 'Does your Dad work at Tesco's?'

Mazzer shook her head in disbelief and went to sit with Jacket.

Rueben thundered in and scowled at Tony, who poured him a pint in silence and added the tally to the Longfield slate. Knowing the harvest to be a particularly stressful time, with hot days matching the hot tempers, Tony thought it best to let the troubled Rueben alone for a while. 'Is no bugger happy today?' Mazzer boomed across the bar. No one ventured an opinion. Tony shrugged his shoulders and went to serve an incomer in the lounge. Mazzer moved from one table to the next trying to shake everyone out of their malaise. ''Ow 'bout a game o' skittles Jimmy?' Mazzer asked.

'Too knackered, Mazzer, ask Milton.'

'He ain't use nor ornament!' she cackled, glancing over at Milton slumped over a table. 'It's like a bleedin' morgue in ere tonight!' Even old Alf was quiet, too hot in his tweed suit but too vain to remove his coat. Mazzer returned to Jacket's side, her dungarees straining with the bulk of four pints of bitter. 'What's ailing yer then Jacket?' Mazzer demanded to know.

'Whole bloody season wasted on the wotsit peppers!' He snarled.

'Ay?' Mazzer said, quite baffled.

'Set whole bloody tunnel o' bell peppers. Beautiful an' ripe they were an all, just ready for harvest. Nice little earner they were gunnu be.' He ranted

'What's the problem then?' Mazzer asked impatiently.

'Whole lot were bleedin' holla, that's wot! Jill's trod em in for me!'

'You daft bugger!' Mazzer squealed.

'Wha'?'

'They 're s'posed to be holla! You eat the outta flesh!' Mazzer collapsed in fits of laughter at the crumpled old man by her side. She bought Jacket a consolatory pint of best bitter and said, 'Ne'er mind, Jacket, least you got yer health!'

'Not much else can go wrong I reckon. Me van packed up this morning an all.'

Steven sauntered in, his hair glistening wet, sporting an inane grin. He clasped his hand on Rueben's shoulder. 'Wha' you having brov?' Steven said smugly. Rueben shrugged his brother's hand from him and moved away. 'What's got your goat, you moody bastard?' Rueben grunted, got off his barstool and turned to face his brother.

'Did you have a good trip to the bank?'

'Yeah! I reckon.' Steven frowned. 'What's up?'

'I saw you Steven! I saw you with my Olivia!' Rueben yelled. The Bull cleared a space rapidly.

'She ent yours, yer daft lad!' Steven said in patronising tones as he grinned at the audience.

'I were gunnoo marry her!' Rueben wailed.

'I can't help it if I'm a better shag, can I?'

Rueben swung violently, making his huge fists connect with Steven's Neanderthal forehead, knocking him to the flagstone floor. 'Hey lads, not in the bar! Take yer fight outside please!' Tony said, firmly but politely.

'Sorry Tony mate!' they chorused. Rueben helped Steven to his feet and ushered him outside to continue their squabble. The locals at the Bull were quite used to the frequent brawls at harvest time and the majority could not be coaxed away from their seats to be spectators under the sultry evening sun. Only Rick the Shop, for whom harvest time was still a novelty, Mazzer and Jimmy Earlem went to view the cabaret.

Steven deflected a few punches and threw a few too, but on the whole, was definitely suffering a great deal more the Rueben. Steven wound himself up and threw an almighty punch, throwing Rueben backwards against the crumbling stone wall bordering the car park. Winded, but feeling very little, Rueben took time to right himself. Staggering back to his former position, he found Steven had run to his pickup, tucked away in the corner of the car park. 'You don't get away that easy, yer bastard!' Rueben yelled, running to the cab of the JCB. It started immediately. Shoving the levers, the JCB lurched forward, bearing down on the pickup as it tried to reverse out of its space. Rueben trapped him, the digger blocking the only passage safely out of the car park.

Slamming the pickup into first gear, Steven dropped the clutch and sped around onto the pub lawn, weaving a slalom through the picnic tables. Rueben tried to follow and head him off, swinging the JCB around 180 degrees, a manoeuvre which churned up most of the turf and bounced the rear bucket off a couple of the customers' vehicles. Steven was clear of the lawn and had just mounted the patio when Rueben knocked one of the levers in the cab. The huge mechanical arm leapt forward, smashing the rabbit hutch and kiddies' swings. Panicking, Rueben shoved the digger into reverse, which then lunged directly into the side of Jacket's 1950's classic Massey Ferguson and attached trailer. Mazzer scampered into the bar, stifling a cackle. 'Ere Jacket? You know you said that nowt else could go wrong today? Well you'd best come an' look for yersen me darlin!'

Shuggy had barred Rueben and Steven permanently, till old Jed Longfield went to the Bull on the Monday with a large cheque for the damage and a new pet rabbit after the old one died from shock the following day. After all, the Longfields were the best customers the Bull had ever known. Various insurances covered most of the damage to the vehicles in the car park. 'Can I claim on your insurance for my Reliant Kitten, Steve?' asked Mazzer, whose car had escaped the Longfield's rampage but looked more battered than the rest of the cars put together.

'Yer might as well, Mazzer!' said Steven ruefully, 'Every other bugger has!'

Rueben delivered an old tractor of Jed's, that he was going to trade in, to Jacket's gully with an offer of a small piece of land to lease on a peppercorn rent next season, while Olivia made herself busy in her father's stables wearing her second best jodhpurs and brandishing her riding crop with Notch Underwood. The Longfield brothers were suitably chastised by their long suffering mother Esme, who forced reconciliation between her sons and made them vow to never fight over a woman again.

CHAPTER 6

October

After Hours

Marge Henderson's girdle creaked and groaned under the strain beneath her crimpline, 'A' line skirt, as she prepared herself for a trip around the village. Since many of the locals were gradually being replaced by incomers, Marge had noticed that her monthly tote round was not harvesting the volume of gossip achieved in the heydays. In consequence, Marge had volunteered her services, most insistently, to the Christmas Auction Committee.

Sticking her head out of an upstairs window to check the weather, she found her straw-like hair rapidly accumulating debris and leaves from the surrounding gardens. The sun tried to peep out from a fast moving cloud, but on seeing Marge, dived for cover. Sonny and Bronwyn were out manicuring their front lawn just opposite Marge's semi, halfway up Wesley drive. Sonny had stopped strimming the lawn's border, for the sixth time in half an hour, as the chain link fence snapped the strimmer's wire. Sitting cross legged on the path, he fiddled with the plastic casing, trying to avoid eye contact with Bronwyn.

Earlier in the day, Sonny had left his dipso father alone in the house while he popped to Rick the Shops for a newspaper. On his return, he discovered that the frail old man had downed two and a half pints of a home-brew kit straight from the barrel, spilling a further three pints on Bronwyn's new kitchen carpet. The fireworks which accompanied Bronwyn's Welsh temper had Sonny, his father and their fifteen year old son, Mick, scampering to each corner in the house. Later, when a deathly hush had fallen on 8 Wesley Drive and Bronwyn's mop had taken up most of the froth and scum, Sonny sneaked outside to his territory, the garden, where Bronwyn rarely ventured.

Marge waved out of her bedroom window at Sonny and made like she was about to run down the stairs to engage him in conversation. Thinking rapidly, Sonny decided a screwdriver from the barn was required for his task and so he hid, mouse-like, in his sanctuary, smoking an illicit cigarette.

Marge yanked a purple comb through her locks, straightened her bosoms and grabbed a handful of fliers on her way out of the backdoor, leaving her husband staring at a hot mug of tea, silent and shell-shocked. She crossed the street, leaned on Bronwyn's gate, just as Sonny had predicted and handed Bronwyn a flier with a few words of greeting.

'What's all this?' Bronwyn chorused in her melodious accent. 'You do too much Marge! You'll wear yourself out!'

'Well what can you do, Bron? I couldn't really say no, could I?' she lied.

'Same as last year Marge?'

'No actually, Bron. The Parish Committee decided that the auction favoured the Bull's profits too much, so its gunnoo be alternated with the Oak. All the profits will still go to the pensioners' Christmas hampers – that ain't changed, just the venue.'

'Won't they lose the incomers' support though?' Bronwyn said, who never for one moment considered herself a non-local, since she married Sonny, a true local. She was generally well liked and the locals were not so rude as to correct her.

'Not if we publicise it well, and it'll help the Oak's trade a bit 'an all.' Bronwyn masked a snort of laughter with a pseudo sneeze and excused herself.

The Oak stood in the adjoining village within the parish, beyond the brook and near to the forest. No non-local had ever successfully entered and finished a pint in Alf Burrow's long memory. It stood opposite the old hangman's house and boasted many secret passageways and hidden corners. The toilets still lay fifty feet from its backdoor in a structure resembling a pigsty, emitting foul stenches reminiscent of Dickensian times.

One time, a new village bobby and his wife entered and walked in total silence to the bar. The whole place stood still, glaring at him. They got halfway through their drinks and, sensibly, the policeman's wife urged a rapid retreat. The second the door opened for them to leave, the noise returned to its original boisterous level. Since then, neither policeman nor incomer had ever frequented the pub. Most people from the village walk the half mile to the Bull for their evening entertainment. Some locals did begin their nightly beverages at the Bull then staggered to the Oak for last orders, knowing full well that nine times out of ten there would be a lock in after hours.

Marge made no comment on Bronwyn's obvious

amusement and decided to move on to the next house. Sonny re-emerged with perfect timing. Looking skyward, Bronwyn said, 'I wonder why Marge's house is the only one without moss growing on the roof?'

'Shouldn't think it dare!' Sonny growled and returned to his strimming.

★ ★ ★ ★ ★

Dave Honey brushed the palm of his hand across the leather skirt of his 35 year old cousin, Sue. She'd agreed to step in after the last barmaid in a series had fled The Oak and Dave Honey's advances, vowing that should he touch her ever again he would meet with a tragic accident involving garden shears. Sue did not flinch, as he had expected. Relaxing a little, Dave pressed his luck and reached over her in the confines of the bar and connected his knuckle with her buttocks for the second time. Pa Earlem was propping up the bar with old Alf Burrows and, witnessing this spectacle said,

'Old Honey the Bunny's at it again Alf!'

'Even I admit to me limits man!' Alf grunted in disgust, 'Unhand that poor girl!' Honey, puffed up by his ego, mistaking the comments for admiration, grinned at his customers.

Dave and his brother George Honey were adopted children of a moderately wealthy family from Adderstey. Their parents' idealism vanished soon after taking on these city children, who ran rings around the simple folk. They gave up trying to keep the young hoodlums on the straight and narrow when the elder of the two, Dave, turned 21. The boys had their adoptive parents placed in care after bribing a bent doctor to sign a statement to the effect that they were no longer able to care for themselves. Selling their farm and land, Dave split the proceeds unevenly and bought the Oak. In the quiet backwater of Henridge, surrounded by fields, the forest and a 'no through' road, the core of the locals could hide undetected from reality.

Honey the Bunny had remained the landlord of the Oak for 30 years – had been divorced twice and sired two legitimate and two illegitimate children. The 60's and 70's yielded high profits for the Oak and secured Dave a healthy bank balance and a long list of mistresses. The strict drink drive laws of the 80's almost sent Dave to the wall, but prudence and careful, if not slightly dodgy management, kept him hanging in to the present day. The majority of his evening's takings were accrued when the curtains were drawn and the back doors locked at 11pm, particularly if a game or two of cards were underway.

★ ★ ★ ★ ★

Jacket ambled up the gully, shut up the poly-tunnels and parked his 'new' second hand tractor in the far corner of the smallholding next to the allotments. The runner bean vines had browned and dried like rope, binding together the hazel pole wigwams. Large areas of soil had been turned over ready to weather down for next spring and all that remained were the stubborn stems of the brussel sprout plants, pale and scaly in the crisp autumn sunshine. Looking up to light another woodbine from the one he was smoking, Jacket noticed

Amos digging an allotment nearby. Puzzled by this recent foible of Amos's, Jacket went to investigate.

'Wha' yer doin?' Jacket squinted through smoke filled eyes.

'Diggin, yer stoopid prat!'

'Amos, you ain't got an allotment!'

'I ent so daft as I am cabbage looking, Jack. No it's old Jimmy Denby's. He ent so hot on his pins no more so I thought I'd help him out like.'

'That's reet good of yer Amos, but old Jimmy is younger than you!' said a frustrated Jacket.

'Fine figure o' a man ent I?!'

'Do yer wanna bit o' tea Amos, wiv me an' Jill?' Jacket sniffed humbly.

'Are yer goin to the Bull later?'

'Nah, the Oak. There's a bit of a game on tonight!' Jacket winked.

Turning the last spit of dirt over in a row, Amos anchored the spade in the earth then grabbed his coat from the rusty fence and followed Jacket back to his home.

Jill was cooking up a storm when they arrived, red faced and thirsty. Bacon and onion clanger, mashed spuds and broad beans, which Jill had blanched and frozen by the sack load, all covered in a rich parsley sauce. The smell hit the old men as they entered the steamy kitchen.

'Alright, Amos? You stopping to tea?' she said, blowing a curl from her fringe away from her eyes.

'Wha' we got?' Jacket enquired, his sense of smell only extending to cigarette smoke and a good ale.

'Clanger.'

'I wish you'd teach my old girl 'ow to make that Jill!' Amos leered.

'Simple really, bit o' suet pastry wrapped around bacon, mushrooms and onions, then boiled in a pudding cloth for a couple of hours,' Jill preened.

They washed down their repast with a pint of tea each from chipped blue and white ringed mugs and mopped up the last of the parsley sauce with a slice of 'Mother's Pride'. Amos had to loosen the knot of rope holding up his trousers.

'Aah! That's filled an 'ole! You do alright for a townie, Jill!' Amos said, tactlessly.

'Thanks very much, Amos!' she snorted. 'Ere, Jacket, before you slope off, you can take some stuff to Marge Henderson for me!'

'You can bugger off!' Jacket blurted out, emboldened since he'd finished his meal.

'That auction gear's been cluttering up my hallway for nigh on a week and it's gotta go!' she screeched, her blood pressure reaching a critical limit.

'I'll tek it to the Oak tonight lass. Don't blow a gasket!'

★ ★ ★ ★ ★

'Where do yer want all this quality tat, Rob?' wheezed Jacket from behind a mountain of cardboard boxes stacked high with Rudi Valli LP's and broken table lamps.

'Chuck it in the lounge with the other junk, Jacket' beamed Rob Honey, whose takings had seen a dramatic upturn since the announcement of the auction. Like Jacket, many other husbands had taken the opportunity to do a good deed for their wives and furnish themselves with an excuse to visit the Oak at the same time. Amos staggered in with an old gramophone and clanged it against the corner of the bar. 'This'll fetch a good price!' he exclaimed.

'Would have done 10 minutes ago!' muttered a few onlookers simultaneously.

Jacket wandered through the bar to the pool room, sparse and echoing in the glare of the strip lights. The Oak Pool Team was limbering up before travelling to the town for a 'friendly' with the Silver Horse. Milton staggered in with a chicken sandwich in one hand and a pint of Guinness in the other. He was greeted to muffled titters from the Pool Team, following the circulation of the story that Milton had been arrested for aggressive behaviour in the town the previous night.

'Ere, Milton! What do you call a judge with no balls?'

'Eh?'

'Justice Dick!' Howls of laughter.

'Eh?' Milton was on his fifth pint of the evening.

'So give us the details lad!' said Pa Earlem impatiently, fishing a fallen cigarette butt out of his pint.

'It were a mistake, that's all,' said Milton, staring through glazed eyes.

'We heard from Rick the Shop you were caught urinating in a public place!' Pa Earlem chuckled, growing tired of the Oak's current inaction.

'Yeah, so what?'

'Well, you're bleeding asking fer trouble, pissing up the back of a police van – yer dense bugger!' Alf wailed, spilling some of his precious liver tonic onto his Hush Puppies.

Jacket and Amos strolled through to give the young 'uns a few tips for their impending rematch with the Silver Horse. 'Nah then boys. You learn some manners afore you gew back there or you'll lose the rest of them teeth. Them's not country lads down that district. They're the leftovers what the East End of London couldn't cope wiv, so swallow yer pride, lose properly and buy all the drinks. We don't want a repeat of last time. Pauly has only just had his pins removed!' Pauly nodded his head very carefully and massaged the healing wounds in his jaw. There was silent agreement from all but Milton.

'Wha's the point o' goin' if not to win?'

'Thick as pig shit!' said Pa Earlem.

'So we stay in the league!' screeched half a dozen team members.

The team, fed and watered, boarded the minibus and made their way to the Silver Horse for a sound thrashing. 'A fiver says Milton gets a good slap tonight!' Jacket chipped in, being a prime candidate for all those organisations that end with 'Anonymous'.

'You're on! You in fer a game later Jacket?' Pa felt he was on a lucky streak since he'd won £50 on the pools the previous week.

'I could be persuaded!' Jacket grinned.

Tony strolled in, smiling with relief to be away from Shuggy and his place behind the bar at the Bull. Behind him, analysing her feet in coyness, was Linda, Tony's long-standing girlfriend, her timidity, stemming from her incomer roots, only began when she entered the Oak. She glanced up for a nanosecond and met the bloodshot eyes of Pa Earlem, whose lasciviousness trickled from every pore. Returning her gaze to the flagstones, she felt the embarrassment rise to her cheeks like mercury. Completely oblivious to his girlfriend's distress, Tony anchored himself to a barstool and ordered the drinks from the ill-fated Sue.

True to form, Dave Honey caught sight of the lovely Linda, who neither dyed her long blonde hair nor required a Zimmer frame to approach the bar, the only two conditions which Dave had when chasing women, and so lunged forward to serve Tony. Genetics have a cunning way of revealing themselves at the oddest moments. Sue, being dubiously linked to Dave Honey, could not control her primeval instincts either, so snatched the money from Dave and engaged her bottom wiggling walk to the cash till, followed by a cleavage flash on returning with Tony's change.

Undeterred, Dave spun around to retrieve a jar of red gobstopper lollies he was saving for a special occasion, like Halloween, where he'd get all the little girls to give him a kiss for trick or treat. 'Hello beautiful lady,' he smarmed, 'fancy a bit of this?' He wagged his bushy eyebrows in a cross between Tommy Cooper and Dennis Healy. Linda shook her head violently, daring not to look at the red stick hovering near his flies.

'I've got a boot load of stuff for the auction, Dave. No end o' people brought their old tat up to the Bull by mistake,' Tony said distractedly. He had finally noticed Linda, frozen to the spot like a mannequin on dope, face to face with Marshall.

No one knew if Marshall was his first or last name, nor did they dare to ask. He only came up from his remote farm in times of drought, be they of the female, alcohol or nicotine variety, it mattered little. This occasion was primarily due to alcohol deficiency, from which he was cured in the first hour following opening time.

Amused with the spectacle of his girlfriend in a stand-off with Marshall, Tony refrained from assisting her and instead shuffled back to a safer distance amongst Pa Earlem and old Alf. Marshall rubbed his oily fingers across his eyes and blinked half a dozen times. Linda was still rooted to the spot, shivering in her lacy white blouse. Wincing, Marshall adjusted his focus manually, moving so close to Linda's nose the peak of his sailor's cap brushed her forehead. She closed her eyes and held her breath as the fumes knocked her sideways. Giggling, Tony shuffled over and dragged her away into a darkened corner to administer medicinal brandy and TLC. Marshall blinked once more before throwing his arms in the air and shouting: 'It's gone! Did you see it? An Angel! Right afore me eyes! It's a warning! I knew summat was wrong this morning when I coughed and shat meself!' He clasped his hand to his forehead and paced up and down the pool room muttering 'It's a warning!' over and over again.

'I'll give yer hand wiv the auction gear, Tone,' said Dave flexing his muscles before a much shaken Linda, who was sobbing on Alf's shoulder. Amos ambled over and patted her on the shoulder,.

'Ere love? Does your Dad work at Tesco?'

Holding her vital statistics, she fled screaming from the Oak and locked herself in Tony's car.

'Not stopping then, Tone?' said a despondent Dave Honey.

'Don't look like it Dave,' he sighed.

★ ★ ★ ★ ★

Marge had distributed all her fliers and was now embarking on her poster campaign. Her first port of call was Rick the Shop's. The little tinkling bell of the door being opened sounded as Marge burst into the shop. Finding it entirely empty, she paced the two strides from the door to the counter and leaned across to peer through to the living quarters. Hearing raised voices and something smashing against a wall, Marge coo-eed at the top of her vocal capacity, which in itself nearly shattered a pickle jar and a bottle of cider. Rick came bounding in, deflecting an onion mid-flight. He went to straighten his hair then remembered its recent dismissal, courtesy of Felicity's dressmaking scissors. 'Old habits die hard,' he thought bitterly. 'Hello Marge, what can I do for you?'

'Can yer stick this poster up for me, Rick?'

'Yeh, no problem. Anything else?'

'Oo-arh, can I have a 'alf a pound o' tea and are you and Felicity getting divorced?' Her recent gossip forage had dissolved any vestige of inhibition.

'That'll be 78p, Marge and yes,' was his pitiful reply.

At the butchers, Marge peered around the corner into the yard where Jordan Maisey was helping Beardy unload a couple of sides of beef from his pickup. Marge waved at them both, panicking Jordan, whose irritable bowel syndrome had returned with a vengeance. 'Square up later, Jordan, alright?' said a shifty Beardy.

Smiling broadly, Jordan ushered Marge into the shop. 'What'll it be?' he said rubbing his frozen hands together. Frowning at Jordan's unease she looked down at her shopping list, which read; a pound of mince and a bit of rump steak. She said 'Two pork chops and a quarter pound of haslet please!'

★ ★ ★ ★ ★

Pa Earlem pushed two tables together and with some showmanship, removed the cellophane from a new deck of cards. Jacket was buying a round in and Sue and Dave were exchanging dangerous glances at each other. 'You in?' Pa said to Marshall.

'It's a warning, I tell yer!' He twitched nervously, 'I'd best gew home I reckon.'

'Well, that leaves us short,' Jacket coughed through tar stained dentures.

'I'll play!' Amos piped up. They laughed, choked and thumped each other's backs.

'No disrespect, Amos, but you never could play cards,' said Pa.

'Well, it'll be easy money for yer, wun it?!'

'You ain't got no money, mate,' said Jacket, rather unkindly.

'Got me pension!' Amos was getting shirty.

'Your missus will kill yer!' Jacket persisted.

'Ne'er stopped you – now are you gunnoo deal or what?'

They started with a few gentlemanly games at £1 stakes, hoping Amos would get bored and retire from the game. Far from having a poker face, Amos would get as excited over a pair of two's as he would over a royal flush. At one point Jacket thought he could detect the slight air of a bluff and called Amos's hand only to find he had four tens.

The stakes were rising with every hand and each player was becoming more serious and engrossed. Through sheer luck rather than judgement, Amos was slightly ahead.

'Dink would call it a night at this point,' thought Jacket as he fondly remembered his old companion since childhood. 'What an old woman he was!' Snapping his mind back to the game, he saw Amos had already drawn one card and was waiting for Pa Earlem's decision. Pa drew two cards. They raised the stakes. Amos was grinning from ear to ear and fidgeting madly on the chair.

Last orders had been called and the doors locked. The Pool Team had made it back, barely in one piece, and were supping on their beers and shovelling up the last of the smoke dried chicken sandwiches that had doubled as ashtrays since 7pm that evening. Pa shouted over to the team, 'Did Milton get a slap then?'

'Very nearly,' said Pauly before returning to the straw which delivered his beer to his fractured jaw. Jacket pushed a fiver across the table to Pa in payment of his lost bet.

'This fiver's 'bout all I got left!' said Pa, whose wallet had taken a severe beating. 'I'll call it a night.' He picked up his pint and staggered towards the Pool Team, who had remained to watch the game.

Amos was grinning again but as his back was against the wall, no one could see his hand. Most of Pa's money was in the middle and Jacket was down to his last few quid. He fanned out his cards, slowly revealing four kings. Smugly, he thought that now Pa was out of the way he'd easily clean out Amos and, for once, be in profit.

Jacket raised the stakes and placed his cards neatly in a stack on the table awaiting a decision. Amos shoved all his winnings in the middle and smiled at Jacket. Frowning, Jacket lit one of Pa's cigars and took a long draw on it. He looked at the meagre pile of cash by his side, then at Amos. He had to call him, but what else could he bet? Theatrically, Jacket slung the pile of small denomination notes into the middle and said 'That 'an my tractor will see yer!' and for added effect, he thumped heavily on the table. The Pool Team, Sue, Dave and Pa Earlem all leaned in and held their breaths as Amos placed a neat fan shape of four Aces down on the table. Jacket visibly shrunk. His eyes closing, he visualised the scene when he told Jill how he had lost their livelihood.

Pa had to prize Jacket's four kings from his hand to confirm the outcome. Amos shrieked wildly and shouted the pub drinks before kicking out time at 12.30am. Pa slapped Jacket's back and offered him another cigar. 'P'raps Marshall's Angel was a warning for you, yer daft bugger! Now wha' yer gunna do?'

'I don't need a tractor Jacket!' said Amos kindly, 'You keep that an' I'll just tek the money!'

'Nah then, you know as well as me, a bet's a bet!' Jacket snapped.

'Well we'll work summut out,' Pa said, 'P'raps you two could be partners, like Clint Eastwood and Lee Marvin in 'Paint Your Waggon'!' Jacket spluttered in the froth of his Theakstones.

'That were a woman they shared, not a bleedin' tractor!'

'T'ent much difference,' beamed Amos, 'Both make a lot of noise and cost too much to run – what do yer say?'

'Bloody stoopid idea,' grunted Jacket, but he knew he had no alternative.

★ ★ ★ ★ ★

It pelted with rain in the morning, but Amos still rose early, put Benny Boy's lead on and took him for a drag around Jacket's smallholding to survey his new venture. Satisfied with his little victory over his patronising friends, he began the slow walk down the Ghost Chase and across the Lands to Adderstey. Pausing on the footpath to let his Jack Russell off the lead, he noticed the last knockings of blackberries rotting in the rain, uneaten. 'Sad state of affairs, Benny Boy! None of these posh folk know bugger all about good food!' Benny Boy was not listening. He was busying himself with the backside of a springer spaniel belonging to Big Mazzer.

'Wha'd hoe Amos!' she bellowed.

'Ello my darlin'!' said Amos joyfully. 'Ah see the brook's well swollen's morning'.

'Not suprizing wiv all this bleedin' weather!' boomed Mazzer. Benny Boy yelped as Mazzer's springer spaniel, Jess, became tired of the pestering and had trodden on Ben's neck, pinning him to the floor. She started to bare her teeth, whereupon Benny Boy peed himself.

'Ta-ra Amos. Don't stand around in this weather or you'll catch yer death! Come on girl, leave Ben alone!'

Turning onto the Main Road, Amos caught up with a

striding Marge Henderson, on a mission. Panting as he tried to keep up, he attempted to engage her in conversation, but she marched on faster saying, 'Not now Amos I need to find out who has died recently.'

'Eh? You what?' gasped Amos, shocked.

'I need the exact number of pensioners in the Parish for their Christmas hampers!'

'Hadn't you ought to wait till nearer the time. Old Betty Henshaw's on her last legs and Louie Kilpin's not too hot either!' Amos shouted at the disappearing giantess, but once she got going she was harder to stop than a ram at tupping time, which would account for her husband's ill health.

Not wanting to return to his missus with her bionic mouth and lists of chores, Amos trudged to his favourite dry den, Piggy Wilde's hay barn. Piggy had recently abandoned rearing livestock on his land when animal activists from the next Parish freed his pigs and set light to their barns. Being adjacent to the Main Road, Piggy Wilde was inundated by complaints from Death Row as the pigs foraged happily amongst old Adolf's zinnias and relieved themselves on the old folks' front paths.

Amos climbed up a few bales, nestled in the warmth of the rick and lit a cigarette. 'Good things come to those who wait,' he muttered, 'An' now I'm sounding like Jill! I'll atta watch that, Benny Boy!' Finding Ben chasing a farm cat right into his kitchen, Piggy paced across the yard to find a familiar picture.

'Oi, Amos! Bugger off out of my barn!' he yelled.

'Bugger off yerself!' Amos replied nonchalantly, 'I were 'ere afore you were born lad – and don't you forget it!'

Shaking his head, Piggy started to walk away. 'Well at least put that fag out! The insurance company will never believe a second claim!'

★ ★ ★ ★ ★

The day of the auction had arrived and Marge was busying herself with the catalogue numbers on an old 1930's pram and a table lamp reported to have once belonged to the Duke of Bedford. Dave Honey was cleaning the pipes in celebration of the event. 'Can't grumble, it's been six months since they were last done,' he said to Sue. Amos was settling himself down at a table near the bar, reserving adjacent seats for locals only.

Tony filed in with his sister Ann and offered his assistance to Dave. Rolling up his sleeves, he found himself once more behind a bar, despite it being his first night off in weeks. Ann turned to Marge with a large basket of fresh fruit, veg and eggs from her parents' garden, which she added to the basket of meat donated by Jordan Maisey and the selection of wines, beers and spirits from a begrudging Shuggy.

'Nought from you this year, Jacket?' Marge said rudely.

'Bit short this week, Marge, I'll buy summat later,' he growled before settling down next to his new business partner.

Sue lit the scrunched up newspaper beneath the pallet wood sticks and skilfully balanced coal onto the young flames as Ann was deputised by Marge to act as Porter for the sale. 'Is Marshall's Angel joining us tonight?' asked Dave Honey hopefully.

'No, she ent, couldn't persuade her at all!' laughed Tony, 'but her Dad said he'd come and check out the auction.'

'When will it start?' Ann asked politely.

'Not till they're all beered up, my darlin'. Then they'll part wiv more cash.' Dave rubbed his bony fingers together and winked at Ann. She giggled at his feeble attempts and returned to Marge – *Mien Fuehrer*.

The locals piled in first to reserve the best seats and order in long lines of beer in anticipation of the queues later so enthusiastic to begin that they had demolished their stockpiles and were just re-ordering as the fretful and timid incomers arrived. Each was duly respectful of their place and asked politely if any of the seats were not taken. All seats and table space had been reserved unofficially and was monitored by head-splitting scowls from the local crowds.

Linda's father arrived as promised and eagerly shook Tony's hand nervously at the bar. Being Tony's friend was enough for Pa Earlem, who yelled across at the meek dentist and beckoned him to a seat next to Jacket. Tony winced at the prospect of his future father-in-law becoming a fully paid up member of Pa's gang. Mazzer barged into the Oak and pushed her way across to the bar where Tony had her usual waiting for her, a pint of Guinness and a bag of ready salted. 'Better do us another, Tone, this wunt last long,' she breathed through gulps of froth.

Bronwyn was bullying Sonny to lend a hand, so he excused himself under the pretence of visiting the gents and instead wove between the young farmers and hid in the Pool Room, leaving Marge and Bronwyn in a heated debate over the morals of that young Sue Honey. Mazzer grabbed her third pint and found a vacant seat next to Beardy. He smiled submissively and felt his spine fall out of his bottom and cower beneath the table.

Pa Earlem leaned across the table and offered his hand to Linda's father. 'Call me Pa!' he said shaking the man's hand vigorously.

'My name is Dominic Fagus, well just Dom really,' he stuttered warily.

'You ent local are yer?' Jacket said, fixing a beady eye on Dom.

'No, I'm not. My family and I moved here about 25 years ago. We live in Adderstey'.

'Wha do yer do?' Amos piped up, joining in with the interrogation.

'I'm a dentist.'

'A poncy bleeder, eh?' said Pa laughing raucously.

'Not really. I'm an NHS dentist. Not private.'

Jacket pushed one of his lined up pints across to Dom. 'You're all right!' he proclaimed patronisingly.

'Ow do yer know Tony then?' Pa persisted.

'Tony has been seeing my daughter for nearly a year now'

'You could do a lot worse than Tone,' said Jacket defensively.

'I quite agree,' replied Dom quickly.

Jimmy and Donny fell through the Oak door closely followed by Milton and the Longfield lads. They had been warming up at the Bull earlier and were hot, sweaty and smelled repulsive. They were ushered into the pool room and served a tray load of bitter by Sue, who managed to escape them with just one ladder in her stockings.

Soon the Oak was heaving and there was barely room to even stand. The non-locals had been relegated to the back, near the pool room, and there they had planned their emergency escape routes in case the natives became aggressive.

Marge yelled through to the lounge, where Ann had busily been putting the lots in order. Marge grabbed her borrowed gavel and thumped it down heavily on the table in front of her. 'Right you lot, we're ready to start, so get your wallets ready for a sound fleecing!' she screeched, really getting into the part. 'Lot number one, Ann!' Marge bellowed, whereupon Ann appeared through the doorway carrying a Wedgewood teapot with only one hairline crack. 'Who'll give me 10 quid?' ordered Marge.

'I'll give yer a tenner for Ann, Marge!' yelled Rueben from a safe distance, 'She's an effin 'nine' !' Steven elbowed his brother sharply in the ribs.

'Shuddup you moron, that's Tony's little sister!'

'Oh, sorry Tone, mate!' Rueben shouted, signing the thumbs up to Tony behind the bar. Tony smiled good-naturedly, willing to overlook Rueben's little outburst. Tony also knew that, as small as his little sister was, Rueben would come out worse if he tried to tackle her. Pity though, he would have liked to have seen that.

The auction started slowly, but with encouragement from Marge and jeers from the young farmers, the old pieces of junk were being sold for ridiculous prices. The next lot was Jordan's meat tray. Jacket and Pa's ears pricked up at the offer of cheap meat and they began their bidding at £25. Beardy caught Pa's eye and, frowning, he shook his head. Pa grabbed Jacket's cuff and lightly tugged at it. Gaining his attention, he nodded towards Beardy who was still gently shaking his head. The bidding stopped abruptly and was won by a dapper old chap from the new housing estate for £50.

'That stuff could cook itself it's so hot,' muttered Beardy to Mazzer through the corner of his mouth. The auction paused for 15 minutes while the punters stocked up on their diminishing alcohol and Marge did a quick sweep of the remaining lots.

When the auction resumed, Ann appeared in the lounge doorway with lot 34, a pith helmet. 'Ere Milton, you could buy that. It'd protect you head when you fall over pissed!' Jimmy Earlem yelled.

'It'd be a piss helmet!' yelled Donny Earlem, shrieking with laughter.

'I'll tell you what,' said Amos, 'That 'ud do my Missus for when she's on the back of my motorbike!' Pa nodded slowly, knowing it to be foolish to argue the point.

'Who'll give me £5 for this lovely, genuine, authentic helmet?' Marge boomed officially. Amos jumped up, waving his hands and shouting.

'Me Marge! I will!'

'Good on yer lad,' bellowed Mazzer, slapping her gelatinous belly.

One of the incomers piped up from the back of the room, a collector of period costume. 'I'll give you £25 for it, Mrs. Henderson!'

'Nope!' said Marge, 'Amos wants it, so it goes to him for a fiver!' and with that she slammed the gavel down. The non-locals were forming a crowd, plucking up courage to defend their outspoken leader.

'But I bid fair and square – £25!' he complained.

Marge stood up and folded her arms. She sighed deeply and looked towards the young farmers for support.

Steven and Rueben leaned over towards the foolish upstart and said in unison, 'You heard Marge, Amos wants it!'

The numbers of incomers to locals was about even but none dared to tackle the unknown strength of the beer swilling natives. 'There's always one who spoils it ent there?!' Pa slurred to his new found friend Dom the Dentist. 'You ent bought owt yet lad. Don't yer fancy any of it?'

'Actually, Pa,' hiccoughed Dom, staring through puce eyes, 'I quite like the look of that Autoclave over there. It would do as a spare at my surgery.' Dom was beginning to slide down his chair.

'Yeh, I've always fancied one meself!' said Jacket sarcastically.

'Who'll give me £20!' Marge resumed.

'My mate Dom 'ere will!' said Pa, equalling Marge's volume.

'Sold!' said Marge without waiting for further bids.

'Silly old fool,' muttered Tony to Alf Burrows, who had spent the entire evening propping up the bar.

'What's that, Tone?'

'Dom just bought back an autoclave which he donated last week!'

'More money than sense I reckon.' A gloomy Alf replied.

'What's up Alf, you ent yerself tonight?'

'Me piles are back again. This bleedin' weather don't help 'em I'll swear!'

With only two more lots to go, Ann and Marge were preparing themselves for the task of collecting the cash and handing over the goods, while Dave and Sue called last orders. 'Better play by the book tonight, Sue' he said slyly, 'Best not risk a lock in with them new folk here.' He winked at Sue and thought to himself that he was in for a good night with her later.

Dom collected his new bargain, which had formally sat in his own garage for about five years, and finally staggered towards the door. Pa grabbed his coat, balanced his cigarette in his mouth and steadied his new friend on his feet. 'I'll walk with yer Dom. I fancy a bit o' fresh air.' While Dave was kicking out the remaining stragglers, Tony and Ann helped clear up, Marge totted up the proceeds and added to it the percentage taken from the bar profits and Sue made the team hot drinks.

'A successful night was it, Marge?' asked Tony inquisitively.

'I'll say!' she said in her deepest baritone, 'I reckon we've got enough to buy 'em all a tot of alcohol wiv their hampers an' all!'

Outside, the rain had stopped and the grass and tarmac glistened beneath the street lights. Worms and snails were committing suicide on the road and most of the autumnal leaves lay in heaps, rotting beneath the mature trees. Amos and Pa started to sing as they hooked an arm either side of Dom to prevent him from becoming better acquainted with the pavement. 'An you'll never – walk – alone, you'll – never

– walk – al – one!' Dom, suddenly bursting with self-confidence, said;

'Thanks chaps, but I can manage on my own!' He stood up and began taking big strides, straight into Henridge Brook.

Sometime later, Amos and Pa dragged Dom and his precious autoclave out of the swollen brook, coughing and spluttering and complaining about the bitter cold. Pa and Amos picked him up again and marched him to his doorstep, where they leaned him against the door and rang the bell, running away giggling like school children.

Linda opened the door to find her father, who promptly fell in on top of her, dripping wet. Dumbstruck, she let him fall to the floor before closing the door and going straight to bed, leaving him prostrate on the hall floor for all to see. 'Had fun did we?' said his angry wife Caroline, 'And why did you bring that pile of junk back home?!' Too angry to wait for a response, she stepped over her sodden husband and followed her daughter up the stairs.

Tony and Ann offered Marge a lift back to Wesley Drive, which she readily accepted. On their way past the church, they saw the unmistakable silhouette of Marshall, kneeling in the graveyard, hands clasped tight in prayer. 'What's that silly old sod doing?' Marge demanded, pressing her nose against the side window of Tony's car.

'Dunno, Marge! P'raps he's found God!'

CHAPTER 7

November

Rick the Shop

Felicity smoothed her cashmere sweater over her hips and fixed a smile before answering the calls from the shop front. Gliding between the ham slicer and the cash till, she recalled the days spent languishing in the comfort of her parental home, pampered and adored. In between returning the change to one customer and serving the next, she glanced down at her once manicured nails and winced painfully at their shabbiness. Her fingers, liberally adorned with minute paper cuts, perforated the four first class stamps from the sheet and handed them to Lily Underwood.

Lily squinted at Felicity through the scratched perspex screen of the counter and wondered which one of Felicity's eyes was trained on her and which one on the stamps. 'Your roots are showing, deary,' said Lily, turning to prod the Jiffy bags at her side.

'Eighty eight pence please!' snapped a pouting Felicity as she threw the change into the steel tray beneath the screen.

'An' anyway, Ethel,' continued Lily, 'they reckon that Pa Earlem pushed that dentist in the brook on purpose! You could never believe that o' Pa,, could you? Well that nice respectable Dom Fagus should o' known better – getting tangled up with the likes of the Earlems… '

Ethel opened her mouth to add a word or two in Pa's defence, but Lily showed no signs of abating, so she closed it again.

Wearing her usual perplexed frown, Ethel stepped up to the post office counter for her pension to find it unmanned. Felicity had taken umbrage at Lily's comments and was extracting Rick from the lounge to take over. 'Mother was right! Cutting off my nose to spite my face! With a son-in-law like you, I'd have emigrated to Australia too!' Felicity screeched. Lily leaned over the counter and peered into the living quarters.

'Keep quiet Ethel!' Lily said to the still silent pensioner, 'I reckon there's a bit o' trouble brewin'.

'I've taken a hundred pounds out of the till. I'm going into town with the car and I'll see you when I see you.' Felicity rummaged in Rick's jeans pocket, while he was still wearing them, and took the keys to their ageing Sierra. Grabbing her handbag, she trudged through the shop, narrowly missing Lily, displacing the little bell above the door as she slammed it shut.

'Well!' exclaimed Lily and Ethel together as Rick tumbled through the door into the shop.

'And what can I do for you ladies?' he beamed.

★ ★ ★ ★ ★

Outside, Bronwyn was reading the advertising cards with interest. An upright piano, pram and doll's house, all required good homes and were going cheap. Tony tapped her on her shoulder, making her jump several inches. 'Oh, Tony, you did give me such a fright,' Bronwyn gushed, stroking his arm and batting her eyelashes.

'Spotted a bargain, Bron?' he enquired out of politeness.

'There's a pram for sale here, Tony. You and Linda should keep your eyes open for these things!'

'Give over Bronwyn!' Tony yelped, 'We're just going out – not getting married!'

'Not yet p'raps,' she giggled before clambering down the concrete steps into the shop.

Rick was leaning on the counter, head in hands, when Tony and Bronwyn shuffled in. He opened one eye and rolled it towards the ceiling before slowly closing the lid again. Lily had the entire contents of Ethel's shopping bag on the counter and was busy re-wrapping and packing her 1/4 lb. of cheese, box of cornflakes, plain flour and two loo rolls for her while extolling the virtues of a shopping trolley. Bronwyn made straight for Lily and Ethel for a gossip.

Rick gestured towards the second serving counter. Tony followed instinctively. Rick groaned loudly and scraped his hand across his freshly shaved head. 'What made you shave all yer hair off?' grinned Tony, predicting the answer.

'Hell hath no fury, 'an all that!' Rick's skeletal features looked even more pronounced and with all the recent late night boxing matches with Felicity, Rick looked a dead ringer for a Belson Victim.

'She shaved yer head!?' Tony gasped with genuine surprise.

'Nah, she hacked off me pony tail after the Telethon Pub-

Crawl that time, 'an it never really grew back proper, so I shaved it all off.' Rick smarted in his confession to Tony but he figured that it would lessen the impact when he went for his usual Friday night with the lads if he told Tony first.

'Looks alright,' lied Tony kindly, 'I bet you'll be beating the birds off now!'

Rick smiled for the first time that day and said 'You mean I didn't have to before!' Tony took the pint of milk and large pack of Rennies back to the Bull to ease Fat Shuggy's peptic ulcer, while Rick served Bronwyn.

★ ★ ★ ★ ★

Rick's afternoon was filled with a plethora of whining women comparing notes on the dosages of Hormone Replacement Therapy each respective woman was taking, followed by a visit from Mad Glad Arbuckle, sister of Alf Burrows and the local GP's worst nightmare. Glad had suffered an illness or ailment for every letter of the alphabet, and made sure that the whole Parish knew and sympathised about it. Rick's day was only slightly relieved when the school bus deposited 53 children on his doorstep, all demanding four packs of Stella and individual cigarettes to go with their Mars Bars.

One of the school children was Rosie, tall for her young years, peaches and cream complexion and a small lycra belt for a school skirt. Rick greeted her enthusiastically and begged her to extend her Saturday job to include a few hours after school behind his counter. Apart from an invaluable extra pair of hands, there were two distinct advantages to

Rosie's employment. Firstly, it pushed Felicity's nose out of joint when all the local lads and old duffers came into the shop to chat her up and, more importantly, the added bonus of being able to squeeze past her backside to get to the sweetie counter.

'Marry me Rosie!?' Rick whined.

'I will not work after school Rick and that's final!' Rosie grabbed her Mother's loaf and half dozen eggs, helped herself to a carrier bag from behind the counter and joined her friends outside. As the late afternoon sun streaked weakly through the pine trees lining the High Street, Rick wiped the slaver from his chin as she ascended the steps out of the shop, revealing the faintest glimpse of her purple knickers.

★ ★ ★ ★ ★

Felicity had not yet returned from her pilgrimage to the hairdresser and boutique by the time Rick had closed up for the evening. He supposed that she must have gone straight to a friend's house for consolation and moral support. Rick cremated some oven chips, which were shaped like corkscrews, opened an accompanying tin of ravioli for the kids and set about finding a baby-sitter for the evening. 'Go on Rosie, please? You know I'll make it worth your while!' he begged down the analogue telephone line.

'You'd better, sunshine. I'm missing a very important family gathering for you!' She silently raised a prayer of thanks to the Heavens for providing her with an excuse to avoid seeing her relations.

Free of children and responsibility for a few hours, Rick

decided to brave the insults at the Bull and try his hand at a few games of skittles. Tony moved aside the belching Shuggy to serve Rick his pint. 'Any chirpier Rick?' Tony enquired with genuine concern.

'Yeah, happy as a pig in shit, me!' he sneered with more than a hint of sarcasm.

'Here, read your horoscope, always good for a laugh.'

'It'll probably say that I'm gonna meet the raging nymphet of my dreams and win the Pools!' He grabbed the paper, perking up a little at the attention he was drawing from all of two people in the bar. The page was already selected and the paper folded into quarters by the ever-obliging Tony.

Cryptic Zola peered from the top of the newspaper column looking all stern and heavily made up as he glanced down to the section on Libra, the sign of balance and diplomacy.

'*Consequences must be thought out before embarking on unexpected journeys,*' warned Zola.

'There you go, Rick,' Tony said triumphantly, 'you'll be going on holiday with your gorgeous nymphet and Pools winnings!' Rick felt sufficiently cheered to enable him to invite Alf Burrows to join him in a game of skittles.

Two games later, Alf put his back out and, declining a deciding game, he returned to his bar stool. Whistle came in at his usual frantic pace, snuffling back a cold and twitching like a shrew on a night forage.

Whistle had been a resident of a rival Parish for a good 20 years and proudly boasted several generations of localness. On the death of his much beloved father, Whistle and his brother vowed to keep the family building business alive and support their mother in her dotage. Through tireless efforts and careful business acumen, the business expanded rapidly until such a time when they could purchase their own company digger. Whistle learned to drive this treasured family possession and became the only skilled digger driver in the firm. He held his head up high and thought of himself as a regular pillar of the community. People remarked on how he had turned over a new leaf, ate civilised meals out with his wife and sat out of any card games that occurred in his presence.

One day in his village of Draythorpe, he stumbled upon a fight between two young Adderstey farmers, who had strayed into their pub, and four burly Draythorpers. As far as Whistle was concerned, the odds just weren't fair. Without a thought for personal safety, he waded in to give them a fighting chance, knocking one Draythorper unconscious and mildly damaging two more before calling a halt to the madness. Despite surviving the scuffle physically unharmed, his reputation had taken a severe beating. Within hours, the whole of Draythorpe had heard about Whistle turning on his own. Although they did not mention it to his face, bad feelings simmered beneath the surface and local business dropped off dramatically. His company barely survived on the strength of the odd job from the town, but his family could not get past the Draythorpe opinion. Eventually Whistle and his entire family relocated to Adderstey and slowly but surely gained the trust of some of the local residents.

Lifting his elbows up to rest on the bar, he ordered a double Jack Daniels and a bottle of cheap champagne from

Shuggy. Intrigued, Rick made his way over to the bar to enquire of the occasion. Rick had lived in Adderstey long enough to know that subtlety was a polite but redundant method of obtaining information. 'What's the occasion Whistle?'

'Me Brother's 60th do in town,' Whistle sniffed. 'I forgot till today so I didn't get him anything. Only consolation is that the Missus has gone away to our Sandra's so she ain't going.' A greenish trail began its slow journey from his nose before being propelled back into its hairy hole with one long sniff. 'Don't suppose you wanna go, do yer? These family things are deadly on your own.'

'I've had a drink mate and Felicity's got the car.'

'I'm driving. Go on, there'll be free drinks if we get there quick.' Rick mulled over the opportunity of free beer and young, unrelated women for all of thirty milliseconds before agreeing with great enthusiasm. After all, it was a Friday night and you couldn't deny a man the odd night out on the tiles, could you?

Thin veils of condensation blanketed the cars and as the puddles in the car park reflected the clear night sky, Whistle fumbled with his keys and unlocked his van. 'This is my unexpected journey,' Rick said, assuming that Whistle was psychic.

'Wha?'

Rick explained Cryptic Zola's predictions as they drove to the centre of the town, chatting excitedly like old fishwives.

The birthday party was being held at the town's Irish centre, where Whistle's family had loose connections with the centre manager, enabling them to arrange a sizeable discount on the hire of the venue. The downside to this deal was that the centre had its own resident band, which played incessant Irish Folk music, too fast and out of key. When Rick and Whistle entered the hall, Whistle was mobbed by an elderly group of aunts and cousins, all vying for the next dance. Rick sauntered over to the bar and leaned heavily while contemplating the unfathomable appeal Whistle had for women. It was the same wherever he went. Rick tried to look objectively at all 5 foot 7 inches of him. With his hooked nose and Grizzly Adams beard and moustache he could hardly be described as the next Sean Connery. Struggling for freedom, Whistle disentangled himself from his little harem of pensioners and joined Rick.

They downed a couple of drinks and then found the host to congratulate him on reaching his 60th Birthday without any serious criminal convictions. A few more drinks and a couple of dances with a lady of known loose morals, Rick had almost forgotten that he was in possession of a wife and two kids. 'Well, I might not be a Pools Coupon winner,' he said to himself, 'but at least I can still get my hands on a raging nymphet!'

Rick threw himself into the Irish jig with such gusto that he completely missed the young bleached blonde mid twirl and landed right way up on the plastic chairs lining the hall walls. Panting, he turned quickly to discover Bronwyn stroking his absent hair. Normally, such a display of flirtatious behaviour would have had him dribbling uncontrollably, but this was Bronwyn after all and Sonny was sitting next to her. 'I do like this new look, Rick,' she slurred.

'Arrrgggh! What you doing here?' he sat bolt upright and nearly sobered up with the shock.

'Teddy is Sonny's' brother–in–law,' she explained, changing the focus of her attention to Rick's thighs. Rick jumped about a foot into the air and followed it with a pathetic attempt at a jig.

'Who's Teddy?'

'The birthday boy!' she giggled. Sonny sat, head bowed, peeling apart the same beer mat he had begun to dissect two hours ago. His father was engaging in solitary swaying with only his Guinness for a partner, his tweed waistcoat being dowsed with each turn. Rick smiled and nodded politely before legging it to find his nymphet, who had already found someone else to play with.

'Now who of yer will be wanting another drink then?' said Sonny's father generously.

'I hear the tab ran out on the bar, Dad.' Browyn said patiently.

'No matter, no matter,' he stammered in his broad Irish brogue, 'I'm buying!' Sonny's father was not known for his generosity and so after the initial shock had subsided they put in their orders.

'Where's he getting all the money from?' Bronwyn shoved her still static husband for an answer. Sonny regained consciousness for just long enough to shrug his answer, and mutter something about winning on the geegees, before returning to his beer mat.

Rick was reaching his second depressive phase of the day on seeing his nymphet indulging in some very amorous and indiscreet kissing with a pimply teenager in the corner near the fire exit. 'So much for Cryptic Zola,' he thought, 'talks out of her arse that one.' Whistle was holding court at the bar with a cousin who had no idea how close the genetic link with him was and wouldn't have cared if she had known. He tried to explain that they had practically grown up together and lied that he was a happily married man, but she was not listening to him. Partly through jealously and partly because he was a mate, Rick decided to rescue him.

'Gotta get back, Whistle. It's nearly half one and I've left Rosie with the kids,' said Rick, prizing an arm away from around Whistle's neck.

'I thought your Missus was called Felicity?' Whistle frowned and scratched at his beard.

'She is.'

'Whey-hey lad! Got another on the go ave yer? Didn't think you had it in yer!' Rick decided that it was pointless explaining, especially since the misinformation had given him temporary hero status.

They bumped and jostled their way to the entrance and politely said their goodbyes before piling out onto the streets, weaving past other drunks urinating in the gutter. Rick had sensibly suggested a shared taxi back to Adderstey but Whistle was insistent that he was perfectly capable to drive, since he'd only had a couple.

Whistle's blood red van had taken on a pinkish tinge with the growing ice crystals, spreading across the bonnet. He scraped the windscreen with the plastic lid from a can of Tyreweld and tumbled in beside Rick, who was already drifting off to sleep. The van rattled into action, then stalled at the first set of traffic lights. He pulled out the manual choke to full and revved the life out of the engine before dropping the clutch and roaring away. The leafless trees were ghostlike in their silhouette against the strong moonlight and the streets of Adderstey were deserted. Whistle slowed for the bend past the Old Folks' Bungalows and cruised towards the Primary School. The tyres slid on the frosty tarmac and in one long slow-motion scene, Whistle's van spun out of control, ploughed through flower borders and decorative chain fencing and lodged itself vertically up the War Memorial Cross.

Rick awoke to find himself sitting in a makeshift rocket launcher, staring up at the stars.

They could hear the gravelly noise of concrete chaffing against itself as they inelegantly spilled out of the van onto their knees. The main upright of the Cross had been snapped clean in two and was hanging limply by the steel rod that ran through its core.

'Bleedin' 'ell Whistle!' Rick gasped.

'Yeah, I know. That don't happen every day, does it?' He said despondently. 'Oh shit! I've 'ad a drink. If the coppers get involved I'll lose me licence!'

They sat motionless on the icy grass for a few minutes as the neighbourhood houses began lighting up the cool night sky, and doors creaked open in curiosity. 'How about we unscrew the number plates and leave it to the Police?' Rick suggested helpfully.

'Yeah, we're bound to get away with that one, yer stupid bugger!' Whistle replied, turning to wave at the local inhabitants fresh from their beds. 'I'll have to sort it meself,' said a now sober Whistle. 'Make sure they don't call the Police!' he shouted to Rick, breaking into a jog.

The scene was ridiculous to say the least, with Rick staggering around gathering up the decorative chains while trying to avoid a drunk in charge of a JCB. The van was dragged free of the Memorial Cross with such a noise that all surrounding households were soon awake and observing the commotion from their bedroom windows. One or two of the residents actually dressed themselves and walked to the scene to find out more. The house adjacent to the Cross, belonged to Bert Gellert, of bottom pinching fame. On seeing the spectacle outside his front door, he thought it was his duty to immediately contact the Chairman of the British Legion, Bandy Roberts.

Bob Roberts, alias Bandy due to the effects of a childhood bout of rickets, was a calm and charming man who insisted on precision in everything he did. Having spent his early years of manhood as a corporal in the Army, he left to work as a gardener for a large estate in the next parish. Within ten years he had impressed the estate managers so much with his dedication and fresh ideas that they had made him Head Gardener, a position he took very seriously. On retirement, Bandy decided to reduce his workload to tending his third of an acre garden, giving him enough time to look after his ailing wife, Grace. There were few surviving veterans of War in the area, especially ones willing to take on the responsibility of running the British Legion and so he was elected into power without his knowledge. It had taken many attempts at persuasion from the Governing Panel that he was the man for the job, but once he had accepted the responsibility, he took to it with the same zeal that he applied to everything.

Bandy arrived on the scene wearing blue stripy pyjama bottoms and his dressing gown. He surveyed the scene calmly and paused to think about the next logical step to take. Tying the cord of his dressing gown tight, he raised two fingers to his mouth and blew an ear-splitting whistle to halt all activity. With hands on hips, he beckoned the perpetrators towards him for an impromptu committee meeting. Whistle and Rick stopped all activity and seeing Bandy hung their heads in shame.

'Well!' Bandy exclaimed, letting out a huge breath. 'What is going on?'

Whistle tried desperately to explain that the accident had nothing to do with his drinking but was entirely due to the slippery roads and the lack of gritter lorries in the district. He also tried to appeal to Bandy's better nature and confided that he and his whole family would lose their home and business if he lost his licence. Rick interjected with the odd comment every now and then in Whistle's defence but seemed to do more harm than good.

Deathly silence followed as the whole neighbourhood watched motionless for the verdict. Bandy scratched his head, muttered something to himself and stood still once more for an age. Finally he said 'This is going to cost you, Whistle.'

'Anything Bandy, whatever you say, only please don't go to the police!' He begged.

'You do realise that its Remembrance Sunday next week don't you? All this needs to be immaculate before then and I shall oversee the sizeable donation to the Legion Funds personally.'

The agreement was made, the debris was removed from the road and a makeshift sign was erected around the memorial cross. With nothing more to see, everyone returned to their homes to catch a couple of hours' rest before daylight.

If Rick had been in trouble before last night it was nothing compared to the explosion that ensued that morning. Spitting fire and flailing plastic nails, Felicity was, as expected, in full battle mode. 'But darling,' he hissed, shielding his face from her new talons, 'I couldn't leave a mate in distress!'

'I'll leave you in distress in a minute,' she screeched. 'You left poor Rosie to cope on her own till a quarter past two in the morning!'

'I thought you didn't like Rosie, now you're defending her! And where were you till a quarter past two?' Felicity stopped her attack for a second while she thought of a feasible excuse for her evening out with a driving instructor from Draythorpe.

'You had upset me so much last night that I had to seek solace with Dawn at her house, in town, all evening.' She was flustered and, taking advantage of the cease-fire, Rick made a dash for it and locked himself in the bathroom. A little later, he heard the shop bell tinkle, which afforded him the opportunity to slide out of the house virtually undetected.

'If it wasn't for the fact that she is an unhinged, schizophrenic psychopath, she could be quite a nice person,' Rick thought to himself as he marched briskly towards the home of the Earlems.

Pa was tucking into his usual oily repast as Donny lay asleep, farting and scratching himself on the living room sofa.

Ma Earlem waved Rick through the open back door towards Pa, who was licking runny egg from his knife. Rick nodded towards the unconscious, festering mass on the sofa.

'Couldn't make it up the stairs last night,' Pa explained, between gulps of tea as thick as sump oil. 'To what do we owe this pleasure my man?'

'Did you hear 'bout last night?'

'Certainly did! There's nothin' that escapes Ma and Dink Winterfield's old lady!'

'So you know about Whistle's problem?'

'Yep, an' I've been having a think about that. If the boys get together Milton, Beefy and a couple of the others for the labouring and you organise the materials, reckon it could be done afore the 11th.' He said casually, shovelling in a chunk of fried bread dripping in ketchup.

Ma plonked another greasy plate piled high with black mushrooms, fried beans, bread, eggs and tomatoes in front of Rick and patted him affectionately on the head. Everything seemed in hand, without even canvassing for support. Rick sat stunned for a while before tucking in to the meal with relish and thanking Ma profusely.

At the shop, Rosie was holding the fort single-handed while Felicity was holding her driving instructor, Seth Crowe in the living quarters.

'He'll be gone for ages,' squealed Felicity, grating her new nails against Seth's trouser zip.

★ ★ ★ ★ ★

Sonny walked into his kitchen, bowed low with a terrible

case of post-party liver dysfunction and an incurable bout of ultrasonic Bronwyn, who herself was swallowing large quantities of Ibuprofen for the pneumatic drill in her head. This morning's crisis had stemmed from the late night discovery of Mick, their 17 year old son, tucked up in their double bed with Araminta Blythe-Brown, which disgusted the proud Welsh Bronwyn with her devout Christian ethics. Mick had wisely scarpered as soon as Bronwyn was rendered unconscious by the five Barcardi and cokes and three Gin and oranges, to leave his browbeaten father to cope with the fall out.

'He's your son!' she shrieked, 'Talk to him! He's too young to be doing that sort of thing. Especially with one of those… those TARTS!'

Sonny nodded sagely and wandered out of the back door, while Bronwyn ranted on about moral wastelands to Joey the family budgie.

Wandering up Wesley Drive to Pa's house, Sonny found that many of the local menfolk had already gathered around the Earlem pickups and tractor. Ma had prohibited entrance to so many muddy booted louts but was not averse to feeding them the odd jam turnover to keep the growing lads going.

Pa was standing in the back of the pickup, flailing his arms about, summoning the men around him. Feeling important, he said, 'I've seen them do that on the films! Paint yer Wagon, I reckon, or summut similar p'raps. 'Cept I'm not gonna burst out singing or owt like that.' He grinned broadly and took a dramatic deep breath before addressing the crowd. 'It's good of yer all to want to lend a hand to poor old Whistle, who is, at this moment down wiv Bandy negotiating terms and conditions for the British Legion's silence. Pretty cut'n'dry really. What ain't so certain is our ability to keep the nagging old trouts of the parish quiet on this matter.' Pa waved in the general direction of Lily Underwood's house just a few doors away.

The men murmured and nodded agreement. 'Any suggestions lads?' Pa said enthusiastically.

'How bout a large dose of strychnine?' shouted Rick to rapturous laughter.

'Don't you have to be human for that to work?' sniggered Jimmy Earlem – more titters.

'Come on lads, serious stuff now please,' interjected Pa, coming over all official.

'Ow 'bout a carribean cruise? Get her out the way like?' Beardy suggested.

'Nice thought mate, but who'd chip in cash to pay for that old cow to enjoy herself?' Pa said stoically. 'Mind you, keeping her occupied ain't a bad idea.' The cogs whirred in the old man's head till it started to hurt. The crowd remained silent till his idea was formed. 'Ere, where's Bert Gellert?' Pa was fit to burst.

'I'm down 'ere, lad!' A bespectacled Bert croaked nervously.

'Got any decent aftershave, Bert?' Pa grinned mischievously. Bert groaned loudly as he cottoned on to Pa's plan.

'Ow are yer at the tango, Bert?' Shouted Donny above the sniggering and giggling. The condemned man shuffled off to shit, shower and shave, before returning in his best bib and tucker to face Lily.

'It's a far, far better thing I do now, than I have ever done… ' quoted Tony, as they watched poor Bert disappear down the Drive.

'Eh? You what, Tone?' muttered an illiterate soul. Pa drew the meeting to a close by inviting everyone to bring whatever building supplies and equipment they could spare with them to the hanging lump of concrete, masquerading as a memorial cross.

★ ★ ★ ★ ★

Rosie was trying to placate old Alf Burrows in one of his indecisive moods while serving Agnes a quarter pound of jelly babies.

'They're Beefy's favourite.' She flushed a putrid pink colour. Mad Glad Arbuckle was talking the hind legs off a donkey about her latest ailment while sounds of Seth and Felicity's passion reached a crescendo in the room next door. Rosie recognised the sound of breaking cups on tiles, guessing that the sofa had migrated across the floor and hit an oversized coffee table. Doing her best to cover for the flagrant act of infidelity and the desire to keep her job, Rosie turned on a radio she and Rick often listened to in the shop, but which was forbidden by the odious Felicity.

A few minutes later, Felicity reappeared, slightly dishevelled and grinning like a weasel on ecstasy.

'Turn that bloody racket off girl!' Rosie shot her an icy glare before marching off for her lunch break, leaving the radio switched on. Felicity leaned across and pulled the plug on Terry Wogan and his dulcet tones.

'Right then Felicity, my dear, what have you got in your garden to donate to the cause?' Mad Glad demanded, suddenly taking on an officious air.

'Cause? What are you talking about?' Felicity was still reeling from her encounter with Seth, who was now gathering up items of clothing from around Rick's living room and dressing himself rapidly before leaving to pick up his client for her 10 o'clock pre-test driving lesson.

'Haven't you heard about Whistle then?' Mad Glad said, shocked at her ignorance.

'Oh, God yes!' sighed Felicity, turning to walk away. 'What do I care what that silly little man gets up to with my husband?!' Mad Glad pursed her lips and took in a long, deep breath. Narrowing her eyes, she stared at Felicity for a moment and judged that she was entirely serious in her indifference. The shop became uncomfortably silent. Agnes, Alf and Mad Glad all looked at one another briefly and left the shop immediately.

Bert had dowsed himself with his best 'Brut' aftershave and smoothed the few remaining strands of white hair over the liver spots on his bald head. As he approached Lily Underwood's front door he hitched up his polyester grey trousers at the back and took a deep breath before knocking. He had no idea how Lily would respond to his overtures and he felt totally unprepared in how he should handle the situation. Why on earth had he agreed to this ridiculous course of action? Through the door he could hear Lily approaching, her solid footsteps echoing in her small hallway. She swept the net curtain of the hall window aside to identify the caller. Her perplexed frown rendered her silent for a moment as she opened the door to the familiar Bert.

'Hello there, Lily,' he said politely as he handed her a small bunch of chrysanthemums he'd bought from Rick the Shop's. 'You must be wondering what I am doing here?' Bert could feel his brain hurting with the speed at which it was working.

'Too right! What's all this silly nonsense, Bert? You haven't given me flowers for 52 years! And you didn't have your way with me then.' Lily, half grinning and flattered and half shocked by Bert, snatched the flowers from his hands and began closing the door.

'Wait!' Bert yelled, holding open the door just enough to peer through to her. 'There is a reason I am here. I was hoping you would do me a favour?'

Lily paused. Where was her Christian spirit? A friend in need is a friend indeed and he had been a friend when they were children after all. She opened the door a little further and said, 'Go on, I'm listening.'

'Well it's like this, you see. You know how I've always loved to dance and how we all used to go as a big gang to the dances in town of a Saturday night?' He looked at her for some sign of encouragement, but there was none. 'Then after all those years wiv me dodgy knees and all, when I couldn't barely walk, let alone dance. Well I thought I'd never get the chance to ever again.' Bert put a finger up to his eye to wipe away a dry tear for effect. 'But God must've been smiling on me Gal. I got me new knees now and I finished me physio, so I'm as good as new!'

'And you wanna go out dancing do yer Bert?' she said, finishing his dialogue for him.

'It just so happens that there's a dance in town this

arternoon. I should be very honoured if you would accompany me'. She thought for a few moments, staring up at the cloudy sky. 'Why not?'she thought to herself, it would be a chance to wear her new black patent shoes and she had just had her hair rinsed a delicate shade of purple.

★ ★ ★ ★ ★

Bandy stayed right next to the memorial cross, sitting in a deck chair supervising and instructing all the volunteers. Many of the local wives had raided their gardens and outdoor pots for the few remaining flowering plants and winter blooms and were waiting to plant them in the borders as soon as the main shaft of the cross had been repaired. It had proven trickier than Pa and the Earlem boys had originally planned. The bent steel core could not be straightened and so it had to be drilled out and a new rod cemented in its place. Following this, Whistle had used the arm of his JCB as a crane and lowered the concrete top above the broken pillar, enabling a team of able builders to quickly add fresh cement, sealing the join. While the cement dried, a makeshift support was erected from scaffold poles and joints by Donny and Jimmy Earlem and a fine layer of sand and grit was patted into the join to blend in. The ladies got to work on planting the shrubs and flowers while Rick struggled with the decorative chain fencing. Despite a superb job in mending the shaft it still did not look right.

'It looks newer than the rest of the cross' Bandy said, puffing on his pipe. 'Needs a bit of ageing somehow.'

'S'alright Bandy, we already thought of that!' Jimmy

Earlem and his brother stepped forwards with a Tesco carrier bag and a trowel. From the bag, Jimmy pulled out a number of large tubs of plain yoghurt. 'Might not work in this cold weather but it's worth a try.'

Bandy looked puzzled as Jimmy and Don began smearing the yoghurt over the newly cemented join. 'Should start to go mouldy in a couple of days, just right for the ceremony on Thursday.'

The ten past two bus sailed past the memorial cross at a steady pace, indicating and pulling out on the other side of the road to bypass all the commotion surrounding the cross. Lily could just make out the scene through the condensation on the windows of the coach.

'What in the name of our Holy God is going on there?' Lily was shrieking at poor Bert.

'Did I ever tell you how much I have admired you over the years, Gal? Is that a new hairdo Lily?'

They all stood back and surveyed their work. The scaffold was still supporting the cross while the concrete set but on the whole it was a fine job. Everyone present looked towards Bandy, who stood frozen for a moment. All held their breaths till a broad smile crossed Bandy's face in approval. Lots of hand-shaking occurred for a while until Whistle, overcome with emotion stood on the steps of the memorial and shouted to gain the attention of the whole gathering. 'Erm... I just wanted to say... Erm... Well... I don't know how to thank you all. You have all been so incredible, so supportive and well, bloody marvellous in my book. I'd like to say a proper thank you and buy you all a drink down at the Bull.' The womenfolk sauntered home for a nice pot of tea and a slice of 'summut special' and the menfolk threw their tools in the back of the Earlem's pickup and clambered in after them while Whistle followed in his JCB.

Bert and Lily returned on the last bus, giddy but exhausted. Lily had been wined, dined and danced into acquiescence. Despite his aching knees and apprehension, Bert had enjoyed himself too and on the ride home he moved his hand over hers and gently squeezed. For once, Lily just smiled.

CHAPTER 8

December

New Year's Ball

'Pregnant!' Olivia's father screeched. 'How the hell can you be pregnant?! You haven't even got a boyfriend! How much shame are you going to bring on this family? And so close to Christmas too. You wanton little whore! Who is the father of this creature? Eh?' He stopped to draw breath and stomped across the room to lean on the festively decorated fireplace.

'Oh Dad! Have you any idea what you sound like? It's the 1980's not 1880's! No one gives a rat's arse about getting knocked up these days. I quite like the idea of having a child. I can dress it up in beautiful clothes and teach it to ride and...' She trailed off as her father turned to face her, the pulse in his forehead pumping rhythmically and dangerously fast.

'You will not bring up a little bastard in my household! And to think that it could end up my heir! Oh your poor mother, God rest her soul. Have you no thought for her memory?' He paused just long enough for a slug of his brandy before continuing unabated. 'I won't rest till I know who the father is. He will marry you and do this properly or you will have to get rid of it!'

'Father!' Olivia gasped. 'How can you say such a thing? It's my baby, no one else's, and I am keeping it!'

'Then be cut off without a bean, my girl! Your choice!'

'You are massively overreacting!' It was a scene directly from a bad soap opera.

He was as adamant and stubborn as his daughter. He stormed off into his study and slammed the door with such ferocity, that a lead crystal vase of chrysanthemums on the sideboard was knocked over by the blast.

In his study, he slumped into his antique leather chair and delved into a wooden box on his desk for a cigar. How could she? His darling little Olivia, knocked up by some local farm hand or tradesman. He had heard rumours that his girls were a little free with their affections amongst the local boys but you just don't discuss that sort of thing with your daughters. That had always been their mother's responsibility. After two more brandies and half an hour of pacing up and down the well worn Axminster, he charged out of his study to locate his daughter. He found her in the kitchen, helping herself to a smoky bacon crisp sandwich with pickled onions. She stared up at him, her mouth poised to bite into the white bread, waiting for him to initiate conversation.

'It's no use girl,' he said vehemently, 'I have to know who the father is. You must tell me. Please!' He started to sound desperate. Olivia put her sandwich back on the plate and took a deep breath.

'The truth is, Daddy…' She paused and briefly contemplated his high blood pressure and the size of her inheritance before saying, 'I really haven't the foggiest notion who the father is! And that's the God's honest truth!'

★ ★ ★ ★ ★

The rain was icy cold and a northerly wind whipped up and stung Jacket's reddened face. Amos was tucking into half a pork pie, crouched in a little hollow next to a hedge while Jacket reversed the tractor and trailer up the narrow lane to the Henridge end of the forest. Reaching the most difficult part of the manoeuvre, Jacket bellowed a command to Amos to assist in directing the trailer through the overgrown gap in the trees that was barely the width of a pair of horses passing on the bridleway.

'Tell me agin wha we're doin'?' Amos said, spitting wet clumps of pastry on his waistcoat.

Jacket sighed slowly, climbed down from his tractor, adjusted his sodden tweed cap and said,

'We're collecting a bit o' foliage and stuff to sell for Christmas decorations and that. You know, mistletoe, holly and the likes.' Jacket drew deeply on his woodbine, the greying fragments from the tip being blown by the wind into his eyes. They heaved themselves between the trees into dense and un-trodden territory, cursing and swearing at the brambles as they snagged their skin, drawing blood. Jacket produced a billhook from a large canvas kitbag and began slashing at the undergrowth with large expansive swipes, creating a safe passageway for them to pass unharmed. 'I fink it would be better if we split up like. Get more collected that way,' Jacket said, handing Amos a shiny new set of clippers and a hessian sack. From the kitbag, Jacket drew out a small bow saw and looped it over his arm and onto his shoulder.

'That's a strange choice o' tool for a spot o' pruning ain't it?' Amos sneered. Jacket grinned broadly and headed into the darkness, occasionally flailing his billhook at overhanging branches.

★ ★ ★ ★ ★

Mazzer was at The Bull, propping up the bar with her usual post-lunch snifter. All the dribbling crones at the old folks' home had been fed and watered and it was her turn for a little repast. Tony was emptying the overflowing drip trays, polishing the ashtrays from the bar and listening to Mazzer wax lyrical about the forthcoming New Year's Ball at the Village Hall. She had planned on getting a red taffeta dress made up with a big starched bow sewn on the back to cover her larger than average rump, but after the fiasco with her 'bestest frock' at the telethon earlier in the year, she had all but decided against a dress altogether. Mazzer had been rummaging around in her mother's attic recently, looking for some spare chicken wire that she was sure had been stored for safekeeping and had happened upon a large trunk she recognised as her father's. Prizing open the lock, she had found his army call up papers, a couple of bent medals and some of his well worn clothes. She was almost overpowered by the stale stench of naphthalene from the moth balls and saddened by the derisory quantity of belongings that had embodied her father's life. Wiping her eyes and the trail of snot on her cuffs she sifted her way through the demob suit, military police arm band and some woollen long johns before finding a full black dinner jacket with tails. By the dim lamp light, Mazzer shook out the folds of cloth and held it against herself. 'That's not half bad!' she said to herself, before kneeling once more to locate the matching trousers.

As a child, Mazzer was often mistaken for the eldest son of the Henridge Gellerts, even on Sundays, on the way to church, wearing her whale bone corset beneath her petticoat dress. Her close cropped black hair refused to be tamed and never reached below the nape of her neck. It was as though it had sensed the tide mark of grime beneath her collar and was repelled by it. She spent her days locked in combat with the local lads over a rugby ball, while her mother toiled long hours cleaning at the big house to feed her two offspring in the absence of her husband Jethro. Mazzer had long known that her father had been more sinner than saint on his return from the War. Her memories of him had been tiny punctuations through his long term absence, usually when he was too poor to get drunk or had tired of one of his many mistresses. He would return to pocket any trinket he could find to pawn or tap one of his many brothers for another loan. Eventually, Mazzer's mother had summoned enough self respect to send Jethro packing one day, forcing him to shack up with his current mistress from Draythorpe. Old Janet had never found the courage to dispose of his belongings, even after he had tried to barter his way past Saint Peter's Pearly Gates. Despairing of Mazzer's masculine lifestyle, her mother tried to educate her in more feminine pursuits, teaching Mazzer country crafts traditionally associated with women such as needlepoint and jam making. Mazzer had tried so hard to please her weary mother but the only thing that she found she had flair for, other than hedge laying, was cookery. Determined to foster this talent, old Janet scrimped and saved and sold what few remaining possessions she had to send Mazzer to catering college as soon as she left school at 16. Mazzer found herself alone and scared in digs in the suburbs of Bedford. It had been hard for Mazzer, both emotionally and physically, but after two years, she graduated with her diploma in catering and miraculously, a distinction in kitchen hygiene. She soon found a job as an assistant chef at a hotel in Bedford, working double shifts and being promoted rapidly. Her tenacity to master new dishes and learn new techniques left her little time for socialising, and much less time to visit her poor old mother and little brother back home. She also found that the lack of personal time meant that her spending was reduced to a minimum. This enabled her to send money home to her mother as well as building a nest egg up for the future. It was at her third job as sous chef at an exclusive restaurant in Sandy, Bedfordshire, that she met Mad Patrick.

He had been delivering flour and dairy products to the restaurant kitchens in a beaten up grey van when he saw Mazzer whisking egg whites for a meringue. Something about her strength and intense focus made him stop suddenly in his tracks to watch her. His mouth gaped open and his dribble stained cigar dropped to the floor. Mazzer had noticed this contravention of kitchen hygiene and had shouted:

'Get out o' my kitchen you filthy bugger!' Chastised, he felt both bemused and self-conscious and immediately returned to his van, whereupon a number of kitchen hands were sent to the car park to retrieve the ordered ingredients.

Patrick had made damn sure over the following months that he always took the delivery round that serviced Mazzer's restaurant, despite it being a far more tiring and arduous route than any other. Before taking in her delivery he would smarten himself up, extinguish his perennial smoke and wipe his hands clean on a rag kept especially for the purpose. On one such occasion, Patrick had overheard Mazzer explaining to another kitchen hand that she was due some time off work, but since she had been working flat out for weeks, hadn't had the opportunity to plan anything to fill her time. Taking his cue, Patrick had stepped from the shadows where he had been lurking and invited Mazzer on a veritable buffet of activities. She had given the matter a mere moment's consideration before readily accepting his offer. They had been dating for a couple of months, whenever her job allowed, before Mazzer announced that she wanted to get married. It wasn't so much a proposal as a warning for Patrick to attend the church at the specified date that Mazzer had booked and to look respectable. Patrick couldn't really see any major downside to this course of action; good wholesome food cooked for him, regular sex and someone to clean up after him. What was to object to? They married in the spring, just four months after they had first met, Patrick arriving in his crumpled, mud splattered suit in his delivery van, dragging a part conscious and inebriated brother behind him as best man.

The rather lack lustre honeymoon in a Cleethorpes caravan park left Mazzer with child, which propagated into another soon after. Suddenly, the full burden of earning a crust and supporting a family fell entirely on Patrick's shoulders, a responsibility which more than scared him. His evening forays to the local pub increased, which had a dramatic effect on the amount of housekeeping money he could give to Mazzer and in turn lead to spectacular arguments and lengthy absences from home on 'special deliveries'. It was history repeating itself. Mazzer had no other option but to relocate her children back to Adderstey and to call on the assistance of her tired old mother and extended family to help her care for the children while she went out to work. She had been the chef at the old folks' home for nigh-on 15 years, putting all her culinary expertise into slopping warmed baked beans over mashed spud on a daily basis. Every few years, Patrick would charm his way back into her life on the pretence of being a better father to his two children, but his absences were more frequent than his presence.

In her mother's attic, with her father's old suit pressed against her, all these memories flooded back into her mind, with the resultant conflict in emotions. Should she make do and mend the suit she clutched to her or splash out on a new gown? She pondered momentarily, weighing up the pros and cons of the suit; more money for booze, less likely to get ripped in an amorous tussle, no need to shave her legs, versus looking a bit masculine and perhaps less likely to pull… hmm… tough one.

★ ★ ★ ★ ★

News travelled fast from the stables to the post office, from the bus stop to the village school and finally to the Bull. Olivia was four and half months pregnant. Wives and girlfriends gasped upon hearing the news, then rapidly calculated an estimated date of conception. Some barely even waited till they were unobserved on the bus to town before ferreting in their handbags for pocket diaries, tracing the whereabouts of their spouses or lovers around those fateful predicted days.

Pa Earlem was itching to bring the tidings to the Bull, on a clear and frosty evening a week before Christmas. It had crossed his mind on more than one occasion since Ma had informed him of the news, that there was a remote chance that Olivia might be carrying another grandchild of his. Despite that possibility, Pa was excited at the prospect of breaking the news to the entire bar. He swaggered in through the rear entrance, which faced the full length of the bar, timing his entrance to coincide with the greatest audience of locals at the end of a long day. Tony served him a pint of bitter, which Pa virtually downed in one gulp. Alf Burrows was scowling on his bar stool, shifting uneasily from one hip to the other, his haemorrhoids painfully throbbing and perpetuating his cantankerous mood.

Pa licked the froth from his upper lip and turned to Alf. 'I hear Olivia up at the big house has been knocked up! It weren't you were it Alf?' Pa grinned, a semi toothless, tar stained grin, while Alf snorted his stout through his nasal hairs. Spluttering, he said;

'Am about the only bleeder in this place who it couldn't be! More's the pity. I reckon I could still teach even her a fing or two!' Alf winked lasciviously at Pa who cackled wildly.

'You already knew about it then?' Pa said a little despondently.

'You kidding? Rick the Shop is running a book on who the father is!'

'Bugger me! That was quick work. And there was me thinking old Ma was the dog's bollocks with the village grapevine.' He turned round and shouted over to Rick the shop, 'What odds 'ave yer got on me being the dad Rick?' There was a roar of laughter accompanied by a few choking fits and more splutters from Alf before Big Mazzer chipped in with,

'Bout the same odds as me… And I ain't got the right equipment!'

'You sure Mazzer?' It was brave of Tony, but then he knew he held a 'special' place in Mazzer's heart which protected him from harm – that and he was tucked safely away behind the bar. She jabbed a fist at him affectionately, knocking him sideways,

'Yer little tinker!'

'Well who yer got on the book so far, Rick?' Pa said gleefully, rummaging through his wallet for some notes to bet. Rick the Shop sauntered over carrying a tatty brown notebook, with a thick wodge of banknotes secured to the book by a fat rubber band. Rick fingered the worn notes absently and reeled off the list.

'Your Boys – obviously Pa.' Pa nodded sagely and resignedly. 'Ummmm, Steven Longfield, Milton… ' Both Pa and old Alf snorted.

'Who the bleedin' ell bet on Milton?! He can't stay sober enough to get it up, let alone aim it in the right hole!' More guffaws all round.

'Erm… Milton did!' Rick the Shop said with a wry smile.

'Go on… who else?' Pa said impatiently.

'Notch Underwood and a couple of lads from Draythorpe.'

'She can't 'ave had em all at the same bleedin time? Don't none of them know when they shagged her then?' Pa said. 'Three's more than a crowd, well it is for my boys at least!'

Old Alf chipped in at this point, wagging a finger. 'Ah Pa, you can't always say that though can yer? Remember Old Man Gellert and his brother and their wife and their eight children?'

'Hmm… I forgot bout them. Queer carryings on at that farm if you ask me,' Pa mused.

'Well anyway, she's four an' a bit months' gone,' Rick the Shop said with a wink, 'and you have to remember that none of them lads passed maths at school!'

Pa rubbed his chin stubble with a thumbnail for a while; it bristled like static. Clutching a fist full of notes, he led Rick by the elbow into a quiet corner to negotiate odds. They spoke in hushed tones, inaudible to all but the wily old Alf, who had been perfecting his lip reading skills for years after the air-raid that had left him partially deaf during the war.

★ ★ ★ ★ ★

The following morning, Araminta Blythe-Brown was revelling in the glorious news of her sister Olivia's disgrace. They had always had little regard for each other and had fought endlessly over everything from dolls to horses and more recently from cars to men. Her father would think her behaviour positively angelic after this latest scandal. She would never be so stupid as to get knocked up before marriage. That was a sure fire way to lose your share of Daddy's estate. Araminta was far more discreet in her assignations with the opposite, and occasionally same, sex. Daddy's fortune was too grand a sum to lose for her planned future of idleness and travel, especially since the old man had kept his will a closely guarded secret for years. Making her way over to the drinks tray in her father's study, she inadvertently scattered a stack of papers on his desk with the hem of her jacket. She poured herself a double brandy and, gulping greedily at the smoky liquid, her eyes wandered to a letter that bore the tell-tale NHS heading. It was addressed to her father. She read the note from the specialist twice before it made any sense to her. She felt hot, anxious and confused. Should she tell Olivia of her discovery or ignore it and hope the problem might disappear? She could hear Olivia approaching the study door, the distinctive sound of her riding boots on the parquet floor mixed with the clatter of dog claws following her. Instinctively, Araminta shuffled the papers back into a pile, making sure to conceal the letter, and moved away calmly.

'Minty? Have you seen my green silk scarf? You know which one I mean?' She breezed in and studied Araminta's expression. 'You look suspicious, what have you been up to?'

'That's rich coming from you! Guilty as charged and no idea who the father is! You are such an old slapper Olivia!'

'It takes one to know one!' Olivia was indignant.

'Stop behaving like a child, this is serious. Daddy will never forgive you this time, you do know that?'

'Oh, I'll bring him round, I always do,' she grinned

broadly, turned on her heels and flounced out again, the devoted labrador padding laboriously after her.

'If you have time to bring him round that is…' Araminta muttered under her breath.

Her dark brow was furrowed with concern, her eyes welling up with the thought of her father's prognosis. Despite constant battles with her father from a very early age, she was still a daddy's girl and it stung her deeply to face his mortality. The fact that Olivia was upsetting him again just added another reason for Minty to dislike her sister.

Olivia had dressed in her riding gear and was heading to the door as the bell rang. The golden Labrador started barking furiously and jumping up at the door, so Olivia grabbed him by the collar and dragged him into the sitting room and shut him in. Peering through the leaded windows beside the grand oak door she spied a miserable looking creature, fists clasped deep in his jeans pockets, hunching his shoulders against the cold.

'Oh Hell! What does he want now?' Olivia toyed with the notion of getting Minty to pretend she wasn't at home and sneaking out the back door, but it was too late, Rueben had spotted her. She opened the door just wide enough to peer through at him, but not to give him the impression he was welcome. 'Yes? What is it?' She was curt and officious with him. He took no notice and launched into the speech that he had been rehearsing all morning.

'I know fings weren't exactly perfect between us Livvy and I know about Steven an that and I know I ain't, well, you know, I have got a bit of a temper, like, but its my kid so I wanna do the right thing by it.' He sighed, relieved she didn't interrupt his train of thought and make him mess it up entirely.

'And if it isn't your kid? What then?' She was cold and dispassionate, staring at him directly in the eye without a flicker of emotion.

'Of course it's my kid! Over four months gone they said! Has to be mine. That's when we were together ain't it?' Even Rueben's slow witted brain could determine her inference. He could feel his temper rising, the jealously he had fought hard to restrain, returning in spades.

'It's a lovely offer Rueben but I have every intention of bringing up my child alone. Off you go now, I am late for an appointment!' She tried to close the door on him.

'It is my child. Olivia, say it's my kid! We were an item then. It's my kid, Olivia, say it!' He was pushing against the door, preventing her from shutting it. She relented, looking heavenward and rolling her eyes.

'All I am saying is that it might not be your child. So would your offer still be valid then? Eh?' There was a lengthy pause while Rueben assimilated this information 'No. I thought not. Now if you'll excuse me… ' She took advantage of his dazed state and quickly closed the door, just as he came to his senses.

'You bitch! You mean you were tarting around even while I was living with you? You said I was the only one! You dirty bitch! You can rot in hell with the pox for all I care!' He turned and booted her Mercedes, leaving a boot shaped dent in the middle of the passenger door. 'Bitch!' He wailed again, before jumping into his pickup and roaring off down the drive at some speed.

Minty appeared in the hallway holding Olivia's green silk scarf.

'Don't look at me like that Minty, the man's a fool!'

'Better a fool than a bitch'.

★ ★ ★ ★ ★

The wooden panels of Jacket's tractor trailer were bowing with the sheer volume of trees; big, small, tall, short, spruce, fir and pines of every dimension. The day was drawing to a close and the light was failing. Mist was forming rapidly in the valley around Henridge Brook providing ample cover to get the load right through the village and to the edge of the parish.

'Ain't a bad harvest for a couple o' old timers, ay Amos?' Jacket ached like he had never felt before. The joints in his hands were burning with arthritis and his lower back had locked up an hour before, but still he lumbered on.

'I still ain't sure this is right, yer know.' Amos said, scraping out the grime from beneath his nails with his penknife and flicking it onto the tractor cab floor.

'Don't gew gettin no guilty conscience on me now! That land belongs to the people o' Britain and we is the people of Britain! Besides, you want to give yourn missus a good Christmas don't yer?' Amos nodded obediently. 'We'll then yer daft bugger, shut yer bleedin whining and drive us up to Adderstey garage. I am gonna have a bit rest in the trailer.' The needles poked through his donkey jacket and pricked his skin, but he was too tired to care. The smell of oozing pine resin filled his senses and mingled with the cigarette smoke in the evening air. It was eerily quiet, save for the tractor engine and the rattle of the metal latches holding up the tail gate of the trailer. The shrouding mists had hushed the noises of Adderstey as they made their way to the garage.

Jacket was just picking a couple of spruce fronds from his collar when he heard Amos hammering his fist furiously on the rear window of the tractor cab. Clamouring to his feet, Jacket steadied himself, clutching at the moving branches, and peered over the heap of foliage at a panic stricken Amos. Slowing the tractor to a snail's pace, Amos pointed frantically at a parked police car in the lay-by next to the garage and a uniformed man standing in the road gesturing for them to stop.

'Oh bugger!' said Jacket, squeezing the life out of his cap and slumping back down between the greenery.

★ ★ ★ ★ ★

Craigie had finished bottling up and stacking new boxes of crisps for the evening shift at the Bull and had cycled back home to Big Mazzer's beef stew and dumplings. He liked it best when Mazzer was flush and could afford a bit of roasted belly of pork to go alongside, but with Christmas fast approaching, belts had to be tightened. He made do with a serving bowl piled high with stew and spuds and a hunk of bread the size of a man's fist. Craigie glanced up at his reflection in the mirror above the fireplace. The ride through the fog had moistened his bleached hair into loose curls which lay flattened against his forehead. He let out a disgusted moan and left the table mid-mouthful and bound up the stairs for his styling mousse and hot tongs.

'Oi! Don't let yer dinner get cold! I slaved over that for you!' Mazzer shouted after him, tutting loudly. She took her son's dish back to the kitchen, balanced it over a pan of simmering hot water and covered it with a second bowl to keep it warm.

'Mum?' Craigie yelled from upstairs. 'Are you going to the Ball this year?' He was applying sticky mousse from an aerosol canister in precise upward points to his hair.

'Yes dear, of course I will. Why?' She twittered, her maternal instincts piqued by her son's attentions to her.

'Ah nuffin. It's just I were thinking 'bout going an all.' Craigie, much preened and coiffured, descended the stairs to retrieve his dinner.

'That's nice dear,' Mazzer said, absent minded, her arms drenched in soap suds in the sink.

'Only I ain't got nowt to wear. Not that's proper like,' he continued. Mazzer put down the dish and cloth and turned to Craigie and said;

'Wha' you driving at? Coz I ain't got money ter burn yer know! I can hardly keep us under a roof, let alone going off spending on fripperies!' She was glowering through her bushy eyebrows, her chin buried deep in her chest.

'Nah I weren't after you to pay, Ma! I was thinking how I could get summut nice wiv me savings'. He had wriggled a consoling arm halfway round Mazzer's waist and had snuggled his face into her bullish neck. She melted in an instant to his charm and wiped a blob of soap foam on to his nose affectionately.

'Great idea lad! A quality suit will stand you in good stead for the future.'

'Right then! I reckon I'll gew wiv cousin Golfball and choose one. Might gew ter Milton Keynes or p'raps London even to get me a nice suit. Wha' d yer think?' He was still nuzzling her gently like a partially weaned pup.

'Wha' ever makes yer happy boy!'

★ ★ ★ ★ ★

PC Williams paced to the rear of the trailer, paused to briefly unbutton his top pocket, remove his notepad and lick the end of his pencil before saying;

'Go on then Jacket… let's have it!'

'Have what? Dunno wha' yer getting at!' A certain childish insouciance had materialised.

'Come on, don't give me that! You telling me you got them trees from your smallholding?' PC Williams was a veteran when it came to interviewing the locals. Some cases he cracked, but most times he failed to prove any of his suspicions. He had come to terms with those odds many years ago for the sake of his sanity. Jacket simply shrugged defiantly and then stole a glance at Amos to warn him to keep his mouth shut. 'You and I both know they belong to the Forestry Commission! It's plain and simple theft! PC Williams rubbed his eyes and then his forehead before sighing. He knew there was no way he could prove where the trees came from and this endless cat and mouse game with Jacket had been rolling on unresolved for more years than he cared to admit. He was tired and fed up and about to give in and go home for the night when Amos leaned out of the cab and exclaimed;

'They're from the Longfields' land!'

Jacket groaned. How many times had he told Amos to keep his trap shut? Just one rule to follow and he couldn't even manage that.

'Is that so?' said PC Williams with renewed interest. 'So if I go to see Old Man Longfield, he'll back up your story will he?'

'Umm, no. The deal was with Steven. Old Jed dun't know 'bout it'. Jacket was thinking on his feet. Oh Bugger, he thought. Now they had to get to Steven before the copper could. He'd better take the wheel as Amos was too slow to catch a cold.

'Don't s'pose you know where I can find Steven do you?'

'Oh yeah! He'll be down The Bull by now, chugging his third pint o' Guiness,' said Jacket, knowing full well that he'd seen Steven's pickup just minutes before heading in entirely the opposite direction.

'Hmmmmm! P'raps I'll try at the Longfields' Farm first' PC Williams said suspiciously.

★ ★ ★ ★ ★

Olivia zipped up her trousers and stooped down to pick up Steven's brushed cotton shirt from the straw bale near the entrance of the barn. She threw it at him as he lay naked save for a rough horse blanket covering his modesty.

'Stay a bit longer, Livvy, I can feel my dander rising again and there ain't no better girl to settle it than you!' Steven said, reaching out to try and grab her. Olivia side stepped his grasp and peered around for her silk scarf and riding hat. He rested his head on his hand and watched her get ready to leave him. 'So is it mine?' As soon as he said it he wished he hadn't. If it was his, she might make him take responsibility for it, perhaps even stay with her full time. He couldn't have that! The affair had only been kept alive for as long as it had due to its illicit nature. Despite that, he also wanted to know if she was carrying his child, perhaps a son, in her belly – his flesh and blood.

Olivia didn't answer but instead grinned at him, pulled the elusive scarf from beneath his back and kissed him lightly on the lips.

'I'm late,' she whispered.

'I'll say!' he retorted. Unamused, she swung the reins of the bridle over the horse's head, mounted him and guided the stallion out into the failing light of the day. Momentarily disorientated in the mist, the horse kicked and tried to canter off, but Olivia held tight and jabbed at his sides with the heels of her boots. After a short struggle, Olivia managed to settle him into a calm trot as they left the field next to the forest. She kept as close to the grass verge that flanked the narrow road as she could, but the horse was still acting up, dipping his head low and pulling at her grip. Olivia realised that she had stayed for too long with Steven in the hay barn. Daylight had all but gone, but she figured on getting back to the stables across the fields. She just had to get to the end of Henridge Lane, cross the Main Road and join the bridleway up to the manor.

It was only a few days ago that Olivia had consulted with her doctor about any potential risks of riding when pregnant. He had reassured her, but had given her a warning to go easy, no cantering and that it would probably be best not to risk it after five and a half months. The bump beneath her straining trousers was growing rapidly and it dawned on her that it might be the last chance she had to meet up with Steven. She was under no illusions about his feelings for her; he was as shallow and fickle as she was. They were a pair well matched. She was just lamenting what she considered to be the end of a fine romance as horse and rider reached the memorial cross where the lane joins with Adderstey Main Road. The fog had thickened and the deep growl of an approaching engine grew louder.

Jacket wrenched the tractor steering wheel to the left and steamed down past the memorial cross, skimming the curbside in his haste. Olivia's horse, already spooked, reared up once, making a loud incessant squeal as Jacket steered in time to miss them. Olivia held her breath, fighting to stay in the saddle but the stallion reared again and threw her into a rocky and overgrown ditch. The tractor screeched to a halt and with unaccustomed urgency, Jacket jumped down from the cab and lumbered back to the tangled heap that was Olivia. Blood poured from a gash at her temple and a jagged and splintered bone protruded from her shin. He peered over her, relieved to see her conscious and breathing.

'Oh, Jacket! Where's my horse?' She was panting heavily.

'Ee's bolted me duck! Don't you worry none bowt that. Ee'll find his way home!' Those were the closest words Jacket could muster when comfort and succour were required.

'I umm… ' Olivia muttered before passing out.

Jacket stayed at Olivia's hospital bedside all that night and every night through Christmas. She had regained consciousness in the ambulance just long enough to grasp Jacket's hand and beg him not to tell the Longfields about the accident.

★ ★ ★ ★ ★

Christmas came and went with its usual fanfare: the vicar preaching to a congregation of old hags and repentant sinners, with kids of the parish attending the service solely on the promise of free food in the vestry; old Esme Longfield dancing naked in the forest, burning her pagan yuletide log and painting woad on her forehead; Marge Henderson selling raffle tickets door to door in aid of the Princess Marina Hospice and Milton staggering around frightening all the women in the Bull with mistletoe attached to his baseball cap.

Jacket kept his vigil beside Olivia throughout the entire holiday, only leaving her side when her father and sister visited or when she required medical attention and calls of nature. The nurses had asked him to leave several times, but they tired of him loitering in the corridors and sneaking a quick cigarette in their linen cupboards. In the end, they allowed him to sit quietly in the chair by Olivia's bed. On the first night, Jacket had paced up and down outside the emergency room, wringing his cap in his hands when the Police arrived to interview him.

'It were all my fault! If she loses that little nipper I don't know what I'll do!' Jacket gasped before he slumped down on a set of chairs bolted against the wall, rubbing his face.

Astonishingly, Amos was a God-send during those few days before and after Christmas, with none of his usual thoughtless slips and irritating mishaps to bring further chaos to the situation. He found Steven Longfield and cleared up the tree stories before PC Williams exacted what little power he had, he negotiated a favourable deal with a market trader in Waterford to take the entire load of trees off his hands, no questions asked, and collected clothes and food from Jacket's wife and delivered them to the hospital and all without spilling the beans as to what had happened that night to the wrong people, as per Olivia's wishes.

The night of The New Year's Ball was bitterly cold, icicles hung savagely from every bow and branch, eave and overhang. Craigie and his cousin, Golfball, were stuck at Euston Station awaiting the delayed 4.15 back home to Waterford Town, cradling their purchases from the pre-January sales as though they were priceless jewels. Craigie chatted enthusiastically and without drawing breath to his slow-witted and placid cousin, who was distracted by every woman walking past, his tongue lolling limply to one side like a bloodhound.

When they finally arrived at Waterford Station, they found a worried Mazzer, pacing up and down the car park near to her Reliant Kitten, the nylon curlers perched precariously in her too short fringe. The boys approached her cautiously, sensing her irritation and ducked with the precision timing of all sons expecting a clip around the ear.

'Do you know what time it is? You are cutting it really fine, my boy, and leaving your poor old mum no time to get herself all spruced up!' It was fake annoyance that Mazzer showed the boys, Craigie was her little blue eyed boy and could do no wrong. Craigie scuttled across the tarmac and launched his podgy frame up towards her and gave her a big smacker of a kiss.

'Awwww, Ma! You don't need any sprucing!' He sniggered, knowing full well Mazzer could do with all the help she could get.

'Did yer get a nice suit then?' Mazzer enquired, as she heaved her bulky mass into the driver's seat of the Kitten, its suspension groaning audibly. Craigie nodded animatedly. 'Let's take a gander then!' she commanded, shaking the flimsy car as she turned and leaned over the bags in the foot well of the passenger side.

Craigie smacked her hand lightly and said, 'Good things come to those who wait, patience Mother dear!'

★ ★ ★ ★ ★

Fairy lights adorned the stone porch, tinsel moulted glittery rain in the foyer and a single solitary bunch of sorry looking mistletoe hung forlornly above the threshold of the Bradley Winterbottom Memorial Hall. Swathes of locals plodded inelegantly in all their proud finery into the cosy warmth of the dimly lit hall. Mazzer was resplendent in her freshly pressed dinner jacket with tails, looking every bit as manly as Beardy, who was hiding in the cloakroom till the coast was clear.

Trestle tables, reinforced with additional leg rests supported a mountainous buffet, at the centre of which lay a suckling pig, its skin thick and translucent with honey glaze, a traditional annual donation from Jordan Maisey's shop. Either side of the pig were two enormous bowls of murky brown punch, carefully guarded by Tony, who had already prevented Milton from pouring half a litre of cheap vodka into them.

Nervous laughter filled the air and clusters of uncomfortable women, locals and incomers alike, formed in pockets on either side of the hall. The men gravitated towards the bar at the far end, laughing heartily and drinking copious quantities of alcohol at an alarming rate, and gangs of gossiping hags sniggered in hushed tones over every fashion faux pas, or cruelly remarking over the style of any non-locals' apparel.

'All fur coat 'an no knickers that one!' Lily Underwood stated bluntly while pointing at the doctor's wife. 'I've heard she's no better than she ought to be!' Bert sashayed over to Lily and steered her gently by the elbow to the buffet, to everyone's great relief. She giggled and chuckled as Bert surreptitiously wooed her through the vintage fuchsia cocktail dress, last worn at the D-Day celebrations.

After an hour or so of awkwardness, alcohol and good food loosened inhibitions and general mistrust, until Jimmy and Donny Earlem were twirling the night away with Felicity, Rick the Shop's wife, and Bronwyn respectively, each thinking in their drunken stupor that they had pulled a young lady. Jimmy had dragged out his seventies 'Saturday Night Fever' white polyester suit with matching cowboy boots, which still displayed the Snakebite and Black stains from Milton's participation in last year's mistimed Congo party.

Mazzer was just about to physically extricate her daughter's tongue from the mouth of a farmer's son who was twice her age and send her to search for the beloved and missing Craigie, when she was distracted by the late arrival of an intoxicated Rueben Longfield. Rueben fell through the doorway, holding a half empty bottle of Jack Daniels and still wearing his jeans, checked shirt and stubble from the previous day. Seeing the dramatic entrance of his brother, Steven rushed to Rueben's aid just as Mazzer caught him swaying at a precarious 45 degree angle.

'Wha'd ho boy!' chuckled Mazzer, 'Reckon you must have started long afore any of us!' Mazzer handed Rueben over to Steven and remarked, 'S'pose you're relieved ain't yer, lad? Eh? Now Olivia's gonna be alright?'

Rueben's ears pricked up and for the first time since his arrival he stood upright on his own two feet. Steven looked at Mazzer and then at Rueben, then shrugged.

'Oh my Lord!' exclaimed Mazzer belatedly. 'I weren't supposed to say, were I? Cripes, bugger me, old Amos will have kittens!'

'What on earth are you going on about, Mazzer!' Steven said sternly and with genuine concern.

'Ee only told me cause 'ee needed me help with the food an…'

'MAZZER!' Steven interjected.

'Oh sorry.' Mazzer tried to concentrate but the five pints of Speckled Hen bitter had kicked in. Rueben was fully alert and clasping Steven by the shoulder as Mazzer explained all that she knew to the brothers.

The drive to the hospital was treacherous, with already icy roads receiving a hefty layer of snow. Tony, who had mercifully remained sober throughout the evening, had volunteered to drive the Longfield brothers to Waterford

General Hospital, the snowflakes mesmerising as they hit the windscreen. He kept wondering how he would be able to patch things up with his highly displeased girlfriend, Linda, who by now would be avoiding the romantic overtures from half a dozen yobs trying to score a New Year's kiss.

Tony stayed with the car as the Longfields made a dash for the main reception desk.

'Steve, do yer reckon she'll be alright?' Rueben was trying to both smarten himself up and sober up at the same time.

'You heard Mazzer, the baby is ok... she will be fine.' Steven was leading his brother by the wrist through the sliding doors of A&E.

'I meant, will she be alright wiv me?' Reuben was welling up. Steven smiled bleakly and cradled Rueben's shoulders supportively. 'I couldn't bare it if owt bad happened to her...'

They paced briskly towards the ward they were directed to and could see at some distance through the windows in the door, Olivia sitting up in bed with her leg hoisted high and in plaster. They peered at her through the glass as she sat chuckling heartily at Jacket, who was trying to understand an article Olivia had insisted he read in her *Cosmopolitan* magazine about 'New Men'.

Rueben started to push open the door but Steven clung to his sleeve.

'Good luck bruv. Am gonna stay out here. Don't wanna... Well you know... get in the way.' Steven handed Rueben a polo mint to disguise his alcoholic breath and held the door open for him. Olivia's face dropped on seeing Rueben and Jacket kindly made his excuses, left the ward and went to sit with Steven.

'What the hell are you doing here?' She drew breath and nearly passed out with the stench. 'Christ, you could have showered, and you stink of whisky.' Her contempt could not have been clearer.

'Please don't, Olivia. Why didn't you tell me?' He took two attempts to sit on the edge of her bed, the first try nearly landing him on the floor.

'It was none of your business! Besides, you think I'm a bitch – remember?' Her belligerence was hard to maintain. The fall and nearly losing the baby had made her think long and hard about how vulnerable and lonely she had become. Being a free spirit definitely had its drawbacks. Jacket had spent many hours regaling her with stories about his life with silly old Amos and with his long suffering wife Jill, to whom he had remained steadfastly faithful to for his entire marriage. Suddenly, the prospect of being a single mother didn't sound so appealing.

'You hurt me, Olivia. You said it ain't my kid. Then you gew 'an get yourself thrown off that poxy horse and all mangled up and don't even tell me!' Rueben looked at her with his glazed eyes and she softened.

'I guess I thought you didn't care about me anymore.' She was welling up too.

In the corridor, Steven and Jacket were trying to make small talk and be sociable. Steven guessed that Jacket must have played some part in Olivia's accident for him to have a forged such an unlikely friendship with her. Gradually, Steven prized the full story out of Jacket, even the part about the illicit tree collection and PC Williams.

'Talking of police,' said Steven, 'Did they give you a hard time over the accident?'

'Well that were the funny thing…' Jacket confided, 'They questioned me as soon as Olivia came in here. I told 'em it were all my fault, I were driving an that and I were right sorry 'an I thought that were it! I was gonna go back inside… lose me licence at the very least!' Jacket was pacing the corridor floor recounting his story.

'So what happened?' Steven was curious.

'Well, the Old Bill waited around till they could interview Olivia, which were a long time mind, cause they did lots of tests and scans and that and checked her over proper thorough like… then that were it. They said I weren't to blame! I reckon Olivia had words wiv 'em. You know, blamed herself, God bless her.'

Steven peered through the windows to see his brother cradled in Olivia's arms, weeping.

★ ★ ★ ★ ★

Back at the Ball, Mazzer was growing anxious. Keeping tabs on both her wayward children was challenging enough on a normal day, but when she was in charge of catering for the Ball and feeling the effects of too many brandy chasers, it was nigh on impossible. She was aware, however, that her precious boy had not yet made an appearance, despite his excitement and intense preparations, and it was fast approaching midnight. She was just considering being a drunk in charge of a Reliant Kitten to go and find him when he burst into the hall in the brightest, pinkest suit, purple cravat and feather boa. Golfball had slunk in beforehand and asked Disco Dave to play Frankie goes to Hollywood's 'Relax' on Craigie's arrival. Only too pleased to encourage controversy, Craigie, having got the entire hall's attention, proceeded to dance his carefully choreographed routine, lewd gestures and all, right in front of Lily Underwood, Pa Earlem and his unsuspecting mother.

'Well… I never!' harrumphed Lily, disgusted. 'Bert! Take me home – NOW!'

Pa stood and applauded Craigie's routine, cackled raucously and even joined in at one point, making the rest of Pa's entourage fall about in fits of hysteria.

Mazzer stood motionless, mouth agape, transfixed. When the song eventually ended he sidled over to his mother and tried to ascertain her mood.

'You are a… you're… a… pansy?' she stammered.

★ ★ ★ ★ ★

James and Araminta Blythe-Brown were making a surprise visit to see in the New Year with Olivia. They passed Jacket in the corridor and nodded inquisitively at Steven on their way into the ward. Steven jumped up and nudged Jacket.

'Ay ay. Looks like there'll be fireworks for midnight!' Steven muttered as they hot-footed it after the Blythe-Browns.

'Oh Daddy! I am so glad you came. We have some fantastic news! Rueben and I are going to be married!' Olivia's face beamed through the tearstains on her cheeks as Rueben sat beside her touching her growing bump. Taking one glance at his daughter then at the youngest

185

Longfield son, James Blythe-Brown growled something incomprehensible under his breath that sounded suspiciously like,

'Over my dead body!'

CHAPTER 9

January

The Adderstey Players

Wiping away his tears and blowing his reddened nose, Craigie asked for one last chance to prove he could sing, 'I could be happy with you,' on key, to the auditioning panel.

'It's just nerves!' he sobbed, 'I'll overcome them… I promise you I will… give me a chance… please!?'

Seth Crow leaned over to Clive Gellert and whispered, 'Pity you didn't choose to do a panto, he'd make an excellent Widow Twankie!'

Clive, irritated, glared vociferously and re-focussed his attention on Craigie's performance. Seth sniggered into his glass of gin and leered at Daisy, who had been temporarily distracted from painting the scenery. Daisy curled up her lip in disgust and went back to the two dimensional Riviera that was forming on the plywood before her.

Craigie's shoulder hunching huffs slowed till he regained his composure. He nodded to Valerie at the piano to the left of the stage, who began plonking out the tune again from the top.

'Skies may not always be blue… but one thing is as clear as can be… you know that I could be happy with you, my darling, if you could be happy with me!' His arms were

187

wide, his head held high as he prolonged the note for as long as his breath would allow, then bowed low to half-hearted applause.

Clive stroked his freshly grown goatee and stared at the podgy young Craigie with his Brylcreemed hair.

'Why do you want to be in 'The Boyfriend' Craigie?' Clive was trying to affect and air of authority, taking his spectacles out from his new sports blazer and cleaning the lenses with slow and deliberate movements.

'I want to be an actor. It's a simple as that.' Craigie felt buoyed by the adrenalin rush of performing.

'You do realise, IF we cast you, you may have to kiss a girl?' Clive warned.

'I suppose we all must make sacrifices for our art!'

★ ★ ★ ★ ★

'Back it up, more, more, left a bit… the other lock stupid! Keep it coming… Whoa! That'll do yer.' Jordan Maisey banged on the side of the cattle truck forcefully to reinforce his instruction to the driver, Beardy.

'Sorry Jordan mate. I ain't much good at reversin' in the dark no more. Well, not since that last punch-up back in May. Detached retina they said.' Beardy shrugged.

The noise of the frightened cattle was unsettling. They jostled and stamped and heaved themselves against the steel shell of the lorry, moaning a hollow and doleful cry.

'Better get 'em unloaded afore they wake the whole bleedin' village!' Jordan was as rattled as the livestock. He knew full well how often PC Williams had been making his circuits along the quiet areas of the four villages recently and it wasn't to his liking.

'Course, when they messed about wiv me eyes, it buggered up me sinuses 'an all,' Beardy continued, bellowing over the noise of the cows, blowing his beaky nose into a dirty cotton hankie and coughing like a consumptive.

'For God's sake man! Could you make any more noise if you tried? This ain't some bleedin' Sunday arternoon picnic here you know!' Jordan's patience was wearing thin, the painful cries from the cattle were echoing loudly from the stone walls of the rear entrance to the butcher's shop. The night was clear and still, with a sliver of moon sitting above the slates of the abattoir roof.

They shoved and steered and prodded the fated beasts down the extended ramp of the truck and into the holding pen at the bottom of Jordan's land, adjoining the brook.

'Do I have to stick around for the next bit, Jordan? Only it really turns me gut!'

'You get off mate. Best not slaughter at this time o'night on a Sunday. Even that bonehead Williams would smell a rat! Nah, I'll make a start first thing in the morning and get Lard to give me a hand,' Jordan yawned.

'Christ! You let Lard weald a knife? Are you insane?'

★ ★ ★ ★ ★

Valerie teetered across the sprung wooden floor of the Bradley-Winterbottom Memorial Hall in her white kitten-heeled stilettoes, bat wing lilac jumper and straining denim skirt. Stopping in front of Seth Crow, she stooped low, letting her ageing and flaccid bosoms dangle in front of him, picked up his pen lid and placed it on the notepad before him. He winced and turned his gaze back to Daisy's rear end in her old ripped 501's. Unperturbed, Valerie continued her strutting right across the hall, wiggling her generous hips in an exaggerated manner.

Clive was getting into the swing of his role as director now. He had finally cast enough locals and the odd brave incomer, to make a decent attempt at his production. They had all read through the scripts a couple of times, and so far it had been relatively successful, with only one minor hiccough, where Big Mazzer had blustered in to disturb proceedings, insisting that the cast help her to unload her Reliant Kitten of Tupperware and baking trays to the kitchens at the rear of the hall, ready for the 'Meals on Wheels' team to use the following morning.

Lily Underwood and Ethel had been co-opted into altering costumes from the previous productions into the 20's style flapper dresses and blazers and the cricket club had agreed to lend spare 'whites' to the male actors who could not supply pale trousers for themselves. Logistically, things were going swimmingly. It was a different story when it came to rehearsing their first scene.

The lead female playing the character Polly Browne, had accrued some experience with the Waterford Theatre, a budding child actor with the precocious attitude that goes with it. She had been teamed up with Craigie to learn the lines and to try and foster a little onstage chemistry between them, but it was very hard going with the pair of them vying for the limelight.

'Shouldn't we be up step ladders to do this?' Craigie said, flouncing dramatically towards the store room door. 'I've seen that on the telly. Don't all actors start up step ladders?' He was wearing faded denim dungarees with one shoulder strap unhooked and the trouser legs rolled up. Craigie had been experimenting with bleaching his own hair and was now sporting a rather orangey lid to his otherwise mousy locks.

'Don't be an imbecile!' came the retort from the Polly Browne actress, Louise. 'Christ, how am I supposed to work with these moronic yokels?' The outburst silenced the entire hall in an instant and every gaze and glare, from Clive Gellert to Lily Underwood, fell on her. Realising her petulant tantrum was a direct slur on virtually everyone in the room, she immediately tried to backtrack. 'Well, just Craigie… um… not the upstanding locals of the community… oh well you know!' She waited for some sign of forgiveness, some indication that at least the director was on her side. Clive rose from his canvas director's chair, paced over to Craigie and said,

'If you want to use a step ladder for the first run through Craigie you can, but it isn't necessary. Do whatever makes you comfortable.' He patted the crestfallen Craigie generously on the back and then turned to face the sulking Louise.

Feeling the full force of the Adderstey locals against her, Louise flushed a shiny rose pink. Ever the diplomat, Clive decided to rehearse a different scene, one which focussed on the Lord Brockhurst character, to be played rather aptly by the lecherous Seth Crowe. Clive opened his mouth and drew in his breath; ready to call the actors involved, but checked himself quickly upon noticing Seth's absence. He knew he couldn't be far away, as a freshly topped up glass of Gin and tonic and a still smouldering inch long length of Bensons and Hedges lay in an ashtray near to where he'd been sitting. Clive surveyed the hall, looking for more clues, and was surprised to see Valerie shuffling music at the piano. 'Hmmm… ' Clive mused to himself. 'If he's not with her, where the hell is he?' Despite the rehearsal having lasted a mere 40 minutes, Clive thought it prudent to call for a tea break.

Ethel busied herself with the enormous urn of boiling water and a dented aluminium teapot that had served the village's bingo nights and WI meetings for half a century. Clive sat on the edge of the stage, flicking the crumbs of a shortbread biscuit from his fawn tank top and supping lukewarm milky tea from a chipped cup. The cast sat in tight cliques dotted around the room, periodically shrieking with laughter or climbing over one another's legs to collect more food, despite there being enough room to park a small herd of elephants. Craigie minced over and sat with Clive, trying to achieve eye contact and ascertain his mood. Mostly, Clive was a mild mannered, accommodating man, without the slightest hint of mischief or malice, hatred or unpleasantness. He was just Clive, the village's historian, archive keeper and all round good egg. Craigie observed Clive's furrowed brow, the gaunt look and the bags under his eyes, and wondered if Clive could bear the strain of the role he had taken on.

Across the room, Lily was picking a fight with a scantily clad friend of Daisy's, whose blue lacy 32D cups were on permanent display. The teenager had taken exception to Lily's interference and had triggered one of Lily's monologues on righteous behaviour and moral fortitude.

Clive balanced his spectacles on the top of his forehead and rubbed wearily at his eyes. They made a squeaking noise as he pushed too hard at the tear ducts. Craigie sucked on the transparent straw of his cola flavoured 'Panda Pop' and glanced down at Clive's beige Hush Puppies.

'Why don't you 'come out' Clive? You know it's really very liberating and people were so nice to me when I did?' Craigie said innocently.

Clive spluttered, choked on his shortbread and spilt most of his remaining tea down his trouser legs.

'You what?!' he stammered. 'You think I am… you know… um… like you?' Clive lowered his voice. 'I am NOT queer! Got it?'

'Oh it's O.K. Clive, I mean, if you wanna keep it secret, that's fine by me. Not that I am coming on to you or owt. You're far too old for me and Mum said we are cousins or summut so that wouldn't be right anyway.' Craigie finished his drink and crumpled the plastic container between his fingers. 'You're not THAT bad looking I s'pose. You might still pull if you smarten yourself up a bit – you know, decent haircut and get rid of the polyester…' Craigie nodded to himself, jumped down from the stage and sauntered off before Clive could respond.

Craigie's observations stung deeply. It was not the first time that Clive had heard them. Throughout his life, Clive had always struggled to be 'one of the boys'. He was one of the vast clan of Gellerts, whose family spanned many generations within the villages. Being the only child of Bert and Flo Gellert, he tried to play with some of his many cousins from Adderstey, but they were often too boisterous for him, especially Big Mazzer, whose 'cowboy phase' left him mentally scarred and having nightmares about being scalped well into adulthood.

More often than not, Clive would retreat from the childish play and visit his Uncle Arthur. Arthur, an experienced engineer from the more respectable end of the Gellert family, had avoided the grating company of his Glaswegian wife for 30 years by escaping into his model railway village that encompassed his entire garden. His fastidious nature meant that he literally left no stone unturned, no detail missed and no engine part, created by his own fair hand, left unfiled or unpainted. Even the replica stone church had tiny stained glass windows and small speakers, cabled back to the garden shed, where a tape to tape reel of peeling church bells played. It was comforting to Arthur to have young Clive take such an interest in his hobby when his own children had failed to. They toiled long into the evenings, either turning machine parts out on the lathe or checking the points on the tracks at potential collision sites by torchlight. Arthur was a gentle soul, whose patience, tenacity and kindness towards Clive encouraged him to follow in his uncle's footsteps and train at British Timken as an engineer in his own right. With Arthur as a mentor and role model, he found little in common with people from his own age group, and so often conversations quickly became stilted and uncomfortable after the initial pleasantries.

The 1960's came and went in a blur of upgraded

locomotives and new Astroturf for the trackside embankments, while Mazzer and Arthur's sons indulged in experimentation peculiar to Woodstock and the Reading folk festival. When Clive was 18, his mother tried to convince him that he would enjoy seeing a few live bands, meet new and interesting people, perhaps meet a nice girl, but the more performances he attended, the more awkward he felt. The music sounded to him like the clattering of an unbalanced flywheel in complex machinery. Dancing was an even greater ordeal for him. It seemed that coordinating his legs with the beat of the music required him to recognise rhythm from noise. The result was a rather poorly timed jelly-like bobbing up and down with an occasional shuffle from side to side. He persevered for a few years to please his mother, who worried endlessly about him, but after her untimely death, he had little appetite for prolonging the whole agonising experience. Content to bury both his social life and grief in his toy trains and photography, much of his formative years were spent alone or in the safe and comforting company of his father or uncle. Apart from one aberrant drunken encounter with the vicar's daughter in the stables following a harvest ball up at the Big House, Clive's knowledge of women was non-existent. He craved neither male nor female companionship. It was as though something chemical was amiss inside him – a total absence of desire. Somehow it just seemed easier to ignore that side of life and concentrate on the things which made him happy; the trains, his photography and more recently, amateur dramatics. His interest in Am Dram flourished after he was strong armed into replacing a sick actor during the dress rehearsal one night. To Clive's delight and amazement, no one laughed at his short performance and instead complimented him on how natural his portrayal of his minor character had been. After a few more productions where he had been coerced into larger and more complex roles, this shy, retiring man found he had a flair for pretending to be other people. More than ten years of performing with Adderstey's 'Group 8' Players had served to bolster his ego and, indeed, bring his nervous disposition largely under control. 'The Boyfriend' was Clive's debut as Director and the strain was showing.

Sitting dumbfounded on the edge of the stage, Clive heard a loud bump and a muffled giggle. He turned and peered into the gloom of the shadowy backstage storage area to see the brown Dralon curtain moving and a pair of black slip-on loafers with white socks beneath. Clive sighed and cupped his head in his hand, turning back to face the throng of thespians scattered around him. 'Our Lord Lucan appears to have been found at last!' Clive muttered to no one in particular. How was it that a married sleazebag like Seth, could get so many women to fall for his patter he pondered, making no allowance for the quality of women Seth was content to attract. He glanced down at his own appearance; his perfectly pressed trousers with central crease, his buttoned down collar – deliberately left open with no tie to mark this informal occasion and beige socks to match his beige boots.

★ ★ ★ ★ ★

Jordan had arrived at the abattoir at dawn on the following

Monday. The sun was weak and low above the butcher's shop, but the air was crisp and the ground frozen hard beneath his cut off wellies. He had donned his work overalls for the sickening task of slaughter in order to keep his white serving coat pristine. He switched on the Roberts Radio that had sat on the shelf by the entrance for the 20 years preceding his father's retirement and the 20 years that succeeded it, and took a moment to adopt the indurate persona he had striven hard to create. Jordan's detached manner enabled the swift despatch of 15 Charolais bullocks with military precision and maximum humanity and all before midday. The carcasses were hoisted aloft by their rear legs, allowing gravity to assist the skilful swipes of his knife, as the offal fell into the plastic container at his feet. The automaton toiled away in the slaughterhouse long into the afternoon and the fading light, sliding half a carcass from the gutting area on its roof-mounted steel girders and hook along into the cool of the hanging room. He packed and pushed, emptied and re-ordered the enormous masses of sinew and bone until he could not find room to locate all the stock. The air was thick with the rank smell of viscera, which was making all the residents, as far as Rick the Shop, retch and gag and hurry indoors.

Lard latched the door of the butcher's shop, turned the great iron key in the lock and lumbered across the yard into the slaughterhouse.

'Still at it then, Boss?' Lard remarked, master of the obvious. Jordan just raised his head and glowered through his bushy, salt and pepper eyebrows. Desperate to please him, Lard offered to stay late and help Jordan find room for all the meat accrued. In his eagerness, Lard began unpacking the cool store and freezers in an attempt to pack more efficiently.

'Lard mate! Stop! I appreciate your help – really I do, but honestly, I can manage. You get off home to your mum.' Jordan was guiding him by the shoulder out of the door. 'Help yourself to a spot of sirloin for you and yer mum's tea tonight on your way out.' Lard started salivating at the thought of the huge prime cut he would slice for himself before leaving. An hour later, Jordan went back into the shop to make a phone call.

'That you Beardy?' Jordan almost whispered.

'Yeah? Jordan? Wha's up? Did they all escape? Heheh! I know, tasteless joke!'

'We have a big problem.' Jordan's tone was dour and sincere. He explained that the day's work had been more fruitful than he had anticipated and had left 6 large containers of ousted prime cuts of meat. Even with the new beef hanging in the cool room, the older beef had taken up more space in the cooler than originally estimated. They had two options, sell the lot for a ridiculously low price to anyone they could offload it to or to find some freezers.

Beardy ruminated on the problem, the telephone line crackling amongst the silence. The thought of reducing his cut of the proceeds was most distasteful to him but the thought of having to ask the only person who could provide the solution irked him even more. Jordan broke the silence.

'Bite the bullet man and ring Big Mazzer!' He heard Beardy's heavy swallow and pause for breath.

'S'pose I'll af to,' he concluded, as an involuntary shudder ran down his spine.

Mazzer had tried to lure Beardy to her house in order that he could 'pay her in kind' for the favour, but persistence and fear made him articulate enough to persuade Mazzer to meet them both down at the Village Hall after her duty at the old folks' home, where Jordan could act as chaperone. She was one of the few trusted people who possessed the side entrance key allowing access to the kitchens at the rear of the hall. It hadn't been the first time Mazzer had been called upon to support a local's private venture, so she parked further up the lane by her cottage at the top of the jetty, to prevent the blowing exhaust on the Reliant Kitten advertising her presence at a peculiar hour, and walked the rest of the way to meet them.

They all waited in Beardy's van for the last of the girl guides to be picked up by their mothers in hire purchase Mercedes and BMW's before declaring the coast clear and driving the van to the back of the hall.

'Better git yer skates on! I can't remember whether old Ethel said she were gunnoo start her bake tonight after she's seen *Corrie* or whether it were Lily what was gunnoo start the stew for the Meals on Wheels?' Mazzer stopped and scratched her head, then helped Beardy carry the crates of meat. With it safely stowed in padlocked deep freezers beneath the stage, Jordan felt calmer and managed a brief smile of gratitude towards Mazzer.

'You know we'll see you right don't you Mazzer?' Jordan said in earnest.

'You always do my dear… You always do!' She slapped

him hard across the shoulder blades, making him cough.

★ ★ ★ ★ ★

Craigie's words kept re-surfacing in Clive's thoughts during quiet periods, particularly while he catalogued this year's village photographs in his journals. He was only 42, still referred to by his uncle and father as 'young Clive', but he did not feel it. It was almost time to go back to the hall for yet another disastrous rehearsal. He peered out of his bedroom curtains to see a wild and turbulent night, the silhouette of leafless willow trees by the brook swaying in collusion with the storm. He wondered if tonight's rehearsal would be equally as tempestuous and, for a moment, hoped that the weather was severe enough to call the meeting off. The fleeting chance of a reprieve was quashed upon seeing Amos pedalling his boneshaker bike hard against the wind, the peak of his cap folding upwards defiantly.

'Damn! If he can venture out tonight, the others won't think twice either!'

He trudged down the stairs and into the front parlour. It was the only place left in the house which had retained his mothers' feminine charm, with pressed dried flower pictures above the fireplace and delicate porcelain ornaments on the mantel, a chintz chaise longue in the corner and her most favourite of all, a walnut bureau that had been bequeathed to her from her aunt. Clive had taken great care to keep this room exactly as his mother had left it and manage the family finances just as she had done.

Delving into the bureau, Clive checked the statements

from his savings account, his Post Office account and the balance of his current account and felt the first stirrings of a radical idea in his mind.

★ ★ ★ ★ ★

Many of the cast and crew were already at the hall when Clive arrived in his navy blue, mud spattered mini metro. He raised the hood on his anorak, opened the car door and scurried through the deepening puddles of the car park and into the vestibule. Ethel immediately began fussing around him, whipping off his coat and positioning it on the back of a chair next to the cast iron radiators to dry.

'It's a bit blowy out tonight me duck, en't it?' She said, balancing a tray of cherry rock cakes beneath his nose. Clive declined with a courteous smile and mouthed the words 'no thanks', while winking at the shy little lady. He marvelled at her tenacious spirit and boundless energy.

Moving through to the main hall, he suddenly realised why he should have observed his customary punctuality. The scene was total carnage. Craigie was mopping tears from his eyes and pouting like a sucker fish, while Louise repeatedly wagged her finger at him, pointing out how unprofessional he was being. Lily was shouting at some of Daisy's friends for spilling their cola on the floor and sticking their used chewing gum under the edge of the chairs, Golfball was balancing precariously up a temporary scaffold holding a metal stage lamp that looked about half his own body mass and Seth was yelling instructions to Golfball while gawping at the nubile young girls and fiddling with the loose change in his jeans pocket. The noise was cacophonous. Clive stood in the doorway, with his hands on his hips, frowned and sighed.

'Do you think it's time for a tea break, Clive?' Ethel enquired, meekly. Ignoring her kind offer, he paced over to Seth for an explanation. Despite the cast's din and immense self absorption, a profoundly low, thunderous growl stopped them all dead in their tracks. Seth pulled a curtain aside just as a series of bright flashes lit up the horizontal rain. Lily began taking off her jewellery and removing her hair pins, telling everyone to stand clear of the metal window frames. Craigie grabbed Louise in a child-like embrace, terrified, and Seth took the opportunity to place a comforting arm around a grinning Felicity's shoulders.

The noise of excitable adolescents and overly dramatic adults reached a climax around the same time as a bolt of lightening struck the external power cables at the apex of the hall's roof. The deafening bang shorted all the circuits and left the entire hall in darkness. Seth linked his hand beneath Felicity's elbow and shepherded her towards their favourite hideout. Craigie grasped at Louise, then Daisy, then back to Louise again, in blind panic, snot and tears.

'Everyone stay calm!' shouted Clive, above the squeals. 'I'm sure it's temporary. Let's find some torches or candles and at least see the wood for the trees!'

'Oh, for goodness sake!' bellowed Lily, 'It's a jolly good job you young 'uns were not around during the Blitz! Now that was something to fear!' The squeals and silliness subsided following Lily's reproach and Clive was content for her to take control.

Lily politely requested that her loyal friend Ethel should search the kitchen for torches or candles and sent Daisy outside to check to see if anything on the roof was on fire before turning to address Craigie.

'Pull yourself together, dear, this is neither a drama nor a crisis.' He did as he was told. She continued; 'Now be a good lad and telephone your mother. We will need to re-locate the Meals on Wheels food immediately.'

'I'm sorry Mrs Underwood' Craigie replied respectfully, 'me Mum's catering some do over in Bedford tonight, she won't be at home.'

'Hmmmmmm, I see,' Lily said forlornly. 'Well, it will have to be a combination of the vicarage and the primary school!' She rummaged in her bag for her address book and charged off through the darkness towards the payphone, to spur the Reverend and the Headmaster into action and save the day.

'Um… H-h-h-ello?' Golfball stuttered fretfully. 'It's a bit sc-sc-scary up here, can s-someone g-get me d-down?'

★ ★ ★ ★ ★

Throughout the following two weeks, the Primary School became the village's main focus of attention, being booked for everything from Yoga to the Boy Scout Group. The Head Teacher, Mr Bryn-Jones, took on the responsibility of scheduling the evening activities to fit in with those already planned by the school. Dafydd Bryn-Jones was a kind hearted, older man with a thick thatch of iron grey hair that flopped across his weather beaten face like a curtain. In between flicking his hair back constantly and smoothing it down with his hand, Dafydd had a noticeable nervous twitch and a slight limp which he never talked about. Despite his mature years and experience, Dafydd's strengths did not lie in his organisational skills and on more than one occasion, he would double book the ballet class with the cross-stitch ladies or the puppy trainers with the wine tasters. Under trying circumstances, most parties settled their differences amicably, all except the W.I. ladies and the Meals on Wheels team.

The kitchen was where the battle lines were drawn. It was ruled during the day time by a matriarchal battleaxe from Draythorpe and jealously guarded and fought over in the evenings by two conflicting teams of bakers. Invariably, it was down to Big Mazzer to wade in and quell the petty squabbles and attempt to get these ageing war lords to work together, instead of deliberately sabotaging each other's dishes. Ovens were left open to cool cooking cakes and then doors slammed closed, to make them 'go sad' with a doughy uncooked centre; salt was 'spilled' into soups and temperatures turned down on the 'toad in the holes' till the batter failed to rise.

Clive was fortunate that Mr Bryn-Jones also favoured amateur dramatics, since he was able to schedule all the planned rehearsals into the school hall without causing delay or disruption. Valerie charged herself with the task of organising the repairs to the Village Hall, which afforded her the opportunity of liaising with the self proclaimed stage manager, Seth Crowe and the Key Holder for the Bradley-Winterbottom Memorial Hall, Marge Henderson.

She arranged a time for them all to meet at the Village

Hall and invited her nephew along to quote for the repairs. Seth strolled in alongside a very chatty and animated Marge and cordially greeted his former lover, Valerie, in the foyer.

'Oh Seth, Marge, I am so glad you could make it!' she gushed, lunging forward to squeeze Seth's shoulder. She had trowelled on a phenomenal quantity of makeup and had spent the previous two hours drying the setting lotion on the hair wrapped around a number of rollers. The resultant look had her hair teased out so high, that you could see daylight through the highest wisps. 'Come in, come in!' she cooed, 'He's already started to make an assessment.'

'Who has?' Seth said suspiciously.

'My sister's boy… Michael, of course!'

'You asked Milton to fix the hall's electrics?' screeched Marge. 'You have to be joking?'

'I'll have you know he's a trained electrician!' Valerie snorted, affronted.

'Yeah, but that was long before he hit the bottle and he had little success at it then!' Seth chipped in. All three were getting red in the face as they marched through to the backstage area where the fuse box and electric panels were housed.

A surprisingly sober Milton was standing next to the switches and panels with his notebook in hand, listing the minimum requirements for repairs.

'S'gonna take a couple of weeks at least, Auntie Val,' Milton said humbly, 'It's all pretty fried.' His lucidity stunned them all for a few moments, leaving them without the power of speech.

Valerie left Milton assessing the damage to the external

power cables and took Seth Crowe aside. As they strolled into the cloakrooms together her hand slid down his back and onto his left buttock, where she gave it an exaggerated squeeze. Circling him, she pressed her voluptuous body against his and, standing on tip toes, planted a wet kiss on his lips. He neither opposed nor responded to her seduction. He fixed her gaze with a dispassionate stare and said;

'Just what is it that you hope to achieve, Val? You broke it off with me if I recall.'

'Don't be like that, Seth,' she simpered, wriggling her hips and trying to illicit some response from him. He caved in pretty quickly, but after a relatively short embrace, they heard Milton and Marge heading in their direction.

'I promise you Mrs Henderson, I will not let you down – I wouldn't dare! Both you and Auntie Val have always been very kind to me; I'd never do anything to upset either of you.' Milton was utterly contrite. He knew his reputation had plummeted in the village, but he guessed that this could be an opportunity to move on and put his troubled past behind him, make amends and rebuild his life.

'If you let me down Michael Keene, you'll definitely know about it! I'm prepared to give you a chance… But like I say boy… don't let me down.' She wagged a finger at him before turning to Seth, who was straightening his dishevelled appearance. 'Come on Seth, Valerie, we're done here!' And with that, she ushered them out of the building, leaving Milton to plan out the repairs. 'Drop the key off at my house at the end of each day, love,' Marge commanded.

'What? Aren't we going to discuss this? But it's Milton? Marge?' Seth protested, in vain.

The rehearsals gradually became less chaotic and started to resemble an actual performance by the last meeting before the dress rehearsal. Lily and Valerie had noticed that Clive had been uncharacteristically late on several occasions and consequently had begun the rehearsals without him. Each time they questioned his tardiness he was deliberately vague in his explanations.

Craigie, Daisy and all their friends, had canvassed support for the performances by sticking posters up on lamp posts, in the Post Office, Butchers' shops and pubs and posting flyers through letter boxes every evening after school. Ethel had arranged a large advert in the Parish Magazine and Lily had instructed the Vicar to mention the play in his sermon on Sundays. Parents, friends and other relatives had all been coaxed into buying tickets until all three performances were sold out.

Milton had proven to be as honourable and trustworthy as he had promised, under Marge's watchful eye, in repairing the Village Hall's electrics, but with the best will in the world, the job could not be completed in time for the Friday night dress rehearsal. Marge had vouched for Milton's best endeavours and volunteered to break the news to Clive. Reluctantly and with grave concerns, he announced to the cast that the final rehearsal would also have to take place at the primary school. Milton pushed on with the work till beyond closing time that night and woke early on the day of the performance to complete the job and not let his Auntie Val or Mrs H down. His fingers ached and he had bruises on his shins from the step ladders and he longed for a yard or two of ale, but Marge Henderson was not a woman to be trifled with. If he could get on the right side of her, she might put in a good word for him around the village.

Most of the cast and crew began congregating in the school hall around lunchtime on the Saturday. Clive had not requested that they all arrive so early, but past productions had followed similar patterns. Lily had been entrusted with the school keys and the code to disable the burglar alarm, and had arrived at the half chime of 9.30am on the steeple clock, after she had cleaned the church, arranged the flowers in the vestry and baked two sets of flapjacks and some rock hard scones.

It had been another dreary morning of grey skies and icy rain. The wind had picked up pace till it rattled the chains on the playground gates and dislodged chunks of moss from the slate roofs. Clive was late again and everyone had noticed.

'Well, if he en't committed to it no more then I reckon we should vote in a new director!' Felicity piped up arrogantly. 'I reckon Seth would be a perfect director.' She flashed her new veneers at Seth and looked at him and Valerie concurrently with her turn in one eye. Valerie was spitting with fury but determined not to let anyone see that it had riled her. How dare she suggest her lover to succeed Clive? Through bared teeth, Valerie replied,

'What an excellent idea Felicity, my dear.'

'There's loyalty for you!' gasped Lily Underwood, disgusted at the potential mutiny brewing in the air. 'Give the man a break! He's put his heart and soul into 'Group 8' for more years than I care to remember!' As she said it, Clive strolled in, his freshly bleached, streaked mousey hair had been sculpted into quite a flick at the front, Ray Bans poked out of the top pocket of his shirt, just visible beneath the new leather bomber jacket.

Valerie glanced down at Clive's new look, lingering over the pert buttocks in his faded skin-tight jeans. The transformation was quite remarkable; even old Ethel raised her eyebrows, wide eyed in shock. Craigie wolf whistled, the youngsters smirked and giggled and Clive blushed a deep crimson, rapidly regretting his decision to overhaul his image.

'Oh Clive! How marvellous you look! So dashing!' gushed Valerie. 'You could be mistaken for..um… George Michael's brother!'

'More like Shakin' Stevens' Dad!' Seth muttered.

Clive fidgeted uneasily and pulled the leather sleeves of his jacket down from his elbows to his wrists.

'Let's just get this rehearsal done shall we?!' He strode across the school hall floor feigning confidence and called the cast to order, his stomach doing backflips inside.

'Must remember to buy some more antacids,' he thought absently to himself.

It was about 4pm when Milton arrived, exhausted and dirty faced, to give the Village Hall keys to Valerie.

'It's all done Auntie Val. I cleared up as best I could, like, but there might be a few bits of spare cable lying around. I guessed you'd wanna set up for tonight as quick as possible so I'll go back and tidy up the rest after the play.' Milton breathed a huge sigh of relief and handed her the keys. She grinned animatedly at her nephew and congratulated him on his reliability and hard work. She also tried to persuade him to help the crew with the final adjustments of the stage lighting, but he politely declined in favour of a long, hot bath and a pint at The Bull as soon as it opened.

Clive sent the backstage crew directly to the Village Hall to shift the scenery and un-stack the chairs, Lily and Ethel boxed up the refreshments for the interval in the school kitchen, while Valerie and Seth ushered the cast through the final hurried rehearsal. One shambolic and embarrassing performance later and it was time, at last, to re-locate to the village hall and prepare for the opening night. Costumes and props, lead characters and extras all bundled themselves into their cars to avoid the worst of the inclement weather, all except Lily and Ethel, who had trudged stoically in the rain to the school on foot earlier in the day.

Standing under the porch at the school's main entrance, Seth called back inside to the old women.

'Would love to give you a lift ladies, but as you can see, I already have a car full.' He gestured towards his British racing green MGB GT, where Valerie was scowling from her cramped position in the rear of his car like a dog and Felicity was wiping her hand across the condensation forming on the passenger window in the front. 'Clive will give you both a lift in his Metro, I'm sure.'

'I… um… haven't got the Metro any more Seth…' Clive faltered, recalling the response he received over his appearance. 'But I am happy to give you both a lift.'

'Eh? You've got yourself a new car? Wha'd jer get? Let's see?' Seth pardoned himself from the elderly ladies and, braving the worst of the weather, he urged the reticent Clive to the roadside. There it stood, all shiny and black with cream leather seats and its canvass soft top – a brand new

Volkswagen Golf GTI Cabriolet, with additional trim and fairing. A crowd of people had started to form around the car as Seth stood transfixed and aghast. Clive folded and re-folded his arms uncomfortably then, squinting against the sleet that numbed his face said, 'I just fancied a change… that's all!'

★ ★ ★ ★ ★

Milton had enjoyed a restorative bath and donned a freshly ironed shirt his mum had laid out for him on his bed. He smiled with satisfaction to himself, kissed his trouble worn mother affectionately on the cheek then headed out onto the main road for his long awaited trip to the pub.

The smoky warmth of The Bull comforted him and thawed the gnawing cold from his rough finger tips. Eagerly supping at the first pint of lager in two weeks, he felt a sense of pride welling up inside him. Those two weeks of solitary labour and enforced sobriety had given him the time to reflect. 'Things will be different now', he said to himself out loud.

'You losing it again, Milton?' Beardy giggled to Tony behind the bar. 'Talking to yer self? Madness they say!'

'No it's just I'm feeling a bit smug wiv meself at the moment,' Milton said. Tony was intrigued. He hadn't heard Milton utter a coherent sentence for so long, he felt sure he was no longer capable.

'What you been up to then, Milton?' Tony enquired. 'Not seen you in here for ages.'

'I just re-wired most of the Village Hall single-handed.'

Milton puffed out his chest and grinned. 'Reckon I done alright at it an all. Well, Marge Henderson seemed pleased.'

'That's great, Milton, I'm dead chuffed for you – really I am. This mean you'll set back up on your own or are you gunna stick it out with the Earlem Brothers?'

'We'll see, I guess. Mind you, it was just luck really that such a big job came my way.'

Beardy, who had lost interest in Milton's conversation and had been tossing coins into the fruit machine like it was payday, suddenly stopped and listened.

What job you on about, Milt?' Beardy had a dark feeling of foreboding brewing in his gut.

'The Village Hall, when it got struck by lightning. You know, a couple of weeks back during that storm,' Milton said.

'You telling me the Village Hall has been without power for two whole weeks?' Beardy was shaking with temper.

'Well yeah, 'course! Don't everyone know about it then?' By the time Milton had completed his sentence, Beardy was halfway to his van and on his way to Jordan's house.

★ ★ ★ ★ ★

The play had begun surprisingly well. There had been a few last minute nerves from poor Craigie, who had half-filled a bucket with nervous vomit, but had neglected to remove the mop first. This spectacle had whipped the younger members of the cast into hysteria and required the firm handling of Lily to get things back on course. The seating had been arranged too close to each other so that some of the audience could not struggle down the rows to fill spaces, but on the whole, all was going according to plan.

It was getting close to the interval when Jordan and Beardy sneaked into the side entrance of the Hall.

'How the bleedin' ell did you get hold of Mazzer's keys mate?' Jordan whispered conspiratorially, 'en't she in the audience?'

'You REALLY don't wanna know, believe me.' Beardy convulsed involuntarily. They waited in the darkness of the alleyway between the kitchen and the stage door till the coast was clear, then shuffled as quietly as they could inside the storage area housing the freezers, bending low beneath the creaking stage.

Beardy began yanking at the padlocks, clumsily fiddling with Mazzer's bunch of keys to locate the correct ones. They heard hushed voices above the louder cast voices on stage and a 'clunk' as someone shoved past the stage door, slamming it shut and locking Beardy and Jordan inside. The freezer motors had clearly kicked in again and were creating a warm, close atmosphere that discomforted them.

'Let's take a look' Beardy said softly, grabbing a freezer handle and heaving it up.

'No! Wait! It'll be… ' Jordan was too late to stop him.

The fetid, rank odour hit him like a wave. He retched, gagged, choked then passed out on the floor. Hundreds of pounds worth of rotting flesh, sat marinating in a liquor of melted ice, which was beginning to re-freeze. Jordan stepped over Beardy's crumpled body and slammed the lid closed but the vile smell lingered. It seeped through the rickety boards of the stage and mingled with the smell of vomit from the mop bucket.

The front row of the audience caught a waft of the stench and began pulling faces and fanning their programmes under their noses in disgust. Ma and Pa Earlem, who had come to watch one of their grandchildren perform, were the first to stir and make noises of repulsion. Big Mazzer cackled and made some remark about Louise's acting stinking.

Clive watched helplessly from the wings as little miss perfect Louise, balked, stumbled forward and tripped over one of Milton's loose cables, groping maniacally at anything to steady her. She clasped at the brown dralon curtain at the rear of the stage as she fell, dragging it with her to the floor.

Screams and howls of delight roared from the audience as they watched a panic stricken Seth and Felicity speedily disengaging from one another and hastily covering the more exposed areas of their bodies. Bert Gellert cupped a hand over Lily's eyes, Rick the Shop shrieked with pleasure at the prospect of a most favourable divorce settlement and Pa applauded and whistled raucously, enjoying every salacious minute of it.

'Well! Who'd of thought it'd be a damn good comedy?!' Pa exclaimed, 'Encore! Encore!'

Valerie burst into tears at the piano and rushed though the audience and into the cloakroom. Eagle-eyed Mazzer had spotted her co-conspirators venturing into the storeroom beneath the stage earlier and so went to rescue the trapped Beardy and Jordan. She poked her head in through the doorway.

'Ow do boys!' she leered. Beardy had regained consciousness and was sitting back to back with Jordan in the confined space. 'In a spot of bovva again lads, eh? That's another one you'll owe me!' She gazed at Beardy, winked and licked her lips.

Clive stormed on the stage, furious and bellowed 'OH FOR FUCK'S SAKE!' The audience gasped. There was a moment of quiet before Lily said;

'Now then young Clive! There is no need for that kind of language, thank you. What would your mother say?! If foul language is part of your new image, then think again my boy!'

'Sorry, Mrs Underwood.'

CHAPTER 10

February

Strickland

Strickland stepped back against the coal barn door, out of the glare from the kitchen window. It was only 7pm but it had been dark for hours and the first few dry flakes of snow had begun to lie on the frozen concrete steps. The young couple that had moved into number 12 Wesley Drive stood in the warm kitchen cradling each other and their new baby in their arms, surrounded by boxes of packed belongings. They were giggling and laughing at the gurgles and chuckles from their new born, contented in their new beginning in the village. Strickland stayed a minute or two longer, watching the graceful young mother busying herself, before he shuffled quietly back out onto the street.

The bitter wind had driven even the hardiest locals into their homes to warm themselves against Rayburns and wolf down eagerly anticipated dishes of belly o' pork with jacket potatoes or roast beef and potatoes with a steamed treacle pudding to follow. Strickland pulled his polyester mac over his growing paunch and turned the collar up against his neck. His arthritic knee prevented a brisk walk back to his house, but it did give him time to peer at each and every tax disc on the residents' cars in Wesley Drive and make a mental note of all those that had expired.

Entering via the back door, he kicked and stamped the snow from his tan loafers onto the bristle mat, peeled his sweaty coat off and threw it onto the head of his daughter, Tracy. She yowled in disgust and threw it to the floor. Tracy was taking out her aggression on the steaming pan of mashed potatoes, spooning more and more butter into the creamy white mix in the hope that it would hasten deep vein thrombosis or a complete cardiac failure as soon as it touched his lips.

'Is SHE going to eat today or do I chuck her dinner straight in the bin?' Tracy growled venomously. Her father glanced at her smudged black eyeliner and swollen red eyes, but chose to ignore it.

'SHE has a name!' The shrill squawk came from behind a dark pink high backed chair and was partially muffled by the presence of a smouldering cheroot clenched between blue tinged lips. 'Have some respect for your step mother, you malicious little witch!' The thin rasping voice was punctuated by a wheeze and a liquefied cough that turned your stomach when heard. Doreen had been perfecting her frailty for more than 10 years of marriage to Strickland and had taken to the role of evil stepmother with great gusto. She poured herself another schooner of sweet sherry, manoeuvred it carefully to her puckered mouth and gulped down two thirds of the glass in one go.

'Dish me up a small plate girl, I'm feeling well enough to eat a modicum today!' She finished her sherry and tapped her false nails against the glass before announcing, 'I think I will have an aperitif before we dine.'

'Modicum? 'Ark at her with her air's and bleedin' graces!

Who does she think she is… Anna – bleedin' – stacia?' Tracy fumed as she thumped the plates brimming with pork chops and gravy down on the melamine fold out table. Strickland side swiped her across the back of her head. She winced but made no sound, hardened to the pain.

'Show some respect for your mother!' he growled, between forkfuls. Moving out of reach, Tracy defiantly replied,

'She ain't my mother, thank Christ!' He chose to ignore her retort, especially since his wife was drifting in and out of consciousness and concentrating more on keeping vertical than on Tracy's comments.

'Get my mail!' he bellowed. Tracy tipped back on her chair and leaned over the doilies on the sideboard for a pile of envelopes addressed to her father. Still shovelling in the mash and gravy with one hand, he pawed through his correspondence, evaluating the contents of each unopened letter by its postmark. He paused when he reached the cream envelope with a crown and portcullis frank next to the stamp. Tracy also spotted the familiar markings.

'Oh great! One from the Borstal! When is Tommy coming for his next home visit?' She felt a genuine surge of happiness for the first time in months at the prospect of her brother returning to the fold.

''Ere, you open it' Strickland grunted, throwing the letter back at his daughter.

Her elation vanished immediately after reading the first few lines of the standard letter – '*It is with regret that I must inform you that your son, Tommy Strickland, has declined the offer of a home visit from Bedford Reform Unit…*' Her face dropped. She threw down the letter and simply said, 'He ent coming.'

Strickland shrugged his shoulders insensitively, picked up a chop bone and gnawed at it till his dentures slipped.

★ ★ ★ ★ ★

Amos removed his cap, wiped the beads of sweat on a crisp new cotton hankie and replaced the cap back on his head. The ground refused to succumb to the pounding from the pick axe and wreaking bar, so solid was the frozen clay.

'Mr Parting!' Father Bruce gasped as he scurried out from beneath the lychgate. 'I never meant for you to dig the grave! It's much too hard!' He was panting and going purple in the face.

'Well, you said it were needed for Friday and young Kurt is away this week – some wrestling tournament or summut wiv the school.'

'Mr Parting!' Father Bruce repeated. 'Amos… With all due respect, digging graves should not be done by a 75 year old man!'

'You 'fraid I'll collapse and fall in, eh? Diggin' me own grave like!' Amos chuckled. Father Bruce blushed, his dog collar straining to contain his portly neck. He didn't want to offend this proud local man, but also did not want his untimely death through over-exertion on his hands.

The snow from the previous night had failed to settle for long but had left behind a raw Siberian wind carrying the remnants of the storm as sleet. The churchyard was a monochrome photo from an art magazine, with small clumps of bright floral offerings from mourners to brighten the bleak day. Not even the sorrowful yew trees could dampen the irrepressible spirits of Amos Parting, the eternal optimist.

Father Bruce tried to persuade the old man to desist and instead to find a farmhand who might lend a hand for cash, but Amos assured him that all would be well. 'It en't gonna beat me, Father! The day it does will be the beginning of the end!'

Stumped and flustered, Father Bruce could not muster a response and so waddled back towards the Church entrance and disappeared inside, just as Marge Henderson marched out.

'Mind yerself, Father! Once I get rolling it's the devil's own job to get me to stop!' She chuckled, raising her lime green umbrella that clashed with her shocking red hair. 'Ow do, Amos?' She piped up as she passed him at the graveside.

'Ow do, Marge! 'Ere Marge… ?' Amos pondered, trying to recall if he had asked her before. 'Does yourn Dad work at Tesco?'

Her usual brusque manner failed to manifest and she softened upon seeing this crazy old timer digging in such harsh conditions. She stopped and held her brolly above his head.

'It's funny you should say that, Amos, he did before he retired and got sick, yes!' She was expecting him to ask a favour or tell her some obscure unrelated story linked to Tesco in some way. She waited patiently for a response, watching the expressions on his face contort into a peculiar smile. Amos leaned in closer to her and almost whispered.

'Can I ask a personal question, my dear?'

She frowned and glared directly in his eyes; 'You can ask,' she said warily.

'What year were you born my dear?'

★ ★ ★ ★ ★

The washing suds still lingered in the kitchen sink when Tracy removed Doreen's purse from her handbag behind her chair and lightened the load by some five pounds. Doreen slouched passively and comatose in her winged chair, a trail of spittle smudging her fuchsia lipstick in the cracks of her face. The latch on the front door snapped closed with an almost imperceptible click, leaving Strickland unaware of his daughter's escape. He sat in the 'best room' filling in the submission forms for the football pools, of which he had been an agent for some eight years or more. Inhaling the last quarter inch of his cigarette, he stubbed the glowing butt in the conch shell ashtray, grabbed his coat and headed back out into the frozen night.

The sky had clouded over again, shielding both the moonlight and Tracy as she swigged the last vestiges of 'White Lightning' cider before discarding the plastic bottle in Alf Burrows' dustbin. Returning to the relative warmth of the phone box, she wrenched open the door and squeezed into the confined space to share her last two cigarettes with Ben. He levered her flicked fringe, solid with hairspray, away from her forehead to reveal her bruised brow and kissed it lightly.

'Why don't you just leave? We could go to London together and make a go of it?' His hand crept down her back and cupped the cheek of her left buttock.

'Don't be a bleedin' moron! What we gonna live on?' She brushed his hand away like swatting flies.

'What about relatives then? Surely there's an aunt or cousins or someone who will take you in? You can't keep taking a batterin' like that, it just en't right'. Tracy ignored his plea. She had spent many a waking night contemplating her escape, or on really bad nights, concocting schemes that would spell Strickland and Doreen's demise in a tormenting, agonising death. She would lull herself to sleep with vivid images of Doreen convulsing violently, shortly after consuming a cocktail of sweet sherry with a dash of rat poison, or her father being bludgeoned to death by a ravening crowd of locals. By morning, Tracy would temper her plans with the potential consequences of her actions, pour tincture of arnica on her fresh bruises and dress for another school day.

Strickland repositioned himself in the rear garden of the new couple. The barn door had been left ajar, giving him greater shelter from the elements and a better view through the bare windows, as the young mother cradled her baby, and opened the neck of her nightgown to reveal her engorged breasts. Strickland let out a little gasp, then fumbling maniacally, reached for the zip fastening his grey flannel trousers.

★ ★ ★ ★ ★

Amos had been unusually quiet all night at the Bull, had wandered home through the deepening snow sober and sat listening submissively to the customary tirade from his wife about spending their pension money on beer and stinking of ashtrays, without comment or retort. Gertrude Parting drew breath to begin stage two of her marital critique, but stopped to enquire whether Amos was paying attention to her. There was a lengthy pause before Amos snapped out of his solitary reverie.

'I think I have found her, Gert!' Amos stared directly at his wife, his brow knitted in anguish.

Gertrude went silent and closed her eyes. Her heart briefly stopped as she weighed up the possibility that Amos had not found her out, had not discovered the personal letter that she had kept hidden amongst her 'wimmins fings' all these years, had not known what she had known for all this time and had deliberately kept from him. The letter addressed to Amos that Gertrude had accidently opened and read and had subsequently cried herself to sleep after reading and re-reading it for the following few decades. How had Amos exhumed a secret that had remained buried for so long?

'What are you babbling about, you old fool?' She tried to dismiss him, call him a drunken idiot, but he was adamant.

'Gert,' he said quietly as he held her firmly above each elbow. 'I know.'

The following morning was crisp and sunny. The storm had passed, but the snow stubbornly remained. The young father had opened the backdoor to take their rubbish to the bin and was puzzled to find footprints carved into the path from their barn out onto the street.

Amos put his overalls and wellingtons on and biked the half mile up Henridge Lane back to the church. He had been surprised by Gertrude's calm response to last night's revelations. He was convinced that she would become the hellcat she had been when confronted in her youth. Time and age had obviously mellowed or beaten her.

He scraped the inch or two of snow from the tarpaulin that covered yesterday's digging and lowered the ladder back in the hole. He stopped suddenly only a couple of rungs down, facing the glistening earth, every muscle in his body contracting malevolently, his short breaths making him dizzy and sick. Blinking back the tears, he let go of the ladder and fell backwards into the half dug grave. He could see them, all around him, the rotting emaciated flesh of hundreds of men, bones protruding from their tangled limbs, their ripped and soiled uniforms tearing as the bodies were thrown into the mass graves. The face of his best friend, who had been too weak to fight the severe case of dysentery, who had passed away in the Thanbyuzayat base hospital, without medical attention or care; the sergeant who dared to argue with a Japanese guardsman, who was then cruelly beaten till his spleen ruptured, the private he had shared a bunk with whose skull had been smashed beneath half a tonne of falling steel rail. The bulk of the dead were air raid casualties or those that had succumbed to malaria or malnutrition. In that grave, Amos shook himself out of the tropical Burmese heat of 1942 and back into the cold light of 1985. Panting heavily, he sat in the frozen mud, wiping the sweat from his brow and swallowing back the bile rising in his throat. Grasping the edge of the ladder, he slowly raised himself up to face the church porch. A wooden crucifix hung above the door. As his breathing calmed and his heart steadied its pace, Amos fixed his gaze on the cross and muttered, 'If there is a God, thanks for keeping me alive, and look after those boys for me till I get there.'

★ ★ ★ ★ ★

Strickland made his way round the old folks' bungalows and around the bottom end of Wesley Drive, collecting the money for the football pools. He stopped in at the Policeman's house between the primary school and the service road to the kids' recreational ground. PC Williams' wife answered the door and shuddered to see who the guest was. She called to her husband and rudely left the visitor standing on the doormat unattended while she declared a culinary emergency in the kitchen.

'Who is it dear?' Williams yelled before seeing Strickland. 'Ah. And how can I help you this time, Mr Strickland?' He tried hard to conceal the contempt in his voice.

'Just thought you should know, there's a few overdue tax discs in the village you may want to chase up, particularly up Wesley Drive. Pa Earlem's is so old you can't see what colour it's supposed to be!' Strickland attempted a light hearted chuckle but felt uncomfortable when the Policeman failed to join in. He'd been down this route before with Strickland reporting petty crimes and it only ever lead to antagonism with the local residents, or Strickland reporting him to his superiors for failing to carry out his duty.

'Right,' Williams said, with emphasis. 'I'll put it on my 'to do' list…' Strickland waited for more feedback, for some gratitude or some indication of Williams encouraging him to foster a conspiratorial fraternity. Instead, he opened the glass panelled front door and stood holding the door handle. 'I won't keep you, Mr Strickland, I know you are a busy man'. Strickland stammered a farewell and then stumbled over the threshold. 'Mind your fragile 'glass back', Mr Strickland!' The constable slammed the door behind him and hot footed it back to the news and weather.

As Strickland rounded the corner of Wesley Drive, Amos caught up with him on his bike, still wearing his wellingtons and overalls.

'Hold up Stricky!' Amos shouted, 'I've got me coupon on me. Can I give yer it now?' Amos balanced the cross bar of his bike against his thigh while he rummaged in his pocket for the Pools coupon, neatly filled in with tiny crosses in two columns, the same numbers he had submitted week in, week out for years. He handed the paper and the required payment over to Strickland, who made a big show of placing it carefully into a plastic bag, then into his satchel. 'I got a good feeling about this week!' Amos shouted as he peddled away up Wesley Drive, out of Strickland's range of hearing.

The past had been praying on Amos's conscious and subconscious all day. He couldn't remember the last time he had been troubled with flashbacks from his years on the Burma Railway. The sudden realisation that his search could be over had brought his past back in focus. His recall was vivid, his memory infallible, his distress real.

Amos leaned the bike up against the gatepost outside Marge Henderson's house and paced up and down the path to her front door for a few minutes. He could hear her shrill voice calling her husband to the dinner table. He looked at his attire and recoiled at the sight of the thick mud on his boots. He strode around to the back door and tentatively knocked. Marge swung open the door with the same power and speed with which she attacked everything. Her rapid response startled him and rendered him temporarily speechless. He cut a pitiful figure standing there on her doorstep, wringing his cap in his hands and opening and closing his mouth like a guppy in a polluted stream.

'You coming in Amos, or yer gunna catch some flies?' He hesitated briefly then stooped to remove his boots, making little grunting noises as he bent over. The sickly odour of boiled cabbage escaped with the steam through the open door as it sat congealing amongst the burnt sausages and flaky potatoes on the table. He glanced up at Marge's husband as he attempted to place a dollop of glutinous gravy on his plate and stifled a grin.

'Ah!' Amos said, with one boot still on, 'I were hoping for a bit of a chat like, but you are havin' yer tea.'

'Yer more than welcome to a bit o'dinner, Amos, if yer wanna stay?' Marge gestured for him to enter. He thought about the impact of Marge's cooking on his well worn dental plate and replied,

'P'raps just a cup o' tea if you don't mind me chattin' while yer eat?' Amos entered the kitchen and slid over the lino in his grubby socks to the table. Just as he was lowering himself down, Marge swooped in with a folded newspaper to protect the chair fabric from his mud splattered overall just before he landed.

They sat quietly for a while, only the clatter of cutlery against china to break the silence, wondering why Amos had decided to visit them. She poured Amos a pint of tea from a 'brown bessie' pot the size of a football and pushed the sugar bowl across the table in his direction. Unable to tolerate the awkward atmosphere, Marge said,

'So what's got you all flustered then Amos? T'ent like you to go visiting people?'

'Oh, I am sorry Marge. I don't mean to intrude, but I didn't know how else to get the chance to talk to you.' He was stalling for time. He hadn't thought through how the conversation would go, how she might react and, worse still, he had forgotten that her husband might be present when he did finally raise the courage to approach her.

'Spit it out Amos! We don't stand on no ceremony here yer know.' She was intrigued. Amos was never a source of gossip, or even common sense, now she came to think about it.

'It's a bit delicate, like. I'm um… well it's about you… you see… I er… ' He took a gulp of his tea and Marge took a deep breath before releasing a loud, impatient sigh. 'I reckon I might be your Dad.'

★ ★ ★ ★ ★

Strickland finished his Pools round and headed up the hill of Wesley Drive. He paused beneath the street lamp and took a glance about him, peering purposefully into the gloom. His satchel was bulging with coins and notes and the plastic bag of coupons that each household on his list had spent considerable time completing. A low moon and pinpricks of stars were his only company as he veered off the path and onto the service road that stood adjacent to Valerie Jones's garden. Shuffling as fast as his flabby frame would allow, he reached the end of the road, produced some keys from his coat pocket and, in the darkness, went straight to his council allocated garage in the corner of the block. There was a screeching noise as the up and over mechanism grated against itself, making Strickland anxious that he had alerted Valerie to his presence. He knew the layout of his garage well enough to reach the lockbox bolted to the back wall blindfolded, but still he turned sideways and reached down for a torch from just inside the doorway. The carefully folded banknotes were placed in a wooden box, the coins into a large tin and the previous week's coupons stored in a box file for a short duration to counter any potential minor claims. The newest coupons he gave a cursory glance across and selected a few to send off to the Football Pools Head Office, thus ensuring a fresh supply of blank coupons for the following week. Having stowed his weekly haul, he took greater care in closing the garage door than he did opening it, so as not to disturb Valerie or her loathsome dog.

Strickland reappeared on Wesley Drive slightly puffed out and a little more red in the face than usual, just as Jimmy Earlem wandered past on his way to the Bull.

'Looks like your Missus is in a spot o'bother again, Stricky!' He said plainly, pointing with his thumb back over his shoulder. 'Who'd have thought that she would need that ambulance bay they painted for her so soon?!' Jimmy didn't linger for an answer but strolled on by, gently shaking his head. Valerie was at her hall window, twitching the net curtain conspicuously as the blue flashing light reflected off her front room windows.

When Strickland arrived on the scene, he found Doreen being restrained by two burly ambulance men trying to load her via the steel gurney into the back of the wagon.

'Come along, Mrs Strickland! You know the drill, please help us to help you!' The paramedic strapped her arms down and cocooned her in a blanket, which he tightly tucked around her.

'They're trying to kill me!' Doreen slurred.

'Now now, Mrs Strickland, keep calm. No one is trying to kill you.'

Strickland stood by passively until Tracy, slamming the front door behind her, walked to the ambulance carrying Doreen's handbag and coat.

'What have you done to her?' Strickland yelled, leaning over Tracy in an intimidating manner.

'I ain't done nuffin to her. Stupid cow had one too many and fell down the bleedin' stairs again.' Strickland raised his hand up to strike his daughter, but remembering that witnesses were just feet away, checked himself. 'She was at the foot of the stairs when I got home.' Tracy glowered at him, pushed past his shoulder and loaded herself into the ambulance.

'I expect you will follow on, Mr Strickland, in the car?' The ambulance man said enquiringly.

'What? Oh yes! Of course!' he made a few gestures and muttered a few consolatory words before turning and heading into the house, cursing beneath his breath.

★ ★ ★ ★ ★

'You what!? My dad? Don't be daft, I already have a dad! You gone soft, Amos?' Marge was thoroughly amused. Her gormless husband was alternately choking on the floury potatoes and on Amos's candour.

'I know it don't sound possible and I know you have yer Dad, who's poorly and that but… '

'But what exactly?' She was humouring him, with a wry smile.

'It's just there was a letter, an it said I have a kid, an yourn Ma an… ' He cupped his face in his hands and let out an exasperated sigh. Dragging the palms of his hands down his sagging cheeks he looked into her eyes and said, 'Please Marge, let's both go an' see yer Dad. I don't wanna upset no-one, I just wanna set the record straight, like.' He had not considered how this disclosure might affect Marge's family. Ever since he found the diaphanous torn shreds of paper that had been carefully repaired over the years with additional layers of sellotape in amongst Gertrude's elastic bottoms and tops, the secret had etched an acid veil over their marriage, both worn and wary of sharing their knowledge and fears. In between the years of hope and the despair of never having been blessed with children, Gertrude had intercepted the letter addressed to Amos that poured vinegar into her wounds. Initially, he had attributed her sullen moods to the frustration of failed attempts at pregnancy, and then despondency turned into depression and depression into despair. Amos transferred his affections to the continuous series of Jack Russell Terriers, while Gertrude grew more and more introvert. By the time Amos had found the hidden letter, his relationship with Gertrude was already past saving. He fixated on the thought that somewhere in the world, he had a child, and one day he would meet them.

Marge had stopped grinning, her husband stopped choking and the kitchen seemed to pause in time while she digested the news. Amos hung his head, weary from the physical and mental exertions of the day. The silence was uncomfortable, but Amos held his nerve. Her eyes bore into him, trying to ascertain his sincerity while she tried to come to terms with the ramifications if he was indeed telling her the truth. She had no doubt that Amos believed it to be true, but he wasn't exactly known for his common sense and rapier intellect. She looked at the wretched figure before her, recalling their meeting in the churchyard earlier in the day, and once again softened.

'Hmmmm… I'm not convinced Amos, me duck, but if it'll make yer happy, we can go and see me dad together. He'll put you straight in no time, Amos. Besides, he'll be glad of the company – you can have a game of dominoes while you're visitin'!' She made light of the suggestion, but you could see her unease fixed in her posture.

★ ★ ★ ★ ★

Doreen was released from the General Hospital on Saturday lunchtime with minor bruises, cirrhosis of the liver and a small bottle of gin tucked into her underwear. Tracy covered her stepmother's knees with a blanket, placed a pack of painkillers on her side table along with a decanter of port and a large glass.

'There you go, Mumsy dearest, knock yourself out!' The literal meaning was lost on Doreen and Strickland was too busy hunkering down in the best room with his formal complaints, the legal papers from his latest malpractice suit and the pile of pools coupons that did not make it to the main office, to care about his daughter's malevolent thoughts. He prepared a grid on A4 lined paper to mark down the pools results and attached it to a clipboard ready to take into the living room where the TV was blaring out a black and white 1940's romance film to stupefy Doreen into silence. Strickland growled at Tracey to make him a milky coffee before lumbering into the living room and switching channels.

★ ★ ★ ★ ★

Amos was wearing his best suit, which Gertrude had stitched under the arms where the seam had worn, and had flattened his unruly hair down with Vaseline jelly. He smelled of Pears soap and, despite his best efforts to shave, he had missed clumps of white bristles under his chin. He arrived early at Marge's house, keen to make a good impression, with a box of Maltesers for her father and a pink flowering cyclamen for Marge. Taking the plant from him, she muttered a surprised thank you and hurried him towards the family car, where her husband sat with the engine ticking over.

It was a short, awkward journey to the Old Folks' Home just outside the village, with Marge's husband driving deliberately slowly to prolong her discomfort. Amos checked his inside jacket pocket for the presence of his clean hankie and the fateful letter, and finally tapped the box of Maltesers on the back seat of the car.

'This is as painful as having shrapnel removed!' Amos mused to himself. When they arrived at the home, Marge lead Amos into the foyer, before stopping to point out the frailty of her father since his stroke a few years ago. She warned him not to upset him or she would frogmarch Amos out and away before his feet could touch the ground. Amos nodded compliance before straightening his tie and collar and scurrying after the giant strides of his potential offspring.

Marge's father was a small, dapper chap, with a neat short back and sides haircut and a fob watch chain hanging from his pocket. He rose cautiously and rather unsteadily from his chair to greet them both, a peck on the cheek for Marge and a weak handshake for Amos. Marge's husband received little more than a cursory nod before he was allowed to retreat to the TV in the next room.

'It's good to finally meet you, Mr Henders… Oh I'm sorry!' Amos flushed. Marge's father had no interest in making the situation more unbearable and said,

'It's Cross. Mr Cross. That's Marge's maiden name, but everyone calls me Victor or Vic. Thanks for the Maltesers Amos, that was really kind of you.' They sat in a huddle in the bay window at the far end of the common room, trying to keep their words private, but still be audible to each other.

'Right then, Dad. Time for you to put Amos's mind at rest. Daft old bugger seems to think ee's me dad 'an not you!' Marge's brow knitted together and she struggled to keep the tone of her voice light and jovial. There was an uncomfortable silence as Vic swallowed hard and said,

'I've been expecting this day for a very long time'. He glanced at his daughter, his old eyes filling with salty water at her pained expression. He reached out to comfort her, but she withdrew. 'We should ask for some tea,' Vic said with a tremulous voice. They all stared down at the floor. The sound of the TV droning on in the background was the only noise to break the silence. Amos slowly removed the letter from his breast pocket and, with a knowing look towards Victor, and with the merest hint of a nod in unspoken agreement; he passed the beige and wrinkled paper to Marge.

My Dear Amos,

I hardly know where to begin, but if you are reading this, then the worst has happened and my husband has fulfilled his promise to me after I lost my fight against cancer. By now you will be aware that our brief encounter prior to you being posted to Burma resulted in me falling pregnant. Four months into the pregnancy, word reached me that you had been captured and had perished in the dreadful conditions on the Burma railways. Please believe me when I say that I was devastated by the news and I mourned your loss, as many others did who lost loved ones during the War. My predicament was becoming more noticeable daily and my family were disgusted with my behaviour and threatened to throw me out of my home. I was sent away to Norfolk for my confinement, to live with cousins to spare my family from shame. While I was there, the sweetest and kindest man took pity on me and saved my life in so many ways, since I went into labour working in the Norfolk fields as a Land Army girl, where he came to my rescue. The kindness and patience grew into an abiding love, especially since he volunteered to raise our child as his own. It wasn't until we returned to Adderstey many years later that I heard of your survival and subsequent release from the camps.

Initially, I put the thought of you out of my mind. My

compassionate and understanding husband did not ask me any awkward questions and for years we remained a very happy family, with my husband gaining promotion at his work in Tesco and our child doing well at school. It wasn't until I saw you in the village, with whom I assumed to be your wife that I began to feel terribly guilty that I hadn't told you of our child's existence. Over the years, I became more and more housebound with my illness and heard less about you from friends, but I tracked down your address from the phonebook.

I expect nothing from this disclosure other than the peace of mind that I will have done the right thing by my husband, our child and finally by you. I only wish that I had had the courage to inform you while I was still alive.

I hope you will be happy and healthy and live a long and full life.

With kindest regards,
Elsie

Marge read the letter slowly, twice. The tears overwhelmed her eyelids and escaped down her cheeks, leaving bright tracks through the thick layer of beige Avon foundation covering her face. All at once she knew all, understood all and felt the pain of all concerned. A combination of anger, hurt, betrayal and sympathy welled up inside her and with a surprising degree of calm, she returned the letter to Amos' hand and strutted out of the building to the frozen gardens of the Old Folks' Home. Amos jumped up to go after her, but Victor urged him to leave her to simmer down.

There was a loud shushing noise from half a dozen

previously unconscious residents as they sprayed each other with saliva and denture cream in an attempt to quieten the visitors. It was time for the Saturday afternoon Pools results. With the TV turned to full volume and their hearing aids maxed to the limit, they strained to hear the dulcet undulations of the announcer.

'Liverpool 2, Bolton Wanderers… nil. West Ham United 3, Chelsea 2… ' They listened transfixed as they waited for confirmation of the match numbers that all drew in their games. 'And that makes the Pools Draws as follows: Numbers 2, 3, 12, 16, 21, 22, 26, 30, 41 and 43.'

There were the usual moans and groans and dashed hopes audible above the clashing zimmer frames. Amos sat motionless, his eyes fixed upon the screen, mouth agape.

'You alright, Amos?' Victor enquired with some concern at his ashen faced guest.

'I've won!' Amos muttered quietly, stunned, and then again, 'I've only bleedin' well bleedin' won!' much louder.

★ ★ ★ ★ ★

Strickland marked down the last few numbers on his hand drawn chart and yawned. He looked at them again and scratched his chin. He had a gnawing sensation that there was something horribly familiar about those numbers. He stood up to help himself to another tot of whisky, but the nagging suspicion made him put down the bottle and go to his satchel in the best room to search out the pools coupons. Leafing through the pile of odd sized shiny sheets, he froze, dropped the lot and made a dash as fast as he could upstairs.

Grabbing a holdall from the landing cupboard, he began stuffing in shirts, pants, socks, shaving gear and his gout medication, before tripping down the stairs to rummage through the bureau for his passport and bankbook. Tracy heard the commotion and dropped the half peeled potato back into the bowl of water in the sink and stood, hands dripping, at the foot of the stairs.

Strickland shoved her aside, ramming her head against the coat pegs in the hallway, making her cheek swell and redden immediately after.

'What's going on?' Doreen's shrill voice penetrated through the walls and ricocheted off their eardrums. She persisted, 'Where is that girl? Come at once and tell me what is happening!' By the time Tracy had found her trusted ice pack from the freezer and walked to Doreen's side in the living room, all she could report was that her father had gone.

★ ★ ★ ★ ★

Marge had heard the beginnings of a party inside the home. Someone had made it all the way across the dining hall to the piano and was attempting to play 'Roll Out the Barrel' Les Dawson style, while another was pouring the contents of several hidden hipflasks of Bert's moonshine into the residents' cocoa.

Victor greeted his daughter affectionately and entreated her to not make a scene over her news and instead to wait and digest the information in her own time. With ultimate respect she complied.

'So what's the party in aid of, then?' she said, baffled at

the pensioners' merriment. There was a feeble chorus of 'Old Amos has won the bleedin' Pools!'

'Well I never!' she exclaimed, 'What a day! Not only have I discovered that I have two dads, but one of 'em's rich 'an all!' There was a weak laugh from both men, who had been raised to suppress emotion at all costs – the great British stiff upper lip.

Marge stopped the merry making for a moment and said, 'You know what, Amos, you'd better get round to Stricky's as soon as. I wouldn't put it past that slimy bugger to try and claim it for himself, yer know!'

'Good point, Marge – thanks for that and um, well you know, thanks for everything.' His cheeks coloured with speckles of red broken veins.

Marge bundled Amos into the family car and instructed her husband to drive them to Strickland's house, but when they arrived all they found was a hysterical Doreen, and Tracy nursing a purple bump the size of a small egg. Despite potential concussion, Tracy rapidly grasped the situation.

'He's done a bunk. He took clothes and his passport and stuff. He'll be on his way to his garage, where I know for a fact that he has a secret stash of cash in a safe bolted to the back wall, cuz me and Ben broke in last summer for a look. Betcha he's gonna drive to Luton airport. I'll call PC Williams, if you can stop him gettin' out of his garage.'

Marge grabbed hold of Amos by the scruff of the neck and dragged him back to the car. Thrilled as the prospect of showing off his driving prowess, Marge's husband, Rob, flew into action and squealed the car round the tight bends of Wesley Drive and screeched to a halt with a handbrake turn, to place the car across the entrance to the garage service road. They were just in time; Strickland was already in his car and was halfway down the road towards them.

Strickland braked and considered his options. He could ram Marge's car, but there was no guarantee he could clear enough space to get free, he could abandon his own car and try to make it on foot across the icy gardens, but with his gammy feet there was every chance Marge would catch up with him. He chose the third option, to stand up and confront them.

He threw open the door to his brand new gold Mazda and heaved himself out onto the road. 'Get out of my way!' he bellowed, with as much resolve as he could muster. He watched Marge leave her car, roll her sleeves up and charge up the service road towards him. Her nostrils were flaring and her shoulders had hunched up, masking the entire length of her neck. Strickland squared up to her. They were similar in size and stature, but where Strickland's mass was mostly fat, Marge was predominantly muscle.

'You low life, wretched little creep!' Marge began, prodding him repeatedly with a thick index finger in his chest.

'Get off me, woman! I shall have you arrested for assault!'

'Ha! That's rich coming from you, you child beating, garden creeping, fraudulent slimy bloody incomer!' She had him pinned against his car, the prodding finger becoming more insistent with each thrust.

Rob and Amos had also left the car and were standing in support behind her.

'Christ, I hope that lazy arse copper gets here soon or

there will be bloodshed!' Rob muttered to Amos.

'You think Stricky will cut up rough?' Amos gasped.

'Nope, but there's every chance Marge will!'

'You mean… ?' Amos pointed towards his long lost daughter proudly.

'Oh yeah! You ain't seen nuffin yet!'

Marge continued to berate Strickland for cheating Amos out of a jackpot win of at least £500,000, for mistreating Tracy and for being a social misfit in what she termed a 'very forgiving village', before declaring that she was making a citizen's arrest.

PC Williams arrived to intervene before the whole situation turned too ugly and thankfully Tracy was most organised and very obliging in the provision of enough evidence to put Strickland in custody, at least until his trial, set for late summer.

Amos's story was the talk of the parish for a long time after he had come to terms with his mere brush with wealth and fortune. Most people pitied him and bought him drinks at the Bull in some odd way of compensating him for his loss, and he was only too eager to play on sympathies while they lasted. Alone with Gertrude, he was content to confess that he had been more excited about finding his daughter than winning all that money. 'Gert… ' he would often say, 'I must be the luckiest man alive!'

CHAPTER 11

March

The Bell Tower

'Ouch! Can't you move to the left a bit? I have a hassock sticking in my ribs!'

'Shush! For Christ's sake, keep your voice down! I reckon the verger is still in the vestry!'

'Me?! You are the squealer, if memory serves me right!'

'Oh just get on with it, will you, or the others will be finished long before us!'

'We are supposed to be enjoying this experience, not rushing it!'

'Well, yes, but I have just remembered that I left a casserole in the oven and it will bake dry if I leave it much longer.'

'Oh great! That's done it. The little sergeant has gone into hiding now!'

'Thought you butchers were meant to have stamina, or so you told me!'

'Oi! If I wanted a critique of my sexual prowess I would stay at home with me wife!' Jordan Maisey disentangled his wiry limbs from the Oak's barmaid, Sue Honey and banged his head on the prayer book shelf of the pew in front. 'I'm getting too old for this caper,' he said, pulling his jeans up and zipping the fly.

'Nonsense! You are never too old for nookie, although I must admit, the bruises are taking longer to heal and are a bugger to explain away at home!' Sue took a couple of attempts to roll out from between the wooden seats and right herself. Her cheeks were flushed from the exertion and from the electric bar heater directed down from the pillars above their heads. The church had a peculiar orange glow about it, like you were viewing the chancel through a cellophane sweet wrapper. Branches from the shrubs outside were rubbing and squeaking against the panes of the stained glass windows as the gales continued outside.

They could hear Dr Clements grunting away at the furthest end of the North Aisle. He had been a gentleman and allowed the other men to choose a set of house keys from the font after bell ringing practice this week. He had held an admirable poker face as the primary school headmaster snatched his wife's keys first, then Jordan took Sue Honey's keys, leaving him with the intolerable Valerie. Stifling a sigh, the Doctor set his mind to the task in hand, closed his eyes and thought of the receptionist's ample breasts from his surgery in order to get the job done.

★ ★ ★ ★ ★

Father Bruce slammed the back vestry door and scurried to his 50cc moped. Wrapping the excess material from his surplice around his legs, he climbed on and trapped the garment between his knees to avoid it snagging in the wheels. His agility belied his portly frame as in one, well practiced smooth move, he clipped his helmet fast and launched the bike from its stand with an insistent heave. Father Bruce was legendary for two things, tardiness and his unfailing naivety, well that and his expanding girth.

Persistent heavy rains had swelled the brook and water ran in rivulets at the sides of Henridge Lane as the vicar hurtled down the hill towards the rectory. Using his Dr Marten boots against the gravel driveway, he slowed just enough to hop off the moped, lean it against the wall and welcome Olivia and Rueben at the doorstep.

Panting heavily, he thrust out his hand for Rueben to shake, bending low to steady his breathing in order that he could speak, his face, wet and red from a combination of sweat, high blood pressure and stinging icy rain.

'Hello there, Father!' Rueben gushed enthusiastically, 'Good of you to see us at such short notice.' They both turned to look at Olivia as she waddled towards the front porch while shovelling a choc ice into her already full mouth.

'Yes, um, I can see there is a need for some urgency,' Father Bruce said tactlessly, gazing in astonishment at the size of her eight month bump.

'You said on the phone that there was a cancellation which might suit us?' Rueben was using his best manners, reserved only for his mother and his dentist, both of whom instilled a degree of fear in him.

They strolled through the wide, echoing hallway and met Bronwyn just coming out from the kitchen.

'Ah! There you are, Father! I have finished the ironing and your dinner is in the stove. You know you really must at least try not to spill so much of your dinner down your surplice, I just can't get the stains out no matter what I try.'

Bronwyn prattled on mindlessly till she caught sight of the voluminous Olivia navigating the entrance to the lounge room. She shot her a disapproving look, pursing her mouth and narrowing her black eyes.

'Right, yes! Thank you, Mrs Cross. I wonder if you would be so kind as to make us all some tea before you go?' The vicar held her firmly by the shoulders and marched her back into the kitchen before her un-Christian mutterings could be vented too audibly.

Father Bruce returned to the lounge to play host to his visitors where, after a prolonged speech about entering the marital institution for sincere and heartfelt reasons, he pencilled them into his diary. The insinuation was crystal clear to Olivia, who squirmed in her seat, especially when the vicar emphasised the part about bringing a child into the world bearing the father's name. Rueben's attention wavered frequently enough to allow him to remain blissfully unaware of the parson's barbed statements. Reluctantly, Father Bruce agreed to do all he could to hasten proceedings in order that the wedding could take place by the end of the month. He suggested enlisting the help of the WI women with dressmaking, flower arranging and catering, to which they readily agreed and thanked Father Bruce for his help. As they shuffled towards the hallway, the vicar said,

'Have you thought about the selection of hymns you might choose? 'Jerusalem' is always a favourite.' Olivia looked aghast, but closed her gaping mouth respectfully.

'We have decided that we want a modern wedding Father... will that be a problem?' Olivia's question sounded more like a command and ended their meeting on a strained note. They left the vicarage buzzing with excitement and ambitious ideas and scurried towards Rueben's pickup, getting drenched in the process.

★ ★ ★ ★ ★

The following day brought sunshine and showers and a light hearted mood in the vicarage. Breakfasting heartily on a fry-up that could have supplied half the third world, Father Bruce sang cheerily as he packed a box of props and his bible and attached it to the back of his moped with bungee straps. For once he was on time when he reached the Primary School and shook hands with Miss Dunkley, the class six teacher and strident atheist.

'Ah! Miss Dunkley, I presume?' He blustered cordially.

'It is and you are the clergyman sent to brainwash my pupils!' she smirked, making her stinging remark into a joke, but the glint in her eyes conveyed the conviction behind it. The vicar chuckled nervously as she turned on her sensible heels and strode purposefully down the corridor, gesturing him the follow her to the hall.

The vicar slipped on the parquet floor, stained brown with the patina of 50 years of floor wax, before anchoring his heels in. While he busied himself erecting a makeshift altar from stage blocks and old tablecloths, Miss Dunkley drew wide all the curtains at the side of the hall and threw open all the windows. The blast of damp air was preferable to the stale odours of gym socks, cabbage water and school strength disinfectant.

'Did you ask the children to bring dolls or teddy bears

for the ceremony?' he asked tentatively, pausing to glance up at her frowning face.

'I did. Whether they remember to bring them today remains to be seen.' There was another uncomfortable pause. Miss Dunkley could see the Headmaster through the glass doors donning his overcoat and fumbling in his pockets for the whistle with which to indicate to the children to line up in their classes ready to enter the building and start the day. 'I have to go and register my class now. Will you manage the rest for yourself or shall I ask the school secretary to come and give you a hand?' The question was posed out of politeness rather than an actual offer of assistance. She waited for a moment in the doorway for his response before dashing to meet her growing charges at the peg racks.

Miss Dunkley hailed the windswept Welsh Headmaster as he bustled in the front entrance shaking a broken umbrella.

'Mr Bryn-Jones! I really feel I must voice my strong objections once again!' she exclaimed vehemently.

'Duly noted, again, Miss Dunkley,' he replied, wiping his feet on the bristle mat. 'And as I have said many times before, it is our role and duty to provide our pupils with moral and spiritual guidance in order that they should become well rounded individuals!' He continued to walk towards his office, shouting his answer to her down the corridor. Growling beneath her breath, she returned to her classroom to register her children.

When the whole school was assembled in the hall, the Headmaster gave a brief introduction before welcoming Father Bruce to the front. Pupils were encouraged to applaud respectfully, although most hadn't got a clue who the

Reverend was. An infant at the front stood up quickly and thrust one hand in the air and with the other hand clutching the groin area of his trousers, jiggled on the spot. With lightening reactions, his teacher launched herself across the row of cross-legged kids, yanked him out of the crowd and frogmarched him to the toilets. Another shouted out, 'Why is that man wearing a dress?' to which the whole school laughed. Even the stony faced Miss Dunkley softened and allowed herself a wry smile.

Unperturbed, Father Bruce explained his role in the community, his apparel, his vocation and his reason for attending their school that day. With Easter fast approaching, Father Bruce rattled off an abridged reading in which the main character, Jesus, gets murdered by the baddies, so that all men can be saved. A few of the brighter kids in Class 3 started crying, 'They killed him? Sob, sniff. Did he go to heaven like our dog Bill?' The chain of crying pupils grew until most of the girls in Class 3 were red faced and bawling. Sandra Newton of Class 2 sat in a puddle of her own making which only became apparent when the acrid smelling liquid seeped across to Eric Plant of Class 4.

'Eeeerrghh, Miss! Sandra's wee'd herself again!' Eric scooted himself backwards into Neil Simmons, who was trying to crucify the action man he'd brought in for Father Bruce's role play.

The noise was deafening, Miss Dunkley's scowl turned into a wicked smile, followed by an involuntary snort. She clasped her hand over her face and stole a glance up at the vicar and as they locked eyes, hers in amusement, his in dismay, he noticed that she really had quite a lovely face when she was not contorting it like Popeye chewing his spinach.

Jumping in to rescue him, the Headmaster took control of the assembly and thanked the vicar for his inspiring talk. He then dismissed all except Class 6 and Miss Dunkley, who remained behind for a lesson on baptism and marriage. Each pupil lined up with their teddy bears and dolls and Father Bruce 'Christened' the inanimate creatures in turn, giving them the 'Christian' name preferred by each child. It was after the marriage ceremony between Sindy and Action Man that attention spans dissolved and chaos returned once again.

'Does that mean that Sindy and Eagle Eyes Action Man can do sex now?' said little Simon Thompson, most innocently. The vicar spluttered and looked towards Miss Dunkley for assistance. The bloated red face of the reverend at the mercy of Class 6 drew out her maternal side and Miss Dunkley dutifully saved him again.

In the staff room at break time, Father Bruce made a concerted effort to thank Miss Dunkley for all that she had done. He sensed that her coldness towards him was more to do with his religion than a personal attack on his character, but he was determined to show her his liberal approach to organised religion.

'I understand that you want your children to be open-minded and make their own decisions, really I do,' he beseeched, tilting his head condescendingly to one side as he spoke.

'Open minded? Your idiotic religion instructs people in exactly what they must think, say, feel and do!' Her neck and décolletage was growing more and more scarlet and her breathing quickened. Mr Bryn-Jones flashed her one of his resolute glares from across the room, stopping her from launching into a full-out verbal assault.

'I think you'll find that most Christians are flexible, tolerant and broadminded individuals who just strive for the greater good,' he continued, oblivious to her rising anger. She bit down on her tongue, her eyebrows rising impossibly high on her forehead.

'Tell you what, why don't you come round to our Sunday school this weekend and see for yourself what goes on? I think you'll find many broadminded and liberal views amongst the ladies and gentlemen who assist my work there.'

★ ★ ★ ★ ★

At the Bull that evening, the bell ringers sat in the snug to discuss the last practice session and future developments. By their third round of drinks, Doctor Clements' pragmatic façade began to slip.

'You know, I'm beginning to think that all our efforts are futile and perhaps we should all call it a day.' The campanologists fingered their glasses, silently contemplating his outburst, looking carefully at the expression on his face for clues. Sue Honey was the first to break the silence. Leaning forward conspiratorially, showing so much of her cleavage that her rolls of tummy flab could also be viewed from a distance, she whispered,

'Is that code for you wanna give up the nookie sessions?'

The doctor nodded slowly.

'Hell no!' his wife, Jodi, exclaimed. 'I think we are just beginning to make headway! In fact, I think that we could escalate things to the next level or bring in fresh blood to practice with, whichever is easier!' Jodi looked directly at Jordan Maisey and Daffydd Bryn-Jones. The penny dropped, leaving them stupefied as they pondered the possibilities.

'Wha'? I don't get it? We going in for a competition or summut?' Val said, squinting naively.

Daffydd groped about beneath the table and gave her knee a little squeeze before burying his lips in her hair and whispering;

'S&M my dear! Don't you fancy a little spanking once in a while?'

Val squealed with delight and shot a wicked glance at Doc Clements.

'Jodi, sweetheart, don't you think we ought to discuss this in private before we take on… new commitments?' he snarled the last part through clenched teeth.

'I don't see why. You neglected to discuss the point with me before you announced you had tired of… bell ringing!'

Jordan piped up, nudging his elbows into the Doctor's ribs,

'Come on mate, you know the exercise gives you such pleasure.'

'Hmmm, just one I didn't know I would have to share for the rest of my marital life,' the Doctor muttered into his pint glass.

★ ★ ★ ★ ★

Big Mazzer pulled up outside the Blythe-Brown's house and began unloading the cake tiers in vast Tupperware containers.

251

Little Craigie jumped out of the passenger seat of the Reliant Kitten to help his mum and get a good look at the last fitting of Olivia's dress. As they walked through the hallway into the sitting room, there she stood in all her abundant corpulence, wearing her ivory silk dress inside out, with Jill and Bronwyn on their knees before her, trying to reinforce the stitching on the additional panel they had sewn in that afternoon.

'Oh my!' Craigie shrieked, 'You look divine, darling! A veritable princess!' Olivia beamed with delight.

'You don't think the frills on the sleeves are a bit much?'

'Oh no, you look like a brunette version of Lady Diana on her big day!'

Jill and Bronwyn looked up from the hem-line of the skirt in unison and drew in sharp breaths across their teeth. 'Except, of course, she wasn't knocked up.' Craigie continued unabashed.

Araminta sniggered, as Olivia scowled viciously at Craigie. He sauntered into the downstairs cloakroom, catching one of the partially dressed bridesmaids off guard. The bridesmaid squealed, drawing the attention of the entire wedding preparation party as she fumbled to cover her half naked body.

'Oh please! Stop squawking darling! All girls together I say!' he said, flouncing into the bathroom to help her adjust the gown she had been trying on.

* * * * *

Sunday morning saw the usual bustling activity at

Henridge Church; the peeling bells were summoning the villagers to the morning service, Jacket's wife Jill fussed over the floral displays and Lily was ushering her young Sunday school victims into the community rooms at the rear of the church.

Miss Dunkley waited outside the church until a group of gossiping women squeezed through the porch in a great gaggle, then using them for cover, scampered across the breadth of the church and poked her head through the curtain separating one of the ante-rooms. Through the gap in the fabric she could see a collection of children of all ages and sizes, some rolling around play fighting on the rug, some reading studiously as though no world existed beyond the pages three inches from their noses, while other older ones helped a struggling Lily Underwood unfold some rickety wooden chairs around the room.

'Ow do, Miss!' The gravelly greeting came from behind her and made her jump, the spike of shocked adrenalin prompting a gasp of breath as she simultaneously spun around to face the wiry, Brylcremed Marshall in all his Sunday finery. 'Beg pardon me duck – didn't mean to startle you.' Marshall was grasping his flat cap with both hands in supplication and bowing his head with exaggerated humility. Miss Dunkley stood rigid, wide eyed and speechless. With no response forthcoming, he continued, frowning, 'Are you teaching us today, Miss? Only Lily... um... Mrs Underwood normally does for us, like?' He waited patiently for Miss Dunkley to come to her senses.

'Oh no! I'm um... not... um... I'm just visiting!'

At that moment, Lily swept aside the curtain and

announced a protracted and enquiring 'Yesssssssss?' directed at the loitering Miss Dunkley.

Miss Dunkley, who had quite a revered and authoritative presence herself in the teaching profession, felt completely disarmed and stammered her way through a brief explanation of the vicar's invitation to observe her Sunday school class.

'Hmmmm,' Lily growled, without even trying to conceal her displeasure. She then turned on Marshall and berated him for his late arrival.

'Sorry I'm late Missus, I got stuck with one of me heifers. Poor old gel had a breech 'un to deliver. You could hear her wailing like the whores of Babylon right down the lane, yer could.' He threw down his coat and hat, unfolded a wooden chair and sat behind the group of children.

'I hope you had a wash before you entered a house of God, Mr Marshall, and please mind your language in front of the children,' Lily chided. Marshall hung his head low, dropping his gaze away from her penetrating stare rather than answer her.

They chanted the *Lord's Prayer* together, the children's mistimed, high pitched voices blending uncomfortably with Marshall's baritone drawl.

'Today's lesson, children, is about the Resurrection of Christ.' Lily began to preach in her pious manner, raising clasped hands to her chest and slowly closing her eyes.

'Did she say erection? Christ had an erection?' It was little Simon Thompson, who had ruined Action Man's wedding to Sindy. 'Doesn't that mean that God gets boners too?'

'Silence! How dare you?! Little boy, don't you realise that

you'll go to Hell for saying that, with all the other naughty little boys?' Lily Screeched, her pearl earrings swinging violently below her ears as she raged.

Marshall raised his hand cautiously. 'Yes? What is it? You should have gone before the lesson started!'

'Oh no Lily… sorry… Mrs Underwood, it's just, ent the boy right though?' Marshall patted the dumb-struck child on the head briefly before continuing. 'Didn't Jesus go to a prostit… to a um… 'lady of the night'? Weren't she a friend or summut?' Marshall, determined to turnover a new leaf, had been reading passages from the bible every night before bed. 'I could be wrong though, coz I ent as clever or as religious as you, like, 'an there ent half a load of big fancy words in the Bible 'an all but I'm sure they mentioned some bird called Mary Magdalene? Well, that's summut I have got knowledge of, 'an wimmin like that always give me a boner!'

The older kids snorted and sniggered behind their illustrated copies of Bible stories for children while the younger ones sat patiently on the floor shrugging their shoulders innocently.

'Marshall, you are a wicked, wicked man and will never get into the Kingdom of Heaven until you learn to hold your tongue and curb those unnatural impulses you have!' She threw her arms up in despair.

'Mrs Underwood? Can we have some cake now?' Simon's sister Tilly piped up.

'Not until you've all coloured in the sheets depicting the resurrect… showing Christ coming back to life!'

They groaned, but with the lure of cake as compensation for their efforts, they all settled down to quiet colouring.

Simon Thompson was lying on the rug on raised elbows colouring the face of Jesus in red. Miss Dunkley slid off her wooden chair and knelt beside him.

'Why are you making Jesus red, Simon?' She enquired in almost a whisper.

'Well, it's hot there ent it? Jesus'ud have proper bad sunburn, I reckon.' He moved his crayons rapidly without care across the paper.

'Did what Mrs Underwood say about going to Hell upset you?' She leaned in closer to him, hoping he would whisper the response in return.

'Oh, it's ok, Miss Dunkley.' Simon said brightly, 'Jimmy Thomas' mum said that Butlins on the South Coast was Hell so I don't mind, I quite like camping!'

Tilly Thompson had finished her colouring in and was cramming a thick golden yellow wedge of sponge cake into her mouth. Swallowing the mouthful, she paused and said,

'Mrs Underwood? What's a boner?'

A short time later, Miss Dunkley made a rapid retreat back through the curtain into a corridor at the rear of the church. Revealed was a dizzying scene of squawking babies spitting up on young mothers' shoulders, interfering grannies giving unwanted parenting advice, fathers competing over collection plate donations and children well practised in escapology mounting the pews like capuchin monkeys. Lily's friend Ethel sat at a 45 degree angle to the organ as she fought and lost a fight against her reoccurring narcolepsy mid-chorus during 'Onward Christian Soldiers'. Her head, thrown forward, smashed against the ivories striking an interesting chord to accompany the peel of bells ringing out from the steeple.

The mass of noisy and spiritually bereft people began to swarm out of the Church, chanting polite platitudes to the vicar as he stood at the exit to receive his weekly praise. Miss Dunkley tucked herself in amongst the oversized handbags and elbows of the ladies of the parish and attempted to leave unseen. She had just cleared the first marble angel on the left of the footpath when little Simon Thompson flew past on his Raleigh Chopper bike yelling, 'See ya tomorrow, Miss Dunkley!'

Father Bruce caught sight of her scurrying away towards the lych-gate and hurried after her.

'Miss Dunkley, you're not leaving already? I was hoping to have a chat with you.' He held out his hand for her to shake. She twitched awkwardly and jerked her hand out in automatic response.

'I… um… I ought to dash really.' She faltered, having not paid much thought to this inevitable conversation.

'Oh please, I care greatly about your opinion,' he said, holding onto her hand for too long. Something about his cool strong hands and his smiling eyes made her defenceless. She opened her mouth in the hope that an excuse would fall out, but was left mute for the second time that day. 'Please.' he implored 'how about a spot of lunch at the rectory? Bronwyn Cross, the lady who looks after me, always prepares enough for two!' He neglected to mention that he always ate enough for two as well. He was still holding her hand when she agreed politely to join him for lunch.

Completing the final peel in the round, the campanologists began to wind up the tail ends of the cords in the bell tower. Dr Clements peered out of the narrow slit window in the wall, watching the last of the congregation leave from the family service. He felt something press against his thigh and caught the unmistakable smell of his wife's expensive French perfume. His body leaned instinctively back against her bosom and let out a tiny gasp as her hand moved steadily up towards his groin. Glancing over his shoulder, she reached up to meet her lips with his. He responded without opposition until he felt her fingers draw down the zip on his trousers and slide her hand inside.

'Jodi!' he warned, in a deep but playful tone. 'In front of the others?' She squeezed the cheek of his buttocks with her free hand, raised an eyebrow and replied,

'Let's show them how it's done!' She flashed her perfect white teeth at him and kissed him deeply into submission. The bell tower was surprisingly warm for a late March afternoon. Shards of white sunlight stabbed across the wooden floor, capturing the suspended dust particles mid flight.

Jodi began to peel her husband's clothes from his lean body while Jordan, Val, Sue and Daffydd lounged on cushions strewn around the room. Jodi drew some cord from her jacket pocket and tied a slip knot in the end. Threading the Doctor's hands through the loop she pulled it tight around his wrists, making him giggle nervously. He stood, a little bewildered in nothing but his boxer shorts, the fair hairs on his chest glistening like golden thread. She kissed him again fully on the lips and he tried to grapple at her clothes with his tied hands. She stroked his arms, clasped the knot securing his hands and raised it above his head towards one of the bell rope hooks. Playing along with her, he voluntarily attached himself to the hook that was out of her reach. She could feel his excitement as she ran her hands over his muscular torso and down to his shorts.

Stepping away, she played to her small audience, performing a striptease of sorts to reveal beneath her conservative and stylish dress and jacket, a tight leather basque, with black stockings and suspenders. All that remained of her original attire were her three inch stiletto heels. She had curves in all the right places, with her neat but ample breasts perched high up and quivering in the retaining leather. She and the doctor were an impressive couple, to say the least. She turned around to face her husband, caressing and nibbling his body, working her way down to his waist. Slowly and carefully, she removed the last of his garments to a round of applause from Sue and Valerie. Jordan and Daffydd sniffed nonchalantly at his obviously superior manhood.

The doctor began breathing heavily, in anticipation of his wife's next caress, the muscles in his lower abdomen twitching excitedly. To his surprise, she spun back around, dropped onto all fours and started purring, stretching and gyrating like a cat, all the time reversing her well rounded rear into Jordan's face. At the same time, she contorted her head around to kiss the headmaster full on his eager mouth. She teased the two men in front of her husband for a few minutes more before Sue and Valerie grew tired of the one woman show and stormed off in disgust. Doctor Clements watched his wife being mauled under her command by the two men for as long as he could bear it before unhooking himself.

'I'm leaving now!' he said, snorting madly like a bull at a matador. Neither Jodi nor the engrossed men responded. 'This is not what I signed up for when I married you!' He grabbed his clothes from the floor and hastily dressed as he descended the tower stairs.

★ ★ ★ ★ ★

Father Bruce wiped the gravy from his chin with his cream linen napkin and poured Miss Dunkley another glass of wine.

'If you were not a man of the cloth I would accuse you of trying to get me tipsy!' she giggled, flushing red in the cheeks.

'Don't let the dog collar fool you, Miss Dunkley!' he laughed nervously with a wink.

'My God!' she thought to herself, 'What the hell am I playing at? Flirting with a vicar! This wine must be stronger than I thought!'

'Call me Daphne,' she cooed.

Father Bruce paused to evaluate her mood. He couldn't decide if his status in the community was the reason for her sudden thaw or whether it was the wine. Could it be that she was warming to him as a person?

'More roast lamb, Daphne?' He stood and began carving in anticipation of her acceptance.

'I don't know what has happened to me today. I seem to have developed an insatiable appetite.' Realising the ambiguity of her statement, she looked him in the eye and clasped a hand over her gaping mouth and flushed a deeper crimson.

He smiled a slow and lazy grin and rescued her.

'So, has the kind and generous spirit of our volunteers changed your mind about the religious instruction of our local youth?'

Miss Dunkley swallowed a lump of gristle without chewing and contemplated her reply carefully. She was just starting to relax and enjoy herself, but knew that the inevitable conversation would lead to a row. As a delay tactic she said;

'Have you observed Mrs Underwood's Sunday school lessons? I mean recently?' She tucked a carefully folded forkful of Yorkshire Pudding, oozing with gravy and mint sauce into her puckered mouth.

'Erm… in all honesty, Daphne, it has been a while, but I am positive it's every bit as good as the one I saw her do a couple of Christmases ago.' He was smug and confident in his praise, leaning back in his chair with one hand on his glass and the other balancing on his expanding paunch.

Miss Dunkley thought carefully about her response, considering a diplomatic answer that would not upset her courteous host, but then the wine kicked in.

'Well, I think you should go and take another look!' She suppressed a burp that was bubbling up her gullet.

'Oh, Lily can be a little brusque, I'll admit that, but her heart is in the right place and she cares deeply for the children.'

'Brusque?!' Miss Dunkley's voice rose an octave. 'Brusque? She's the living end, man!' Daphne hiccoughed through the last part of her outburst. 'Do you know, she told a little boy that he would go to Hell for speaking out of turn?'

The vicar frowned in disbelief, sizing Daphne up for her potential to over-dramatise matters.

'Hmmm. I'm sure it was taken out of context. Perhaps she meant it as an allegory for something.' The vicar was determined to remain calm, even if the school teacher seemed to be flying off the handle.

'Oh really!' She exclaimed, reaching down for her handbag before rising from the table to leave. 'If you are going to discount everything I say as a lie, why bother asking my opinion?' She strutted out of the dining room and into the hallway, hotly followed by the vicar.

'Really, Daphne, I do think you are exaggerating somewhat. Lily is a nice lady. She does a tremendous amount for the WI and the Parish Council. Why would she frighten a little boy with Hell?'

Miss Dunkley turned from the coat racks to face him. She was a good foot shorter than the Reverend Bruce and a third of his girth, but the blaze of angry fire did not go unnoticed.

'My Good Woman... ' he began.

'Did you just 'Good Woman' me?' Daphne was boiling with fury and taking strides towards him. The vicar tried to take a pace backwards but stumbled and was pinned against the hall mirror on the adjacent wall. Daphne repeated herself, 'Did you? Eh? 'Good Woman' indeed!' she ranted, prodding the reverend in his chest with her index finger. To both their surprise, Father Bruce exclaimed;

'My God, Daphne! You are marvellous!' Then he grabbed her in a passionate embrace, scooping her up to kiss her deeply on the mouth while her feet dangled in mid air.

★ ★ ★ ★ ★

Olivia's big day began with a pink Cadillac convertible festooned with white ribbons and bows leaking oil all over her father's driveway. James Blythe-Brown had been on the single malt since 8am and was chatting despondently to the patient Labrador about his failures as a parent, while he perched on the last two steps of the staircase. All about him whirled the excitable youth and the troubled elders of the village, puffing up hundreds of yards of baby pink taffeta, refreshing carnation button-holes and 'testing' the salmon mousse with mucky pinkie fingers. Araminta appeared to be the only rational and serenely sober participant as she watched her sister waddle down the polished oak stairs, her pregnant bulge partly concealed by the most enormous bouquet of white and pink roses. As she reached the bottom, her father stood up and turned around, grunted his disapproval and stuck out an elbow for his daughter to grasp. With whisky tumbler still in hand, he led Olivia out to her wedding car.

Henridge Church tiptoed at the top of the lane, its spire casting an imposing shadow over the parish sinners. The wind was doing its best to dislodge the newest leaves on the ash trees leading up to the lych-gate, but the graveyard yews stood unperturbed by the chilling breeze in their black-green sombre mood.

Inside the Sunday school ante-room at the rear of the Church, Rueben paced about while his 'best man' Steven smoked a cheeky cigarette hanging out of an open window. Eagle eyed Lily Underwood caught the flash of a pink Cadillac streaking up Henridge Lane and scurried inside to bring everyone to order. She glanced up the aisle and signalled to Craigie to fetch the groom, but could not see the vicar. 'Tsk'ing' loudly to herself, she hotfooted it as fast as her wide-fitting court shoes could carry her, down the back corridor to the vestry. Bursting in she announced;

'Father you must come at once!' then stopped abruptly, aghast at the sight of Miss Dunkley kneeling on a prayer stool beneath the vicar's robes. It was a few moments before the enraptured Reverend came to his senses and halted the motions of the all too eager seductress beneath his vestments.

'You, me and the Bishop are going to have words about this!' Lily screeched, before turning on her heels back to the awaiting congregation.

Olivia nodded at Craigie to turn on the hidden stereo behind the pulpit that connected directly to the PA system and out blared Billy Idol's 'White Wedding':

'Hey little sister what have you done?
Hey little sister who's the only one?
Hey little sister who's your superman?
Hey little sister who's the one you want?
Hey little sister – shotgun!
It's a nice day to start again,
It's a nice day for a… white wedding!'

Matron of Honour, Araminta, gasped and prodded Olivia in the back.

'Are you having a laugh? Seriously?' She hissed.

'We thought we'd use irony!' Olivia snorted.

'Stupidity more like, you dumb bint! Could you be any more insensitive if you tried?' Still shaking her head,

Araminta followed her sister up the aisle to where a sheepish vicar and the Longfield brothers were waiting.

Father Bruce began his pious and well worn speech on the virtues of marriage, emphasising the part about honesty, commitment and being true to the vows they were about to take. There were a few quiet sniggers in the congregation, but not quite loud enough to be heard at the front. Then it came to the part of his speech that was normally rushed through.

'Does anyone here know of any just reason why these two cannot be joined in holy matrimony? Speak now or forever hold your peace.'

The crowd froze, you could have heard a pin drop.

James Blythe-Brown swayed in his semi-comatose state and piped up;

'You mean a reason, apart from them being cousins?' he staggered, clutching a pew to keep him upright. There was a collective gasp of breath. Olivia spun around and looked at her father with a cold, withering glare.

'Daddy! Don't you dare spoil this for me!'

'What?! It's true. Ask your soon to be Mother-in-Law!'

Olivia stared at Esme Longfield sitting nonchalantly in the front pew on the groom's side of the nave.

'Well?' Olivia barked after a brief pause, 'Is it true?' Esme re-arranged her fur stole around her shoulders, shrugged, then nodded slowly.

The Longfield brothers were struck dumb. Olivia was panting heavily and pacing the short distance between her fiancé and her father.

'It ent illegal. Technically speaking,' Esme Longfield

began, 'you are only half first cousins. You share the same grandfather, I suppose that makes me your half-auntie!'

'What!? You dim-witted old woman!' Olivia exclaimed thoughtlessly. 'That still makes us blood relations!'

Lily Underwood sat with folded arms, a thunderous scowl and a murderous glint in her eye, while the congregation enjoyed the spectacle sporting smirks on their faces.

'Would you all like some time alone to think about your course of action in view of this... um... revelation?' The vicar said tactfully.

Steven grabbed his cousin/lover/potential sister-in-law by the elbow and guided her and his gibbering brother to the vestry.

★ ★ ★ ★ ★

Tension was also mounting above in the bell tower. Still furious at the recent turn of events, Valerie and Sue Honey had cried off sick, leaving the rest of the campanologists to manage two bell cords each. They had worked up a sweat ringing the bells to call the villagers to the wedding service and were having a breather, resting on the cushions on the creaky wooden floor.

Jodi grinned shamelessly and unbuttoned her blouse just enough to allow the Headmaster and the butcher a glimpse of her leather underwear beneath. A broad smile crept across Daffydd Bryn-Jones' face in realisation of the treat that lay ahead of them.

Dr Clements tutted audibly and gently shook his head from side to side. He looked at his wife as she postured provocatively on the bed of cushions in an entirely different light. The beautiful, elegant creature he had once captured and wed, who had once shared vows to love and to cherish in sickness and in health, had become this sickening lascivious siren, writhing around for any man's approval in front of him. He felt the acid in the pit of his stomach rise and scorch an embryonic ulcer, the pain sharpening his temper.

They could hear a mix tape of music that Craigie had quickly shoved into the stereo downstairs to drown out the bridal party shouting in the vestry. Just as Tina Turner belted out the chorus of 'What's love got to do with it?' Jordan Maisey whispered;

'Aye aye, better straighten up Jodi, I can hear footsteps coming this way!'

They waited for the clipping noise of metal heels on wood to reach the top of the stairs and there she stood, with fulsome bosoms bouncing in her fluffy angora bat-winged sweater, the young receptionist from the surgery. Doctor Clements jumped to his feet and grabbed both her hands lightly, leading her into the room. 'Don't be shy,' he laughed roguishly, 'we won't bite, unless you want me to?' Jordan Maisey cringed at the line the Doctor had used. The receptionist giggled girlishly.

'Oh, Doctor Clements, you are funny!' She tapped him lightly on the shoulder and then laid her hand on his chest.

'Everyone, I'd like you to meet Sharon, the receptionist at work and my friend.' He sneered and stared pointedly at Jodi for her reaction. 'It turns out that Sharon is very interested in learning bell ringing and has quite an adventurous nature too!' The Doctor clasped Sharon's face in both hands and began kissing her passionately.

'Oh no!' Jodi said, 'I am not having that!' She bounded

across the tower and pulled Sharon off her husband, flinging her backwards with some ferocity.

'Now now!' Dr Clements said, 'Fair's fair. We can't have one rule for me and another rule for Queen Jodi now can we?' Jodi flew at him, first slapping him cruelly across his masculine jaw then scratching at his face and neck wildly.

'Oooh! Is there gonna be rough stuff too?' Sharon enquired calmly, 'Coz I ain't sure I'm into that 'an all!'

★ ★ ★ ★ ★

The music stopped and the bride, groom, best man and respective parents ceased their squabbling and emerged from the vestry to resume the ceremony. Olivia was determined that she should have a husband and a father for her child, regardless of whom that poor fellow was and Rueben cared little for the close proximity of the genetic line. He wanted Olivia and that was the end of it.

The vows were recited and agreed to and the marriage certificate signed and witnessed. Ethel was assisted up the steps to the church organ to play the wedding march for the less than happy couple to walk back down the aisle. Thankfully the organ was loud enough to drown out the peel of mistimed and partially missing bells as Jodi had escorted the bewildered Sharon forcibly back down the tower steps and then left in a fit of histrionics.

By the time the photos of grimacing relatives and smirking friends were complete, the guests were chilled to the bone, huddling at the side of the church porch out of the cool wind. Most were heading up to the big house to help themselves to the Pimms in the marquee, long before the newlyweds had arrived to greet them.

The mood was solemn and unusually quiet, just a mild but cordial hubbub and the odd drunken shriek of laughter from a distant relative as they dined on pheasant and roasted vegetables. Olivia ordered some crushed ice to munch on and a few anchovies to liven up her meal, a penchant she had acquired during the early months of her pregnancy.

The top table braced themselves as the toastmaster rang a small bell and announced that guests should charge their glasses for the speeches. Olivia elbowed her inebriated father sharply in the ribs and motioned for him to stand up and begin the 'Father of the Bride' speech.

'What? Me? I have to say my bit now do I?' he grumbled miserably. 'Well, what can I say? Other than a huge apology to all our guests, who have endured such a shabby affair. Shouldn't have got this far really, my fault, should have put an end to it – didn't – hmmmm – there you go. Thought Olivia would come to her senses in time. What was I thinking? She has no sense, nor common decency come to think of it. Bit of an 'Old Slapper' from what I hear. That's what they say don't they? 'Old Slapper'?' The guests winced, some shaking their heads in disbelief. 'Anyway, pretty clear that she can't be trusted to keep her knees together, so Rueben, best of luck old chap!' He raised his glass and paused while the guests stood alongside him. 'To the Bride and Groom!' They all sipped meekly and sat back down. 'Oh and by the way, Olivia, I'm changing my will. Better that Minty runs the estate when I'm gone, don't you think? Right, good.' and with that he slumped back down in his chair.

There was no applause, no sniggering, just the harsh sound of Olivia's chair legs grating on the temporary floor of the marquee as she shoved it back and scurried in floods of tears through the exit and across the lawn to the house.

Steven looked at his grief stricken brother and then at the expectant guests. No one seemed to be making any attempts at following her. Not even Araminta, her maid of honour and closest relative seemed to warm to her plight. The toastmaster was just about to ring his little bell again when Steven stood, apologised for the delay in the eventful proceedings and bid everyone to charge their glasses again with James's vintage champagne, promising that he would return in a short while. Rueben was rooted to the spot. Steven tried to drag him from his seat, but to no avail. He had no choice but to leave the marquee and go after the Bride.

★ ★ ★ ★ ★

The bell tower was silent and locked up. The Doctor had caught up with Sharon and his wife and had escorted them both home, leaving Jordan and Daffydd left standing by their cars, pontificating on the outcome of the day's events.

'You reckon it's all over bar the shouting then, Daffydd?' Jordan said wistfully as he fumbled with his car keys and leaned his backside against the wing of his muddy Land Rover.

'Oh aye lad, that's it! Without the Doc and his missus it'll all fall apart!' The Headmaster joined the butcher in his doleful preponderances. 'Still, we had a bloody good run at it though, didn't we?' His lyrical Welsh accent always sounded cheery and was quite infectious.

'I don't think I have the time or energy to learn another past-time just to get a spot of extra-marital leg-over!' Jordan sighed.

'Chin up old boy! I hear that the bunch at Mountford Church are short of a couple of ringers and they are a much younger and fitter crew!' Daffydd winked conspiratorially.

★ ★ ★ ★ ★

The following day, Father Bruce received a telephone call from his Bishop.

'Bruce?' The bishop's tone was terse and abrupt.

'Your Grace? How are you?' Father Bruce braced himself for the worst.

'Never mind all that. I got a call from a very irate parishioner this morning, telling me that you run a den of iniquity over in Adderstey and Henridge!' The Bishop drew a wheezing breath past his Cuban cigar. 'What've you been up to over there? Got caught with your frock up eh? Tututut! And with the school mistress, from what I hear!'

Father Bruce gulped. It was bad enough that he should lose his place in the community, but for his poor Daphne to lose her position too.

'Look sir, please… ' Father Bruce implored.

'Oh don't get your cassocks in a twist man. The way I see it you have two choices. Marry the old trout or get out of Dodge!'

'Yes sir,' Bruce replied humbly. Protestations were futile when it came to this Bishop.

'Oh and Bruce… ?'

'Yes sir?'

'Do something about those rampant bell ringers will you before they ruin what little respect is left for the Church!?'

CHAPTER 12

April

Menagè et Trois

Esme Longfield tied a headscarf around her unruly curls and began sweeping the clearing between the trees with a well worn besom. It was more than two weeks after the wedding, April the 13th, and both families were still unsettled and feuding. As the afternoon sun weakened to the west, she gathered a solitary flower from a bluebell stem, whispering her thanks as she did so, and tucked it into the canvas bag at her side. Alternating between singing and whistling whenever she forgot the words to the tune, she happily busied herself collecting wood to build her little fire, adjacent to the clearing and near to the stream, which, later in its journey, fed Henridge Brook.

The sticks crackled and snapped in the yellow flames and the light breeze carried their embers to older logs rapidly. Esme filled a small kettle from the stream and balanced it over the flames before returning to her freshly swept ground. She retrieved a number of items from her satchel, including some string that hooked on her walking pole and unravelled to the exact length of six feet six inches, plus a slip knot in which to secure a second wooden pole. In the centre of her clearing she pushed her walking stick into the ground with some force, grunting through the effort, and unwound her string. Looping the second stick in its end, she traced a circle in the dirt, walking deliberately clockwise till the groove was clearly visible. Removing her walking stick, she placed the bluebell flower, 13 drops of water, a pinch of salt and a small misshapen stone, which she kissed first, into the hole that the stick had made. Finally, she covered the hole with a larger, smoother stone and placed markers outside the circle that indicated the compass points and some rune markings in the soil.

The kettle began to whistle shrilly, sending two crows flapping and squawking up from the trees. 'Get off with you! Nasty lurking creatures!' she shooed, 'We won't be needing your sort around here today!'

Esme used the edge of her tweed skirt to shield her hand from the heat of the handle and lifted the kettle from the fire. She took a little jam jar from her bag containing dried brown fibrous material and popped a generous chunk into the boiling water, giving it a bit of a swirl around before replacing the lid. Cradled in the base of an old oak tree trunk, she drew her shawl around her and waited.

★ ★ ★ ★ ★

Steven brushed Olivia's fringe from her eyes with a tender stroke of an index finger across her forehead. They were in the kitchen of Rueben's cottage on the opposite side of Henridge Lane to the Longfield Farmhouse, unpacking boxes and drinking coffee. Olivia had moved most of her possessions into the house just prior to the wedding and had planned on persuading Rueben to sweet-talk his mother into giving them the adjoining cottage in order that they could knock through and make one larger family home. The previous tenants had been old and frail and had moved into a care home some time ago and the cottage had stood empty ever since. With all the recent turmoil and upset, long term planning seemed to be the last thing on Olivia's mind.

'You know, I don't know what I would have done without you these last few weeks,' Olivia said, choking back bitter tears.

'You have had it pretty tough lately, that's for sure, but everything will be fine now – Rueben will look after you.' Steven's head bowed away from her searching eyes as he said it, as the first stab of jealously crept up and paralysed his lungs, stopping his sentence short. Olivia gently held his face in her hands and kissed him; not out of lust, not out of friendship, but a kiss that was altogether something different and new to them both.

Rueben slung the kitchen door open and leaned in, leaving his muddy booted feet planted on the mat outside.

'Steve, come and give us a hand with that old ewe will yer?' Rueben took in the scene for a moment, his brother's arms clasped around his heavily pregnant wife, her face serene and content for the first time in months. His eyes narrowed and he snorted, before slamming the door closed and running across the yard.

'Oh God!' Olivia exclaimed in genuine remorse, 'He'll think we were… ' She trailed off. Steven was nodding his understanding. 'I have to go after him!' Olivia was scrabbling in amongst the garments on the coat rack as she said it.

'Don't be daft woman! You are in no fit state to go after anyone!' Steven looked out of the kitchen window. 'He ent taken the truck, so he's on foot'. He paused briefly to think. 'I know where he'll be. He always hid up the tree house in the forest when we fell out as kids.' Steven stroked her face once more and went for the door.

'I'm coming too. If he's there it's only a short walk and I could do with the fresh air. Besides, he won't believe anything you tell him when he's like this.' Steven argued for a while before giving in to this headstrong woman for whom he had a new found admiration.

A small flock of noisy finches were squabbling over their bedtime perches in the hedgerows and young rabbits scattered and hid in side ditches as Steven and Olivia made their way to the end of Henridge Lane. It was a long and laborious jaunt up to the forest as Olivia chose her footing with care to avoid the ridges made by tractors and holes left by all the horse traffic over the years. Eventually, they walked the short riding in the forest up to a tiny footbridge over the stream. The tree house was no more than a rickety platform, attached to the beech tree with six inch nails at a point where the trunk split into four branches about twelve feet above the ground. There were some signs of recent repair, as the next generation of village kids discovered the location and claimed it as their own, bringing rusted tools and scraps of wood from their garden sheds to re-commission this secret playground.

Rueben sat cradling his knees, with his head hung down to one side, resting on an arm, his back leaned against a solitary post that stuck upright incongruously from the platform. His eyes were red and puffy but his breathing was slow and calm. He heard Steven and Olivia approaching, their heavy steps clattering on the wooden planks of the footbridge.

'Leave me alone!' Rueben shouted petulantly.

'Come down!' Steven yelled. 'Stop being such a child. We need to talk about this!'

'Darling, please!' Olivia implored. 'There really is nothing going on between Steven and me, you must believe me.'

'Must I? It's not exactly the first time I have caught you two together!'

'Steven was just being kind to me – that's all. Come on love, come down, please?' They waited, just a few seconds, but Rueben made no sign of moving. 'Come down or I will come up! Your choice!' Olivia grasped the sun bleached wooden ladder and placed one foot on the first unbroken rung and hoisted herself up. It gave way with a loud crack and she thumped the two feet to the floor with quite a jolt.

'Ohhhhh!' she cried.

'Olivia! Are you hurt?' Steven said, dashing to her side. Rueben jumped up and peered over the edge of the platform.

'Pain,' she said, as a dark patch of liquid spread across her blue maternity trousers. 'Oh God! I think my waters have broke!' She doubled over her bump and drew breath. 'It can't be, it's not supposed to be for another two weeks yet!' She groaned again, this time from between clenched teeth.

'Oh, Jesus Christ!' Rueben said, scaling down the ladder at speed while Steven supported her as best he could.

'Ah! Thought I could hear you!' Esme announced,

appearing dramatically on the footbridge. 'You are late! I had to heat the um… tea back up, it had gone cold!'

'Mother!' Steven said amazed, 'What on Earth are you doing here?'

'Oh you know, I had a feeling.' Her manner was almost indifferent, but altogether smug. As she turned around to cross the bridge again, she shouted her orders back to her sons. 'Rueben, you're the fastest, go back to the cottage and ring for an ambulance, then wait at the end of Henridge Lane to direct them to the clearing. Steven, carry your cousin… um… sister-in-law over this way. Come along now!' she commanded, 'This baby won't wait!'

★ ★ ★ ★ ★

Esme instructed Steven to enter the circle via the East marker and lay Olivia down on a blanket, resting her head on the canvas satchel.

'For God's sake!' Olivia screamed between contractions, 'What the Hell are you playing at? Carry me to the edge of the forest so the ambulance men can help me when they get here! Arrrrrgggghh!'

'It's too late for that, my dear. My guess is that you are almost fully dilated, he's on his way now!' Esme said calmly, pouring her 'tea' into a wooden cup and taking a few gulps before offering it to Olivia. 'There now, take a spot of this – it'll help you cope with the pain.'

'Mother! You can not give Olivia mushrooms! That's practically LSD!' Steven pushed the cup away from Olivia's face.

'Did you say LSD? Give it here now!' Olivia said, grabbing at the cup and sipping the warm amber liquid swiftly.

'That's enough dear, you only want to numb the pain, not orbit the moon!' Esme instructed her son to bank up the fire and collect more water, then she knelt next to Olivia, raised her hands and looked heavenward, facing a creamy full moon creeping slowly above the tree tops. Then she chanted. 'We begin. A circle within a circle, a life within a life, a universe within a universe. A moment is eternity, eternity is a moment. I declare this circle to be mine and by the divine feminine, Mother Earth, I ask that this mother and child be protected and flourish this night!'

Olivia's long moans and groans grew more frequent until she felt the strong urge to push. Esme stooped down and grabbed the hem of her own simple robe and started dragging it above her head, revealing her aged, sagging and unkempt body in all its glory.

'Mother, no! For crying out loud spare us your nakedness will you?!' Steven rushed to cover his mother's dignity.

'It's part of the ritual!' She pouted, but as the night air was unusually crisp, even with the fire, she relented.

'What are you doing, you mad old crone? Steven, get me out of here!' Olivia heaved between gasps of air.

'It's ok. I can hear the ambulance sirens. It won't be long now.'

Olivia squeezed the life out of Steven's hand, screaming and grunting and pushing till the veins in her forehead were dangerously raised and pulsing and her teeth clenched like a vice. Esme sat cross legged on the corner of the blanket, eyes closed, humming a tune and rocking gently from side to side. Before long, Rueben could be heard scrambling through the thickets and leading the ambulance men with torches to the clearing.

The crew agreed that it was far too late to attempt to move Olivia and that delivery was imminent. Rueben and Steven retreated a few paces and sat on a fallen tree trunk at the edge of the clearing. Esme refused to budge.

'Glad you made it in time, Bruv.' Steven said squeezing Rueben's shoulder.

'Thanks for looking after her. I can always rely on you in times of trouble, can't I?' Rueben replied amicably. Steven's grin completed their reconciliation.

'It's a boy!' The medic cried out, quickly clamping the umbilical cord and wrapping the baby in a clean sheet. Relieved laughter and congratulatory and vigorous hand shaking ensued between the brothers and the ambulance driver.

'Would the father like to cut the cord?' The ambulance man enquired. The Longfield brothers shifted uneasily and scratched their heads. Before either one of them could volunteer their services, Esme woke up from her trance and said;

'The Father ain't here. If I know Jed, he'll be knocking 'em back at The Bull right about now!' They all froze. A painfully uncomfortable silence followed while they assimilated that possibility. Olivia lay with her newborn cradled in her arms, mouth wide open, aghast. Rueben finally grasped his mother's insinuation and turned to his wife with a pained expression carved on his naïve face.

'Olivia?' Rueben begged. She glanced from one face to the next, appealing for divine intervention.

'Don't take any notice of her! Silly old tart has been drugged up for most of the day!' Olivia responded, locking eyes with her mother-in-law in a steely glare.

'I'll um… I'll just cut it for you shall I?' The medic said, making an admirable attempt to diffuse the tension. 'So, any thoughts on a name yet?'

'How about 'Bran' – the Celtic God of Health?' Esme chipped in.

'Yeah, God of Healthy Bowels! Come on Mum, give the kid a break!' Steven chided.

'What about 'Angus' then? The Celtic God of Beauty? We could have a lovely naming ceremony for him right here!'

'We most certainly will not! My family are Christians and we will have a proper Christening at Henridge Church!' Olivia sniffed contemptuously.

'You'd have a problem there, love,' Steven replied. 'Didn't you hear? Father Bruce has done a runner with Old Daffy Dunkley the School Mistress! Turns out he was less than devout after all!'

'Either way,' Olivia yawned as the ambulance men lifted her onto a stretcher and gathered up all their equipment, 'His name is Jack, a good, honest and simple name.'

'Yes,' said Esme, pleased with herself, 'That will be perfect – Jack in the Green, a common name for 'The Green Man', the Sacred Masculine, and he shall inherit what is rightfully mine… The Blythe-Brown Estate, yes, yes, that is how should be.'

Her sons looked at each other and then at Olivia, hoping

for an explanation, but none was forthcoming. Steven pointed at his own ear and drew circles in the air, indicating how batty he thought his mother was, but the seed of doubt had been sown.

The brothers followed the stretcher bearers back towards the ambulance parked at the end of Henridge Lane, Steven and Rueben taking their turns carrying Olivia and Jack to give the medics a rest, while Esme remained behind to 'close the circle', bury the placenta and give thanks. Inside the ambulance, Olivia and Jack were strapped in and made comfortable. The driver turned to the men and said;

'There's only room for one more. It's usual for the um… father to accompany… ?'

'Rueben, go with your wife. I'll fetch Olivia's bag and follow on in the pickup.' Steven pushed his brother into the back of the ambulance, keen for his brother to assert his rightful position.

★ ★ ★ ★ ★

At the Bull, Jed was desperately trying to beat Big Mazzer at skittles but failing dismally. She had won five games in a row and each time Jed had made the mistake of gambling double or quits. Mazzer was already holding 10 of Jed's crisp ten pound notes and was recommending that he call it a night before he lost any more.

Above the cacophony in the pub, the telephone was just barely audible in the passageway between the bar and the private quarters, ringing continuously. Tony left the locals briefly to answer it, sticking one finger in his ear to hear the message.

Moving on from a resounding thrashing at skittles, Jed was challenging Pa Earlem to a game of darts, as Tony reappeared, waving his arms about and shouting across the room, trying to gain Jed's attention. The uproar quietened to listen to Tony's announcement.

'Jed, your wife is on the blower, apparently Olivia's had a little boy. She wants a word with you!'

'Whey hey! Excellent news!' Jed said, dancing a little jig at the thought of another addition to his family. 'Drinks are on me! You can all wet the baby's head!' There was a small cheer, then a renewed interest in the sweepstake that Rick the Shop had been running for the past few months.

'Hey Jed, ask your Missus who the father is will yer?' Milton yelled, before crowding around Rick and his notebook to see how much money he had waged on himself as the father.

Pa Earlem returned to his seat and buried his nose in the froth of his pint. He could clearly see the elated Jed on the phone, his face sporting a euphoric smile as he listened intently to Esme relay the events of the evening to him. After a short time, Pa noticed the smile vanish from his old friend's weather-beaten face and an anxious frown replace it. Jed did not say a word, just gulped hard and put the receiver down slowly.

'Everything alright is it?' Pa asked with some concern.

'Oh um yes. All's well. She had it in the forest, can you believe! The boys have gone to hospital with her.' Jed seemed distracted. Pa thought it was altogether similar to how he behaved when he had rows with his own wife.

'Well?' Pa asked impatiently. 'Did Esme tell you who the father is?'

'Oh yes! Apparently Olivia says it's our Rueben's kid, so everything's worked out for the best! Drink up everyone, I'm a grandfather!'

'Esme said that that Rueben's the father?' Pa frowned, determined to get clarification.

'Olivia said Rueben is.' Jed replied slowly and deliberately.

'Hmmmm,' Pa mumbled.

'What? You have issue with this Pa?' The frivolous and joyful character had all but vanished as Jed turned on his oldest companion in the village.

Pa leaned in close and whispered into Jed's hairy ear, 'I saw you in Norris's minibus the night of the telethon!' He leaned back again and winked conspiratorially, then stood up and wandered over to Rick the Shop. 'So then Rick – who bet on Rueben?' Pa raised his voice to engage the whole bar in the reckoning. Rick poured through his notebook for a moment, double checking all the entries.

'Well, I'll be buggered! No one bet on him, so the book wins! I get the dough!' Rick the Shop exclaimed, astounded at his fortune.

★ ★ ★ ★ ★

A week after the birth, on a blustery and showery day, Olivia, Rueben and baby Jack returned to their cottage to discover that Steven had redecorated the nursery and fitted it with a cot, a multitude of soft toys and a nursing chair for Olivia to rock Jack to sleep in. Esme and Jed kept a respectable distance from the couple, restricting visits to more formal family occasions, such as Sunday Lunches, Birthdays and Christmases.

Over the first few months, Steven became such an integral part of their family, doting on little Jack, showering him with gifts and volunteering for baby-sitting duties, that Rueben suggested Steven move into the empty cottage next door, in order that he could be 'on hand' whenever any of them needed his services. Olivia was particularly happy with this arrangement and surprisingly, Rueben and Steven were also content with their lot too.